Acclaim)

THE COLLE __.vE
UNDERGROUND

Realm Makers Book of the Year Award
Science Fiction Realm Award
Young Adult Caleb Award

"[The Collective Underground] deserves a wider readership due to the quality of the writing, the universal themes, the suspenseful elements, and its examination of faith issues in an intriguing way. Ultimately, it has a message of hope."

— AUSTRALASIAN CHRISTIAN WRITERS

"*The Matrix* meets *Divergent*... Easily the best young adult novel I have read this year!"

— MORGAN L. BUSSE, award-winning author of the Ravenwood Saga and Skyworld series

"A gripping, unpredictable journey... Young paints a beautiful allegory of hope and love persevering through tangled darkness."

— SANDRA FERNANDEZ RHOADS, author of the Colliding Line series

FLIGHT

Books by Kristen Young

The Collective Underground series
Apprentice
Elite
Flight

FLIGHT

COLLECTIVE UNDERGROUND | BOOK THREE

KRISTEN YOUNG

To John and Dad,
faithful men who love Jesus.

WE CAN ONLY BE FREE TO LOVE

WHEN ALL THREATS TO OUR LOVELINESS

HAVE BEEN ELIMINATED.

REPORT HATERS NOW.

–Supreme Lover Midgate

The Love Collective.

LOVE ALL.

BE ALL.

PROLOGUE

ONCE THE SIRENS' UNDERGROUND MEETING is finished, we work the usual anti-surveillance measures to get back to Elite Academy. Step one is to split up four blocks away from Melody's workplace, taking circuitous routes to the dingy hotel in the seediest part of Love City. Hodge and Loa, dressed as rainbow-clad menial workers, head to a secret location to change. I'm wearing a maid's navy-blue uniform, so I travel with Melody to sneak in through a side service door.

Hidden by a large pile of laundry bags, I let the Muse sing to me while I change back into my Elite Apprentice uniform. It's all grey now. No indigo collar to mark me as a Watcher since Crucible let me out. At the time it was a relief. But I am ashamed to admit that sometimes I kind of miss the luxury of the Watcher Dorm. Every time I'm tempted to start feeling nostalgic, though, I make myself remember all the things Watchers had to do, and that's more than enough to make me glad to be a humble Coder. As if being an Elite is ever a humble job.

After hiding my disguise, I leave the hotel and meet up with the boys at the riverside park. An Overcar is already waiting, and we sit quietly while it whisks us home, unwilling to let slip any details that might incriminate us in front of the cameras. It's hard work not talking about the Siren meeting. The Song still rings through my head like a background soundtrack, threatening to spill itself out through my lips.

I bite my tongue, staring out the window in tense silence. When the Overcar spits us out onto the pavement below the Academy, I finally feel myself relax. The late-afternoon light throws a rose-gold hue across the outer Academy wall. Leading up to the entrance, the avenue of trees lining the driveway rustle in a gentle breeze, as if trying to block out the distant hum of traffic.

I slow my walk, reluctant to swap this beauty for the sterile white interior of my home. Birds flit around in the branches, their afternoon songs full of joy and life. I take a deep breath, recording the scent of leaves for later use. Memories like these are helpful when I spend long hours in a semi-darkened Coding lab.

"Nice, isn't it?" says Hodge beside me.

"Mmm," I murmur. I tear my eyes away from the beautiful scene and give him a little smile. His eyes twinkle at me, and for a moment it feels like the world disappears.

"I'm hungry," Loa interrupts loudly. "Let's get some food." He pats his stomach.

A patrol of Love Squad soldiers stands in front of the doors, silent as obsidian. The disappearing sunlight glints off a dozen shiny black helmets.

"What—" I start, confused by the military presence in front of our home. "That's never happened before."

"Shh." Hodge squares his shoulders and draws closer to me, standing protectively on my left. Loa takes up a position on my right. A cold, creeping fear begins to steal over me, despite their familiar presence.

Elite Academy has never needed guards before. Ever.

My companions begin to march with stiff formality, and I follow their lead, feeling as if every ounce of beauty has drained from the afternoon. The long, leafy driveway now feels ominous and foreboding. As we near the entrance, one of the

Love Squad soldiers steps forward. His tall, bulky form is made even more threatening by the armour of his suit.

"State your business here," the soldier barks, their voice sounding robotic and artificial through the Love Squad helmet.

Hodge salutes. "Love Squad detail returning Apprentice Flick from external duty to her quarters."

The soldier looks me up and down, eyes narrowing.

"Authorization?" The soldier says, pulling a small infotab from a pocket at his waist.

I hold out my wrist ID, and the soldier scans it. "Dorm Leader Akela sent me to visit a Collective corporation," I say, trying as hard as I can to keep the nervous wobble out of my voice.

The soldier snorts in a decidedly mocking way. "Get inside," he nods his head back at the entrance. "You should be in the assembly hall."

When we're in the middle of the orange lounge area, Loa lets out a low, soft whistle.

"Where is everyone?" I ask in a quiet whisper so my voice doesn't echo.

"This is big," Hodge says softly. He walks forward with the easy grace of a hunter, ready to strike at any moment.

Far above our heads, intricate mobiles dip and spin in the air current. The concrete waterfall, carved into the wall, is a sentinel over the empty array of orange couches.

We step into the small silvery elevator, and Loa selects the Atrium level button. My foot drums in a nervous rhythm on the floor, while Loa and Hodge stand with tense readiness. When the doors sigh open, Loa and Hodge launch ahead of me to peer carefully around the corner. I catch a glimpse of their hardening expressions when they see what's waiting for us, and my heart flutters into anxious overdrive. Hodge straightens and places a finger over his lips.

Before us, Love Squad soldiers stand shoulder to shoulder

in the Atrium, their bodies forming an impenetrable black fence around a field of grey Elite uniforms. The Elites' pale, anxious faces make it even more clear that this is not an ordinary assembly.

Rows upon rows of neatly lined students stand facing an upper-level balcony. At the front, just below the space where Supreme Lover Midgate's face is projected each night, stands Lover Fuschious. I haven't seen him display this kind of cockiness since the first day I met him. But that was before Akela demoted him, which can only mean . . .

"Salute!" he barks. The entire Academy snaps to obey.

This only seems to displease him. "Not good enough!" His face twists into a harsh scowl. "This whole place has gone soft. From now on, you will remember that you are supposed to be Elite. You will stand like Elites. You will train like Elites. You will live, eat breathe, and sleep like Elites. It may be Triumph season, but you will behave like Elites. Do you hear me?"

"Yes, Lover Fuschious!" The sound of their voices is deafening.

"That's Dorm Leader Fuschious to you," he yells, and I feel the strength drain from my legs. With a superhuman effort I remain standing, and share a frightened glance with Hodge. His hands tremble as he pushes me behind his torso so I am mostly hidden from view.

In spite of the surrounding soldiers, there's a murmur across the crowd. Fuschious's face turns a deeper shade of red. "Silence!" he screams. "You will not leave this room until I am satisfied with your discipline. Do you hear me?"

A murmur ripples across the crowd again, and the Love Squad soldiers bristle. Keeping his face turned toward the nearest Love Squad soldiers, Hodge pushes me gently back toward the lifts. "Go," he says.

"What about you?" I ask. I reach for him, as if his presence can keep me from panicking. He dislodges my hand and takes a step away. I make another grab, but he turns to me, face solemn but eyes gentle.

"Don't lose it now," he says firmly. His eyes point me to the lift door.

"But you'll be punished for being late," I hiss.

Hodge shrugs. "We will be okay."

I can tell he's nervous, so I don't believe him. "If you go in now, you'll just make a scene, and Fuschious will discipline you for sure. What are you going to do if he Realigns you?"

Hodge pauses, his face conflicted. In his expression I can see his Love Squad training battle against his Siren identity. Of course he would want to bravely step up. But what would that achieve? We all remember what happened to Sif after her Realignment.

I look my companions in the eyes. "Either we all go in," I say, nodding to the crowd. "Or we all wait."

Hodge studies my face. Then he nods and turns back to the elevators. "Go," he hisses, ushering me ahead to the waiting lifts.

PART 1

1

A note, as your graduation approaches.

Congratulate yourselves, Elites, for you have endured until the end.

The riches of the Collective now lie before you. Yours is truly the destiny of the Elite. Rejoice, my Lovelies, for those who persevere can finally enjoy the full reward they have worked so long to deserve.

I love you all, I mean it.

Love all.

Be all.

—Supreme Lover Midgate

THEY TELL ME MY NAME IS KERR FLICK, ELITE Apprentice #540/187503. They tell me I belong to the Love Collective—body, mind, and soul—for as long as I shall live. A life that begins and ends at the Love Collective's pleasure.

But I'm not who they say I am. Not the obedient little acolyte learning their Hater-Recognition signs. Not the clean-marching dorm student who gets straight As in every Collective subject. No, I belong to a different place. In that country, my true name is Cadence. In that country, I can soar on wings of Song, high above the marches and the rules and the nightmares. I'm not an Apprentice. I'm a Siren. A daughter of the great Composer of the Universe. And I carry a priceless treasure no government could ever steal.

In the beginning was the Lyric . . .

I won't be what they tell me I should be. And as long as the Composer's Muse sings his Song in my heart, I won't die when they say I should, either.

I SQUINT DOWN AT THE RECTANGULAR GLASS console, trying to bring as much relief as I can to my dry and sore eyes without actually having to close them. My final exam is only a week away. If I'm going to get into the Hall of Love Coding group, I'll need perfect marks. But hours of squinting at a screen is hard. My eyes feel like they're covered in sand.

It's okay to take a break, you know, the Muse chides softly in my head. I snort, then look around to see if anyone noticed.

The seniors' Coding Center is full but silent, save for the soft finger-taps on consoles and the occasional tinny beats emanating from an Apprentice's headset. Nobody wants to be interrupted, which is why I picked this room instead of my usual one. When I'm in the same room as Cam or Chu, they're usually too chatty to let me concentrate properly.

I'm just about to begin another exercise when there's a knock at the Coding room doorway. I look up. Sif is at the entrance, her face stony. When she catches my eye and beckons to me, my heart immediately sinks.

"You know, Sif," I say, closing up my console. "It would be so, *so* nice if you were here because you missed me."

Sif smiles. "You know I'm far too busy and important to miss you." Her words are gruff, but the way her eyes twinkle tells me she's joking. I am relieved. I see her far less now that our accommodation is in our separate cadres. But she comes on these little errands regularly enough for me to see that she's "old Sif" more often.

"What does he want this time?" I ask. We both know who *he* is.

Sif's mouth turns down in a grim frown. "Didn't say."

I sigh. "Let's go then."

Sif leads me in a wordless march down the halls of the Coding cadre, heading for the executive wing. Akela's office is forgotten and abandoned now. Since taking his place as Dorm Leader, Fuschious expanded his quarters into the original leadership wing of the Academy, telling everyone that Akela's taste was too austere for a true Dorm Leader anyway. But that's probably a good thing. I don't know how I'd cope if I had to see Fuschious sitting where Akela should be.

"So how're things?" I ask, breaking the uncomfortable silence.

"Good. Hard to believe we'll be out of here in a hundred days."

"A hundred and six, to be exact. Do you know where you're going yet?"

We pass a small group of Coders, and Sif marches more forcefully down the corridor until we leave them behind us. Then she speaks to me out of the corner of her mouth, still swinging her arms in Love Squad march formation.

"We have to wait for finals to get confirmation. But I'm pretty sure I'll be on street patrols first. Then into Love City Officers' League."

"Will you get those burgers?" I ask, remembering a conversation we had back in our first year. Back before Sif's Realignment. "I hear the officers' league gets pretty good treatment."

Sif starts. "You remember that?" She rolls her eyes. "Of course you would." She smiles wistfully. "I would like to be able to try a burger one day."

Another group of Coders emerges from a nearby console room, and Sif slows her march.

"Flick," she says, glancing around to make sure the others aren't in earshot.

A small flutter of anxiety makes me look carefully at her expression. But I can't see any hint of the militant Sif of old. "Yes?" I say.

She chews at her bottom lip. "There was something I wanted to ask you, but—"

We have reached a small white airlock of sliding doors, which marks the boundary of the Coders' wing of the Academy. The first layer of doors slides open with a soft beep, and Sif shakes her head. "Never mind," she says.

I want to ask her to keep talking, but we are about to enter the Dorm Leader's wing. Fuschious watches every inch of the floors here. Even if all Sif wanted was to ask about the weather, I have no desire to be interrogated for hours about why I prefer sun to clouds. Okay, so maybe that's a small exaggeration. But I still won't speak in this part of Elite Academy unless I absolutely have to.

The second bank of sliding doors whooshes open, announcing our entrance into the opulent quarters of our current Dorm Leader. As we do, we swap the smell of polished concrete for the carefully synthesised scent of old sandalwood and cinnamon. Walls of gold-leaf wallpaper shimmer in fan-like patterns, and the carpet below our feet is a deep, plush black. Fuschious never was subtle. Everything here reeks of luxury.

I keep my facial expression carefully neutral. Fuschious has already questioned me many times, and I'm familiar with his psychotic ways. There's rarely a reason he calls me in. He probably just felt like humiliating someone today, and I was the first to come to mind.

Composer, keep me safe, I pray silently as we reach the reception lobby. The Muse doesn't reply in words, but I'm nudged by a quiet sense of peace. I nearly smile.

At the reception desk near the lifts, a prim, young Apprentice sits in silence like a robot on standby. She springs to her feet as we approach, clasping her hands in front of her. From memory, her name is Nym, and she's been seconded into Fuschious's service for almost a year now.

"Can I help you?" she says, starting forward. Then she sees me, and a knowing look appears in her eyes.

Sif cocks her thumb upward, and the girl nods. "He is in his office."

We march past into a waiting elevator.

My anxiety level rises as we ascend. The lift doors open directly into his reception room, and I take a deep breath to calm myself before the onslaught. Sif is silent beside me, but judging by her expression, I know she's as unimpressed as I am.

Richly decorated, the entire space is designed with intimidation in mind. The room is vast enough to host a hundred people. A long, wide line of polished timber floor forms an aisle down the center of the thick black carpet. Light sconces along the walls beam down on larger-than-life photos. Every image shows Fuschious shaking hands with important people: members of the Executive like Crucible and Munsch, celebrities like Carell Hummer, and even a gaggle of scantily clad Triumph dancers. In between these large, black-lined frames lie glass cases of various weapons, some looking ancient, but all lethal. It feels more like a poorly curated art gallery than the office of Elite Academy's most senior Lover.

Two mannequins on stone plinths stand against each wall at the halfway point of the room. One is dressed in a strange suit made of panels of metal, and the other is dressed in a Love Squad uniform, complete with utility belt and solid black helmet. They loom over our heads as we pass, and I battle against the weird feeling that they're staring at me.

At the far end of the room, Fuschious's ridiculously sized desk sits on a dais. The steps leading up to this are covered with the furry black pelt of an unfamiliar animal. I know it's an animal pelt because a head yawns out at us from the front, all sharp teeth and hostile yellow glass eyes. The desk is covered in gold, with large gold studs around the edges.

The Dorm Leader sits in an oversized obsidian chair that I'm guessing is designed to look like a throne, but which makes him look like a small child sitting in an adult's seat. "You're late," Fuschious growls.

As usual, he watches us approach with his glittering, beady-eyed stare. I notice quietly that his paunch has grown over the years, and the places where his muscles had previously bulged from his uniform are now looking fleshy and soft. If I were more ignorant of his behaviour, I'd take this as evidence he's grown lazy. But I've had too much experience in this office to fall for that.

"My apologies, Dorm Leader," I say, saluting with all the accuracy and primness I can muster. "I came as soon as I was summoned."

"Not good enough," he snaps.

"I embrace myself in penitence, Dorm Leader." I bow my head and wait for the inevitable blade to fall.

Fuschious makes a dissatisfied clicking noise in the back of his throat and leaves me in that posture for a few moments.

"Apprentice Grohns, you may wait below," he says eventually.

"As you wish, Dorm Leader. Love all. Be all." Sif snaps to attention, and then marches back to the elevator with staccato movements. My mood darkens a little when I hear the faint whine of the elevator that takes her away. Just because I know Fuschious's tactics too well doesn't mean I like any of them.

"You know why I've brought you here," he begins.

I do not reply. By now I know better than to try and guess his reasons. It only ever doubles the punishment I have to deal with later.

Soft strains of melody continue to flow through my memory, and I let them fill my thoughts. My body may be in the Dorm

Leader's vast office, but my mind is an eternity away, soaring through the skies with Lyric and the Sirens. I can tell this displeases Fuschious.

His face reddens. "You can't be that stupid, Apprentice."

"I apologise, Dorm Leader," I say, keeping my voice steady. It's not defiant—at least I hope it isn't—but I won't back down and cower before him like he wants me to. "I am ready to hear what you have to say."

Fuschious takes a deep breath, and the fatalistic thought flutters in: *Here we go.*

"You call yourself a Watcher?" Fuschious sneers.

"Coder."

"What?" His voice is as sharp as the crack of a whip.

"I have not been a Watcher for three years, Dorm Leader." I stand straight, holding myself carefully still.

Fuschious's eyes narrow. "Oh yes. How could I forget that? Well." He stands, resting his fists on the table in front of him. "You should know better than to be insolent to your Dorm Leader." His gaze is hostile, and his beady eyes seem to be daring me to try and argue. This is what he really wants.

I don't answer. I know he's going to escalate soon, and if I can avoid purposely inflaming him, perhaps I'll get off more easily than usual.

Fuschious barks out loudly enough to echo in the wide room. "Twenty. Now."

"Yes, Dorm Leader," I reply, dropping to the ground. Thanks to years of hard practice and more than one visit to this office, this command is nothing. I complete them smoothly.

"Forty."

I grit my teeth and reply to the floor. "Yes, Dorm Leader." I guess today's a make-Cadence-sweat day. Better than a yell-at-Cadence-for-an-hour day, though. Or a threaten-Cadence-with-Realignment day. Or worse.

My pace slows.

"More," Fuschious commands again. I struggle through, arms burning and sweat pouring down my face. Whenever I look like stopping, he commands me again. "Keep going."

"How many?" I gasp.

"I'll tell you when you're done."

Feeling a sick, sinking feeling in the pit of my stomach, I begin again. Sweat drips down my back and glistens on my arms. The Song in the back of my head is the only thing stopping me from bursting into frustrated tears. Finally, unable to continue, I collapse to the floor.

A boot lands firmly in the small of my back, forcing the air from my lungs. "Pathetic." Fuschious's voice is harsh and scratchy. "I knew you were a failure the moment I laid eyes on you."

I am too exhausted to reply. The boot grinds itself deeper, and it's only thanks to exhaustion that I don't cry out in pain. After a few agonising moments he lifts his foot, leaving a weird, weightless feeling where it had been.

"Get up," he commands. I force myself into a standing position. Every muscle down my shoulders and arms aches, and my heart feels like it's going to explode from my chest. But I push my chin up, looking somewhere past Fuschious's left shoulder so I don't have to make eye contact.

There's silence for a few moments, then Fuschious begins to walk a slow circle around me, his hands clasped behind his back.

"You're no Elite," he mutters. I bite my tongue.

After circling around me, he comes to a stop behind me. "Weak," he snarls. I remain carefully still, hoping my breathing will slow soon. A small bead of cold sweat trickles down the side of my face.

"Nothing to say for yourself?"

"No, Dorm Leader."

"Figures." His thick fingers suddenly clasp my neck, and against my will I let out a shocked gasp.

"I could snap this little neck with one twist. Do you know that, Apprentice?" His voice is oily with satisfaction. I clamp my jaw shut as his grip tightens slightly. "Just give me one reason. Haters, I don't even need a reason. I'm the Dorm Leader."

"You may do as you please, Dorm Leader," I say through clenched teeth. "But wouldn't the Watchers have something to say about that? You killing a decorated Apprentice and all."

I hate bringing it up, but my get-out-of-Realignment card has always been the award Crucible gave me for averting the Triumph bomb attack. Sure enough, Fuschious's grip loosens, and his hand drops away.

"Get out."

"Yes, Dorm Leader. Love all. Be all." I salute and turn with crisp steps to head for the elevator.

Even Dorm Leader Fuschious is afraid of the Watchers.

2

Without the influence of Haters, the Love Collective is one big, happy family. You are all my Lovelies, and I am your Parent.
      -Supreme Lover Midgate,
            Intimate Diaries of a Loving Leader, *chapter 13*

WHEN I REACH THE FLOOR WHERE SIF IS waiting, I keep on marching, not willing to delay a single second longer than I have to. She catches up.

"That was dangerous," Sif says when we're finally out of the Executive wing.

"Only one hundred and six days until we graduate," I reply.

"Mmmm."

"Can you believe they're sending us out into the world?" I say as we pass another Coding lab. "I feel like I've lived in a dorm room forever."

"Almost," Sif mumbles. Something in her tone makes me turn to look at her.

"What?"

She shakes her head. "Oh, it's nothing."

"Not with that tone of voice," I say brightly. "What's up?"

She slows to a stop, and I hang back. Her expression is thoughtful and sad, and she stares off into the distance. For a few seconds, I see the Sif I used to know: young, intelligent, sure there was something wrong in the Collective. Of course, she was Realigned. But her suspicions had been right all along. There *was* something wrong in the Collective. Something I discovered when my earliest memories returned.

"Are you okay?" I ask gently. I haven't seen Sif like this in years.

She looks up at me, eyes haunted. "Kerr . . . I . . ." A range of emotions flashes across her face: confusion, anger, hopelessness. Then the haunted expression returns, and she looks away. "I'm sorry."

"For what?" I say.

"I think . . . For a while there, I think I stopped being me."

Unsure of what to say, I just wait. Whatever happened in that sterile Realignment lab changed her whole personality into something machine-like and aggressive. Even now I'm not sure I can trust her.

"I should get back to my study." I stare down the corridor, which gently curves away.

After a couple more seconds staring into the distance down the hall, Sif gives herself a little shake. "Yeah. Whatever. I'm sorry for reporting you, anyway," she says gruffly. Then she marches off.

I watch her go, wondering what just happened. Was that a setup? Or did I just miss an opportunity to get my old friend back?

CAM THUMPS WORDLESSLY DOWN INTO HIS Coding room chair, causing it to swivel sideways a little too hard. He rides it back into place like a Haters' Pavilion performer, gripping the sides of his console with familiar expertise while he wheels himself beneath it.

"Okay, where we at today?" He squints at the screen, which illuminates his face in a ghostly grey light.

"Tweaks to the Triumph security protocols," I say, flicking a screen over to him. "There's an exploit in sector 47 that someone might be able to piggyback into."

"Using the Things again?" Cam raises one eyebrow. I nod, which brings a knowing look to his face. "Which one this time?" he asks.

"Popcorn temperature gauges," I reply. "I worked out that they can backdoor into the surveillance system if they hack the remote thermostat."

"Another day, another leak to plug," he remarks. "First one to fix it buys the other one dinner."

"You're funny." I give him a mock scowl. "We both know you'd be the one buying."

"Ouch." He winces. "You know how to wound a guy."

I smirk. "You know who always wins."

"Only for another ninety days. Then you're out in the Collective, and I'm off to an infotab-game company far, far, far away from any of your Coding superpower megabrain things."

"You should have worked harder for last week's exam." I wink at him.

Cam gives me a deadpan look. "Nobody could come close to your marks even if we studied every night for a year."

"Aw, you're too kind." I grin. "I'll miss this banter when we've graduated."

A screen from Cam lands on my display, showing a little cartoon Midgate blowing kisses.

"Not like that," I say, pushing it away.

Cam's voice is resigned. "You gotta give a guy points for trying."

"You should have found yourself a nice Engine Roomer by now, Cam. I've been telling you that for years."

"And miss the fun of our arguments? Not a chance." Cam laughs, but I throw him a worried look, and he shrugs back at me. "Don't mind me. I'll get over you when we graduate and

I'm finally allowed to find some other Elite to settle down with. You're not *that* unforgettable."

"Whatever. I've almost fixed the problem anyway," I say with a wicked smile.

"Ugh. Should have known." Cam throws his hands up in the air. "Why do I even bother?" He sighs, laying an arm across his eyes in an over-dramatic gesture.

I wait for a few seconds longer than necessary before I say, "Done."

"Of course you are."

Closing down the dialog box on my console, I flick over to the task list. "Ha!" I stretch my arms above my head. "Finished for the day and it's not even 1100."

"I'll send over one of mine, if you like," Cam says hopefully.

"Well, I'm supposed to report to the Lovers' desk when I finish, but—"

"They're sick of you," Cam finishes. "Go on. You could use something to fill the time until drill practice."

"You know how they feel about me taking your tasks."

He raises an eyebrow. "Ninety days."

I stare up at the darkened ceiling for a few seconds, deliberating. Take the task, and I don't have to face the eye rolls and exaggerated insults from the Lovers' room. Don't take the task, and I sit here twiddling my thumbs for an hour.

"Send it through." I flick my message app open.

Cam lets out a small whoop of triumph, and then taps his screen. "I knew you'd come through. You're the best."

A little red notification pops up in my inbox, and I open it. But instead of Cam's name in the message, it's someone else.

EXECUTIVE LOVER CRUCIBLE: I hear congratulations are in order. Well done on your final exam.

I stare stupidly at the message for a moment. Then, as if I'm watching myself from a distance, my fingers move to reply.

APPRENTICE #540/187503: Thank you, Executive Lover. May you follow your dreams and find yourself in the universe.

I've barely pressed Enter when the reply swings back.

EXECUTIVE LOVER CRUCIBLE: I am told by a reliable source that due to your unprecedented scores, you are to be assigned straight into the Hall of Love Coding team.

APPRENTICE #540/187503: That is correct, Executive Lover.

EXECUTIVE LOVER CRUCIBLE: Would you like some extra practice in preparation for your new assignment?

APPRENTICE #540/187503: I am happy to obey, Executive Lover.

EXECUTIVE LOVER CRUCIBLE: Oh, come now. No need to be so formal, Apprentice.

APPRENTICE #540/187503: I apologize, Executive Lover.

EXECUTIVE LOVER CRUCIBLE: I am sending you an example of the kind of code you will be dealing with in here. Be warned: the complexity of this code is far greater than most of the material you have been dealing with thus far. But I want to make sure you can handle the assignment.

APPRENTICE #540/187503: I will do my best, Executive Lover.

EXECUTIVE LOVER CRUCIBLE: Don't give me any excuse to be upset with you.

APPRENTICE #540/187503: I won't, Executive Lover.

EXECUTIVE LOVER CRUCIBLE: Good. Find the exploit in this code, and I will be satisfied.

APPRENTICE #540/187503: Yes, Executive Lover.

Shortly after my reply, an attachment arrives in my inbox, labelled with a long, incomprehensible serial number for a name. I move it into my console app and watch as the waterfall of code scrolls down the screen.

For a few minutes I flick it forward and backward, savoring the view as if I'm exploring a new part of Love City. I quickly stop seeing symbols and commands and start seeing the structures behind it. I see locked doors and security code consoles, which begin to give me a mental picture of rooms and halls and camera arrays. Behind the numbers are spaces, the codes a window into a place I have only visited once, but still remember as if it were this morning.

MEMORY DATE: 2282.307 (FIVE YEARS AGO)

Memory Location: Train station elevator

"If it does not trouble you, Executive Lover, I was wondering if you could tell us where we are?" Hodge stands beside me, looking innocently at Executive Lover Crucible. It's only because I know him better now that I can tell he's nervous by the tension in his posture.

Crucible's eyebrows shoot up in surprise. "Did Dorm Leader not tell you?" he asks insincerely. The predatory smile on his face chills me to the bone. "Ah, yes. That's right. She had some ridiculous plan as to how you needed to witness Triumph preparations, blah blah blah." He waves his hand dismissively. "I had a much better idea."

At that moment, the lift doors open onto an expansive glass-and-concrete half dome. Four times the size of our assembly atrium, the far walls curve overhead in a lattice of laser-carved beams. Sunlight streams down on the polished concrete floor like glittering jewels. Opposite the outer dome wall and to our left, a vision screen as high as an apartment block projects the Supreme Executive's faces, intermingled with scenes of Love Collective Triumph and slogans.

Love always Triumphs.

Haters will never succeed.

Love all. Be all.

Outside the dome and across a vast stone courtyard, a blindingly white building towers high above us.

"Welcome to the Hall of Love," Crucible says, his wizened face wrinkling in a wide, benevolent smile.

3

A faithful Lover submits to the will of the Collective.
Learn in quietness, children. Be silent and live.
     -Supreme Lover Midgate

AS I TRY AND GET MY BEARINGS IN THE CODE
Crucible sent, I get an excited thrill. I'm not just looking at the
Hall of Love. I'm looking at a small portion where security is at the
highest level possible.

"Where exactly *is* this?" I wonder even as the answer floats in
front of my face. I scroll back and forth, travelling in my mind's eye
through invisible corridors and door locks. Suddenly, I catch sight
of a small block of code that sends my mind reeling. It's not that
the code is difficult to understand. It's the name that I find there:
MIDGATE.

"What the—" I scroll back and forth again. What exactly am I
looking at right now?

"Have you seen this?" I ask out loud, sending my screen to the
center of the room. The code glows in the air in the center of the
console chairs, drifting downward in slow, elegant streams. Cam
squints at it for a few seconds, then his face goes slack.

"What . . . wait." His voice quivers with alarm. "That's not what
I think it is, is it?"

"Don't worry. It's read-only."

"No way." Cam shakes his head, disbelieving. "Someone actually gave you permission to look at Midgate's security protocol?"

"Yeah." I don't tell him that Crucible personally sent the code to my inbox. My initial excitement has begun to fade into anxious jitters. What is Crucible playing at, giving me this?

Cam swallows nervously. "I'm just looking at supply-chain infiltrations. But you . . ." He shakes his head again. "You went for the center of the entire Collective just for *fun*?"

It's my turn to shrug. "Apparently I need a decent project if I'm going to confirm the Hall job."

"Speechless." Cam stares at the code, wide-eyed and wondering.

"It's not like I'm looking at *her* or anything. It's just the protocol around the edges of her security detail. I can't see people in there."

Cam looks a little mollified. "Still."

"Cam." I tilt my head at him. "Code that stops fanboy nutjobs from tracking our Supreme Leader is not exactly *that* big a deal."

"'Fanboy nutjobs'? What are you—like four hundred years old or something?"

"You're just jealous because you don't get to research Hall of Love code." I turn back to the code fragment I've been working on.

As I flick the code upward again, another small subscript catches my eye. "What's that doing there?" I mutter under my breath. With a single tap of my finger, I take the script off the central screen so Cam can't see what I've just discovered.

"That shouldn't—" *Shouldn't be there*—at least, not in that part of the Hall of Love. I stare at it, dumbfounded. The anomaly stares back. Cold, creeping fear breaks out in a clammy sweat across the back of my neck. I check the script again, just to make sure I'm not imagining things.

Unaware of what I'm feeling, Cam hams it up, slinking his shoulders down and pretending to bow and dip his head. "You keep coding the big stuff, Apprentice Bigshot. Us app monkeys gots to find our supper where's we can."

I laugh a little too loudly. "You're funny." But I abruptly cut the laughter off. "Get back to work." My throat feels as if it's constricting, and I swallow hard to try and clear the fear out of it.

He keeps joking, but I ignore him until his chatter quiets. I'm too busy trying to process.

It can't be. But it is. Why would Crucible send this to an Apprentice? Mind whirling with questions and panic, I lift my hands to dig deeper into the Hall of Love code. Just as my fingers reach the glass, something stops me.

Not here.

Obedient to the warning, I shut down my console and stand.

"Sorry that I didn't get to help you with your list." I smile at Cam. "But I remembered . . . uh . . . something I have to do."

Cam just grunts, and I dash from the room, snatching the console's portable screen as I go.

MEMORY DATE: 2285.011 (THREE YEARS AGO)
Memory Location: Secret bunker

"Hodge, what do we do?" Allegra's voice is tremulous. Her legs jiggle wildly, and her eyes dart from side to side as if the Love Squad is going to jump through concrete walls at any moment.

Fife nods, looking nervously at the door of our bunker meeting room. "Without Akela here, who's going to protect us?"

Hodge's chair makes a little squeaking noise on the concrete when he leans forward. "The Composer will be with us no matter what happens," he says. In the dim reddish light, the scar on his cheek is a streak of shadow.

"But Fuschious will find us and Realign us," Allegra says, voice rising to a high, thin wail. "We can't keep meeting here."

"Allegra, I know it's scary." I reach out to pat her shoulder. "But panic will only make them find us faster."

She looks at me with tearful eyes, and I have a sudden urge to give her a reassuring hug. But she shifts away slightly, so I don't bother. I haven't been her favourite person since . . . well, since Hodge and I started going on City missions.

"You're right, though, Allegra," Hodge says. "We need to lie low for a while until we know exactly what's going on. This will be our final meeting until I'm sure we can get together safely."

"But—" Piccolo blurts. "We need the Song. I need the Song right now. Especially the fragment Cadence brought us last week."

Hodge shakes his head. "It's only temporary."

"It's a coward's way out," Piccolo insists. "I want to keep meeting. The Composer would want us to keep meeting."

"I want to keep meeting as well, Piccolo." I try to keep my voice calm and pleasant. I see Hodge stiffen in his seat, so I keep going quickly. "But Fuschious is on the warpath. He's only been in that office four days, and he's already sent thirty-eight people to Realignment."

"Not even our thoughts are safe," Allegra says miserably.

"It's not that bad." Piccolo leans back in his chair. "Fuschious is all muscle, no brain. We could parade a Siren group under his nose, and he'd never see us."

"Don't be foolish," Fife warns. "If he's smart enough to topple Dorm Leader Akela, he's smart enough to find us."

"The Composer will keep us hidden," Piccolo continues stubbornly.

Fife frowns. "Did he keep our parents hidden?"

"Yeah, Piccolo." Allegra's voice trembles even more. "If the Composer was going to keep us hidden, why has Akela gone?" She pauses, wiping her cheeks where tears have begun to fall.

Piccolo opens his mouth to argue, but Hodge raises a hand to stop him. "It doesn't matter where or why she's gone," Hodge says. "Now that Fuschious is in charge, we take extra safety precautions.

Stick to the Siren message app and be extra careful about accessing it. I will send a message when it's safe to meet again. We're going to need to stagger leaving here tonight, so enact the highest level of caution you can."

Piccolo frowns, but nods. Allegra relaxes a little in her seat. Fife just sniffs, his face downcast and twisted like he's trying not to cry.

"I'm sorry, everyone," Hodge says. "I know this is hard."

"We should sing," I suggest, looking around the circle. "If this is the last time we're together for a while, let's sing our hearts out, so we won't forget."

They agree, and for the next hour, we let the harmonies burst from our mouths and hearts. We're half-hearted at first, overwhelmed by loss and fear. But slowly, surely, the Muse leaves us with the Composer's quiet presence, soothing and comforting. Our voices quake and our eyes are wet, but by the time we leave the meeting, we know we have been seen.

"It's going to be okay," Hodge assures us as we finish. "Even if we have to take the Exodus, we will be okay."

HUGGING THE CONSOLE SCREEN TO MY CHEST, I wander down the Coding cadre's central hallway, seeking a brief ray of sunshine. Thick soundproofed doors line the white-walled hall, their high windows darkened to protect the displays and equipment within. Occasionally students leave a door open, and I catch a brief glimpse of glowing screens and console tables. But for the most part the entire wing is silent.

At the end of the hall, I take the elevator down to ground level and emerge in the Coders' lounge. The colors here are mostly grey, with vivid green pinstripe decorations around the walls and along the furniture. Groups of two-seater couches gather around rectangular console tables, and every armrest contains an infotab charging station. I hurry past these, heading for the tinted glass doors at the end of the room. The hedges beyond the walkway outside are vague, nearly invisible shadows through the smoky glass wall. It's meant to keep the atmosphere perfect for working on screens, but to me it just feels dark and sleepy.

As I reach the exit, Chu enters into the lounge through the rotating door. I step aside to let him through.

"Hey!" He smiles and stops. "Where are you off to?"

Hiding my frustration, I wave my console screen at him. "Need some sunshine, so I'm taking my work out to the grass."

Chu brightens and does a quick about-face. "I only came in because I didn't want to be alone out there. I'll join you."

My heart sinks, but I try and cover it with a smile. "Sure."

We let the rotating doors spit us out onto the footpath, and I cover my eyes. I've been indoors so much lately that my eyes hurt when they meet actual light. When I hurry into the shady, tree-lined avenue, I'm met with a cool burst of air that initially makes me regret leaving the warm rooms inside. But I have to find somewhere to take a closer look at this code, and the overwhelming presence of cameras indoors makes that impossible.

I shiver. "I can see why you were leaving this place," I say to Chu and hug my infotab to my chest again. "It's freezing!"

Chu gestures ahead and quickens his pace. "It's way better in the sunshine."

As we hurry along the shady paths, Chu rubs his arms. "Why is it so cold? It's nearly Triumph season."

Having Chu mention the festival brings another rush of memories.

MEMORY DATE: 2285.348 (TWO AND A HALF *years ago*)

Memory Location: Obstacle course

After lots of hints and too many hours of waiting, I have convinced Hodge to meet me on the obstacle course. My heart is fluttering like a malfunctioning LED, and my instincts are urging me to run away. But I'm not leaving until I've said what I brought him here to say.

"I know you're graduating soon," I begin falteringly. "A-and I won't get to see you after that. So . . . I, uh . . . I was wondering if you would be my Triumph buddy this year," I say, my voice high and reedy with nerves.

Hodge's smile is half hidden in shadow. "Thank you for the offer, but I don't think I'd like to be your Triumph buddy."

It feels as if I've been punched in the gut. "I thought we were . . . I thought . . ." My protest sounds far more desperate than I want it to, and I curse myself inwardly. If he wasn't smiling at me right now, I'd be running in shame for my dorm room.

All this time we've been friends. I thought I had finally worked out that he was interested in me. The way he asked me how I was, the way he always seemed to make space for me in Siren meetings, even the way he kept on looking at me all the time. But now he's rejected me?

He steps toward me. "I don't want a couple of weeks."

"Hey! What are you guys doing?" Fife's voice calls from the distance. I turn to see him heading through the trees. It's almost impossible to see his expression in the darkness, but he doesn't sound happy. "You shouldn't be out here at this time of night. It's dangerous."

Hodge spins to face him. "Just talking," he calls. He turns back to me. "Can we talk later?"

I nod, feeling dejected. "I guess."

Your Supreme Lover desires to bring you the best life possible. You are her only flesh and blood. You, her nearest and dearest Loves.
  –Supreme Lover Midgate,
    Intimate Diaries of a Loving Leader, *chapter 13*

I SWALLOW HARD AND LOOK AT THE WIDE path ahead, dappled with sunlight filtered through the avenue of trees. I can't wait to get out of this place. "Ninety days," I say under my breath.

"What?" Chu asks, startled.

I shake my head. "Nothing."

We emerge from the tree-covered path onto a grassy hill near the center of the Academy. Bright sunlight streams down on the grass. I lower myself to the ground, feeling the soft prickle of turf beneath me. The ground is warm, and my fingertips begin to thaw a little. I open up the console and log back into the script I was working on earlier.

"We're graduating soon." Chu lies back on the grass, closing his eyes with his face turned toward the sun. "You really don't need to keep working so hard."

"What do you think of this?" I ask, handing over the screen for him to see.

He opens one eye. "What do I think of what?" Reluctantly, he reaches for it and blinks at the screen.

I point at a small paragraph. "That section of code. What do you think it is?"

He purses his lips. "Looks like a standard—"

Chu's words disappear under a loud screech from across the field.

"Pathetic. Utterly pathetic!" the familiar voice shouts.

I look over to see a small group of Apprentices standing to attention in two straggly lines. Dorm Leader Fuschious prowls up and down the lines, his face livid. His screech brings back hundreds of similar memories, none of them pleasant.

"What do you think you are doing?" His yell is so harsh that there's a collective flinch along the shoulders of the recruits.

The new Elite Apprentices stand cowed as Fuschious struts along the line in front of them. Even at this distance, I can see the fury knitted into his brows. The flourish of golden embroidery down the front of his linen suit only serves as a sickly contrast to the red flush along the line of his bulging neck.

Looking hungrily at the frightened faces, he gesticulates at them. "You are the worst group of freshers I have ever seen in my life!" I notice a smaller Apprentice at one end of the line who looks like he is about to burst into tears.

"What a welcome." Chu's dry sarcasm is a contrast to the carefully neutral expression on his face. Handing me back the console screen, he sits up and dusts off fragments of grass from the legs of his uniform. "Is it just me, or are there more recruit groups lately?"

"He's bringing them in every fifteen days now. Remember being there?" I ask, watching as the recruits start a vigorous exercise routine at Fuschious's command.

"Glad we don't have to do that anymore. Why so many new ones?"

"It takes a strong Elite to survive Fuschious's training

regimen. My guess is there are lots more dropouts." I'm too busy staring at the infotab screen to say much more. "This code—"

Chu is still distracted by the new recruits, so he's slow to turn and look. "Oh, that. It's standard AI boundary protocol, isn't it? Keep the robot in their proper playpen. Can't see any errors in it, if that's what you're asking."

"I'm not. It's just—"

A note in my voice brings Chu's attention sharply to me. "What?"

Quickly shutting off the console, I bite the inside of my cheek. "Nothing."

Out of the corner of my eye, I can see Chu staring at me, but I don't turn toward him. I shield my eyes, pretending that the freshers' exercises are suddenly the most fascinating thing I've ever seen.

"Flick, exactly what are you working on?"

I put on my best reassuring smile and pat him on the knee. "Nothing you need to get all worked up about," I say. "So don't start imagining things."

His eyes narrow. "You're not hacking into secure records, are you?"

I don't have to pretend to be shocked. "Me? No!" I gasp. "That's illegal!"

Chu relaxes, but he doesn't take his eyes away from me. "Good. Because I'd hate to have to report you."

I laugh. "I'm not going to disobey the fundamental Coding rules," I say. There's a tremble in my voice that I wish I could stop. "You'd have to have a death wish to even try that."

He relaxes back into the grass, letting his legs stretch out in front of him. "I just had to check. That's all."

"You're a good citizen. But so am I." Doing my best to slow my racing heartbeat, I count to one hundred in my head, then quietly stand. "Anyway, I think that's enough sun for this afternoon. Catch you inside?"

Chu nods. "Sure."

"Don't you have coding to do?"

He closes his eyes again, face up at the sun. "I've already started my posting. They're taking me out to the warehouses this afternoon."

"Oh. Well, have fun then." I leave him leaning back in the grass.

Chu's words have only confirmed the scary suspicions I've had since that code came in. To be honest, I don't know what I was expecting, exactly. Maybe something that looked after her private quarters, entrances in and out, personnel shifts, and so on. Instead, I find something that shouldn't be there at all.

Why does the Supreme Lover's security look more like it's protecting a server room than a human residence?

Lyric, what did I get myself into?

MEMORY DATE: 2285.009 (THREE YEARS AGO)

Memory Location: Secret bunker

Hodge, Loa, Yip, and I gather together in Akela's underground office, which seems unchanged apart from the load of trash that has been strewn across her desk. Papers are piled high on the mahogany surface in untidy heaps. Books and ledgers are spread among them, lounging against the piles in a haphazard fashion. It looks as if it was dumped in a hurry.

Hodge sits in Akela's chair, staring at a spot just beyond the end of her desk. Loa leans against the wall, his arms folded and head bowed dejectedly. Yip walks slowly along the bookcase at the back of the room, dragging her finger across the surface of the shelves. She rubs the dust between thumb and forefinger, then flicks it away.

"A transfer?" Loa asks.

Yip nods. "That's what they told us. Crucible sent her down to a Nursery Dorm out in one of the backwater regions."

I flop down into the visitor's chair, leaning back against the seat cushion and staring up at the concrete beams above my head. "So what now?"

Since Akela's always been the one with the answers, nobody responds. We just keep on staring. The absence of our leader is like a presence of its own in the room. It forms a whole bunch of spaces where she should be, but isn't. It's even behind the door that leads into the bunker residences, as if she's standing back there waiting to make a grand entrance. But we've already searched in there, and she wasn't anywhere to be found.

"Is there even anything we can do?" Yip asks.

"Nope," Loa says bluntly.

Hodge lifts up a few papers, letting them fall slowly through his hands. "We could look through these."

"Why?" Loa asks. "They're not likely to tell us where she's gone."

Yip doesn't look happy with his answer. "So we just wait for the Squads to arrest us?"

"At least she had time to hide them here," Hodge says, pointing at the piles of paper.

"Which is fine unless she's been arrested," Loa retorts. "Then even this place is going to be found out." He glares around at the concrete walls.

Yip starts up at that, fuming. "She hasn't been arrested."

Loa's look is withering. "You did listen to that speech of Fuschious up there, didn't you?"

Her eyes flash. "Fuschious would say anything to smear her reputation. Everyone knows he's a psychopath. She's been transferred." Yip is so angry she looks as if she's going to stamp her foot with impatience. Or punch Loa in the face, which I decide is more likely, given her personality.

"How about we have a look at the documents, just for the sake of it?" I suggest, standing. "If Akela left them here, it probably means she wanted them to be found by us. The least we could do is look over them."

Hodge sits up in Akela's chair. "Great idea."

Ignoring Loa's protests about Embracement, we start to file through the documents. After half an hour, Hodge suggests a kind of sorting system, and so we content ourselves with trying to organize documents into piles. We work in silence. Most of the pages are accounts and financial documents, but there are the occasional letters and pages of notes, which stops us all while one person reads out the contents. There's no mention of Lyric or the Sirens in any of them.

"Cadence!" Yip calls out after about an hour has passed. "This has your name on it."

Looking surprised, she holds out a thick envelope to me. I stare at it, a long and tedious accounts document still in my hand. Yip waggles the envelope at me. I reach out for it, dropping the other papers. The envelope is yellowed with age, but still smooth. Made of a good-quality vintage paper, it feels weighty in my hand. The name CADENCE is printed carefully in block letters on the front, but there's a small paragraph of handwritten scrawl beneath it:

> Your mother asked me to deliver this to you when you were ready, Cadence. If I'm not handing this to you personally, I am sorry. I have failed you. —A

My hand trembles. The thousands of memories of my Before

start to tumble through my head, and I'm transported back to my earliest childhood, watching my family through eyes that had seen no violence or loss.

"It's—it's a letter from Mumma," I manage to stammer. I look up at three faces, all of them looking back with sympathy. I feel a sharp prickle of tears at the corner of my eyes.

"Open it, Cadence," Loa says. "It must be important."

Hodge is around the side of the desk in a flash, guiding me to a chair. "You don't have to read it in front of us if you don't want to." He leans over to support me as I sit back in the seat.

I glance up at him and meet such kindness in his eyes that I want to hug him. "No," I say. "I think I need to read it now."

He nods, moving back to give me space.

I rip open the envelope and remove its contents. A small chain of silver snakes out of the envelope into my lap, pooling on my uniform. A familiar pendant lands in the middle of the pile, a flat circle of silver, containing a laser-cut tree with a small, stylized figure of a person's shadow on it.

Lyric's tree.

My heartbeat quickens, making my hands tremble a little more. So it takes me longer than necessary to unfold the pages of the letter. Eventually I manage to get it open and smooth the folds carefully against my leg. It is several pages long, scrawled in a hasty but neat hand.

My darling Cadence,
    If this letter is coming to you, it means that I must hand you into the care of the Composer, who loves you more than even I ever can. Do not grieve too much for me, my darling. For if you have this letter, it

means that I am gone into the care of Lyric himself, far from pain or suffering, with your father at last. It is sad to miss you growing, but I can trust in the Composer's goodness that he will not forsake you. One day we will meet again, and for that I am truly grateful.

Many of our people have joined the Exodus and have fled to safety far beyond the Collective walls. Your father and I decided to remain of our own free will. Your father paid dearly for our choice. But he did so, knowing that this life is not our forever home. There is a better country—Lyric's country—waiting for all of us if we persevere. Remember that.

There is so much more I want to say to you, sweet one. It breaks my heart to think that I may not have the privilege of seeing you grow into a faithful, strong young woman. But these are dark times in which we live, and so I must trust the Composer's strength. Remember Lyric always, my love. For in him alone is the true way.

Much love, my darling.
— Mumma xox

The words are already seared into my memory, but I read the letter several times more. Each time, I hear my mother's voice until it feels like she is here, speaking to me. Tears blur my eyes and stream down my cheeks. The words are precious and painful.

While I sit and feel sorry for myself, the others have been standing around in a little group, giving me space to read and cry. They flinch when I stand up in a rush.

"We can't let her just disappear," I say, voice hardening. "This isn't fair."

Yip steps forward, face alive with enthusiasm. "No, it's not. We need to take Fuschious down." Her hazel-colored eyes gleam with excitement.

Hodge seems unmoved. "That is not a good idea," he says, leaning against the desk with his arms folded.

Yip lets out a frustrated gasp. "But we can't just let him win. No matter what's happened to Akela. She should be standing up there, not him. He's used the squads to take over. Unless we do something, we'll never see her again. We need action."

Hodge stops her. "Yip, you know how well that went for Wil. You want to go down his path?"

She rubs at the stubby hair on top of her head, looking torn. "He failed because he tried to do it alone. If there were more of us, we might stand a chance."

"Wil didn't fail because he was alone," Hodge replies. "The Composer wouldn't let him kill all those people."

"Hodge is right," Loa says. "Akela wouldn't want us to start a rebellion."

"But if we do nothing, they'll win," Yip persists.

"Akela played the long game," Hodge reminds her.

"Yeah, and look where it got her," Yip argues. "Some little backwoods Nursery Dorm out in the boondocks."

I put the letter onto the desk. "We're not getting anywhere."

I turn toward the door. "When you guys have decided whether we're going to do anything at all, let me know."

I walk away from the table, my emotions in a complete mess. For so long, I've worked hard to place my feelings about my family into a neat little box—to seal them all away so I can function in Elite Academy. This letter has punctured my heart and left me bleeding.

"Cadence?" Hodge stills my hand as it reaches the doorknob.

I turn, feeling irritable that he's trying to stop me from escaping. "What?"

He holds up a silver chain, with Lyric's tree dangling from the end. "You forgot something."

"What do I do with that?" I ask. "It's not like I can wear it."

"Put it under your uniform," Loa says.

It's Yip's turn to scoff. "And then what? Get busted by the cameras?"

"What should we do with it?" Hodge asks me.

"Put it with Akela's copy. It's no use to me now."

"Wait. Akela had one of these?" Hodge asks, surprised.

I nod. "She showed it to me one day in her office. Back when she was testing my memory."

Loa lets out a low whistle. "It's not anywhere here."

My head feels heavy. I shrug and turn back to the door. "Well, when you find it, leave that one with it too."

5

And Lyric said to them,
"Sing, children. Sing.
You will never be enslaved while you have my voice."
Song Fragment 78.2

AFTER DINNER, WHEN MOST OF THE SENIORS
are celebrating their night off in the Coding atrium, I decide to
take a closer look at the Code. It's early Triumph season, with
all of its annual weirdness. In all the common areas, the air
crackles with a kind of nervous electricity. Apprentices, who are
normally forbidden to fraternise, are sizing one another up as
potential Triumph buddies, flirting and parading around. It's a
relief to walk away from all of that and head for the unoccupied
classrooms.

High in the Coders' wing, the specialist VR labs line a
central hallway, hidden behind soundproof doors with no
windows. Using my wrist ID, I scan the panel beside the first
door I find and enter. The lab is cool and quiet, save for the low
whisper of air through the climate-control vents.

Feeling strangely guilty, I step up to one of the vacant
stations. There's a console-sized slot in the wall, and I place the
glass rectangle I took from the Coding room into it. A small
dialog box flashes in white on the glass:

INITIALIZING SEQUENCE.

Fitting the slim grey VR glasses over my head, I step onto the platform, leaning back into the suspended saddle-like chair. Then I slide the gloves over my fingers and wait for the room to disappear.

Sure enough, the boot sequence flows across my screen, and then I'm in a dark cavern-like space, watching a waterfall of code in front of me. Soon, I'm in an acrobatic-like dance, moving fragments of code around the room with swirls and swishes of my hands. A pinch of my fingers here, and a small block of code changes color before enlarging. With a sideways nudge, I send it back into the waterfall, letting it pass by again.

The exploit that Crucible told me to find is almost too easy to spot, and I enlarge it in the air. It's only a tiny flaw, but with the right hacking skills, someone could sneak in to spy on the Executive's living rooms. Figuring that this is what Crucible wanted me to find, I copy it into the message system and send back my answer. But the rest of the code is so unsettling that I am reluctant to close it down just yet.

I let the code flow past several times, waiting for some kind of inspiration to tell me that I'm not seeing what I think I've seen. Yet every pass only reinforces my growing unease.

Holding both hands in front of me, I halt the flow, then use my hands to pull out another fragment. When I flick this fragment into the distance, it converts the commands into a rudimentary schematic. Soon, I'm standing on a virtual floorplan, and the placement of personnel and cameras shine in small red and yellow stars along the various routes. I avoid placing names on the spaces but I can tell what I'm looking at, anyway.

The uppermost floors of the Hall of Love are devoted to the living quarters of the Supreme Executive. I can tell by the coded labels attached to various security details. Cameras cover the halls so well that not even an insect could get near the doors without being seen. There are interesting blind spots in the inner rooms, but the schematics give every impression of a vast interior space for each member of the Executive. Far larger than the Watcher Dorm ever was.

The more I look, the less I understand. A huge amount of electricity is directed toward Midgate's quarters, but small amounts of space. It's the kind of thing a Coder would expect to see from a bank of large consoles or a server room. It looks nothing like the smaller energy drain I'd expect to see from a large human residence.

I'm imagining it, I think to myself, stepping away from the VR station and shutting it all down.

MEMORY DATE: 2287.036 (SIX MONTHS AGO)

Memory Location: Secret

Danse straightens in his spot in front of us all. His black, tightly curly hair is tinged with grey. Deep brown eyes that sparkle whenever he talks of Lyric wash over our faces as he takes a couple of moments to smile at us all. His presence brings a kind, gentle leadership that always puts me at ease. Akela introduced me to Danse's group a few weeks before her disappearance, and even now I can't sit in these meetings without thinking of her.

Yet again, I push away the memories and the grief they bring, and try and focus on the Sirens meeting. It's been two years and twenty-eight days since I last saw Akela, and it still feels as raw as that first day of returning home to find Fuschious in her place. They told us it was a transfer, but it's hard to know anything anymore.

We sing together. Then for a few minutes, Danse asks the group questions about the fragment, explaining and expanding on the words to help us understand. Finally, he lifts both his hands over everyone's heads for the blessing. "Go out in the Composer's love through the sacrifice of our Lyric and in the power of the Muse."

Seats are pushed back against the wall, and the few tables are rearranged into standard conference-room configuration. Within minutes there will be little evidence we were even here.

When most of the Sirens have trickled away, Danse beckons me over. "Cadence, you look troubled."

"You noticed?"

He nods. "Do you want to talk about it?"

I look away, bombarded by memories. "There isn't much to say. I'm always reminded of Akela here."

"You're grieving."

I shrug. "It's nothing, really. I should be over it by now."

Danse folds his arms. "Grief doesn't play by time rules, Cadence. It's okay to still miss her."

"CADENCE, THESE PEOPLE WANT YOU TO forget."

With the words of a dream still ringing in my ears, I open my eyes. The room is warm, and the sleeping bodies of my Coding roommates lie undisturbed in their bunks nearby. I lie there for a moment, my face hidden in the alcove of my bunk. Mumma's words echo around my brain, knocking away any remaining stupor.

Through circular vents in the ceiling, I hear the whirring sounds of the heating system, which tells me that the morning wake-up call isn't far away. I roll over toward the wall, too tired to get up, but too awake to be able to rest again. My mind seems to want to run through a marathon of thoughts, even if my head feels too heavy to lift off my pillow.

Maybe it's because graduation is coming closer, or maybe

my mind is just starting to freak out about being out in the big wide world for the first time. Whatever the reason, my thoughts reject anything cheerful, choosing to focus on everything sad, traumatic, and frustrating that's ever happened to me.

My parents are long gone. I was stolen and forced into this life of regiment and blandness. Sif was Realigned. Wil betrayed us. Akela left. Hodge graduated. To make it worse, I can't shake this gnawing sense of dread that I'm going to be arrested for something that Crucible asked me to do in the first place. Lyric knows I've tried to fix my problems many times, but I'm too small and too useless to do anything much.

Wouldn't it be better to sit back, relax, and settle in to doing the work of the Collective? Wouldn't it be easier to forget? To go along with everyone else, never fearing that I would be caught and imprisoned?

Before the thought has even finished thinking itself, I'm already pushing it away, feeling a little stab of guilt. Of course I can't forget—not with my memory freak ability. Besides, everything I've seen and sung has been true. It's the Collective that time and time again has shown me they're full of lies and deceit. I couldn't walk away unless I was content to live those lies forever.

I just . . . I just wish life could be easier sometimes.

Why can't I make anything happen for myself like I want it to? It's so hard to think without Akela around me now. Before, I could always go to her with any questions, and she always knew what to answer. She could be stern, sure. She could be aloof and distant sometimes too. But I knew she would always be there to protect us. Everything was going to be alright as long as she was around. Until she wasn't around anymore, and then all I felt was lost.

So who were you depending on, really? a small voice in the back of my head whispers.

I sigh heavily.

I remember the sweet moments in my first year, when Lyric first appeared to me.

I am calling you, Cadence.

As if I'm seeing the vision for the first time, the sounds and sights flow freely again, and I am back there, being visited by Lyric in my dreams. Finding Lyric was like discovering oxygen and realizing how much I needed to breathe. I would have given anything to have that moment last forever.

"I can't do this by myself," I whisper in my head.

A small, sweet refrain sings out from deep within, one of the Songs about Lyric that Danse taught me a few months ago. It carries a quiet peace along with the words.

Though we struggle, we are not lost
For his life is lived in us.

It strikes me all of a sudden that I have been wasting my time trying to solve a problem, instead of giving it to the only one who has the power to do anything. So I begin to pray. Slowly at first, then everything in a rush. I tell the Composer about my fears, my worries, and my hopes.

Alone in my bunk, talking in my head so no one can hear me, I bare my deepest feelings to him, confessing how stupid I've been, and how much I want things to be different. Then equally slowly, like the first glimmers of dawn, the Muse comes to reassure me. Before long the words are flowing so fast I can barely keep up, and as I think them, the weight I've been feeling is lifted and carried away.

When the morning alarm goes off an hour later, I spring out of bed, feeling lighter than I've felt in years. Nothing in my circumstances has changed. But the music in my head makes me know for certain that I won't be facing the future alone.

6

Hate, as I have said before, masquerades in many forms. Sometimes it bears an obvious, ill-tempered aggression. But on other occasions, it wears a far more subtle cloak.

–Supreme Lover Midgate, Intimate Diaries of a Loving Leader, *chapter 14*

FOR A FEW WEEKS, I CAN DO NOTHING except sit on the explosive information I carry. I can't talk about it to anyone. Who would believe me? Even if they did, I know that what I'm thinking is treason of the highest order, and that's not something you let yourself even whisper.

Final-year Elite Apprentices get a city pass once every thirty days, so I try to line up my visits with Siren meetings as much as possible. It's not an easy feat, but I manage to get there most times, thanks to the coded message that arrives in my Siren app, telling me when and where to meet.

I've planned today's excursion for over a week: early-morning Overcar to the riverside park, then an hour of walking around the streets like a tourist on my way to my changing point at Melody's hotel.

Today's meeting is in a building three blocks back from the riverside in a quiet, neglected part of an ancient city area. Cameras are scarce here, since nobody in their right mind would bother lingering in a place with this stench of sulphur and paint thinner. Any cameras that do exist have been rerouted, thanks to Viola's coding expertise.

Melody and I travel together down the dilapidated alley, which bears marks that seem to predate the Collective's rise to power. Occasional graffiti peeks out from beneath long-forgotten paper posters that flutter like tattered flags on the walls. Mounds of dust and rubbish spill over the sides of the gutters like snowdrifts. Rats don't bother scurrying away from the rubbish heaps, too bold in their numbers to run as we approach.

"Up ahead," Melody whispers.

Fife is sitting beside a rusted dumpster, blending into the scenery so well that I could easily have missed him. Although he graduated into a health center somewhere last year, today he is wearing brown overalls, his cap pulled low over his face. His back rests against a brown brick building that looks like it once might have held offices. Most of the windows are boarded up now, and the large, steel double doors stand askew on their hinges.

Even in the early morning it feels spooky. Melody walks straight toward the building's entrance, passing Fife without a backward glance. I resist the urge to nod at him, and I pass by into the dim, musty hallway.

After scurrying past dusty and derelict rooms, we reach a brown-stained door bearing a faded label: STAFF ONLY. The door hisses like an airlock when Melody turns the handle to let us both in.

Most of the group are already here, and a small circle of chairs has been set up, facing one wall of the room. The door closes behind me with a solid *thunk*. When it does, the dozen or so Sirens relax and return to their conversations.

A couple of familiar people wave from the other side of the room. The old Academy crew are hanging together in a little circle down by the boarded-up windows. Loa and Viola are there, chatting. Hodge is there too, sitting in one of the chairs with his back to the entrance.

Loa looks up and sees me hovering near the entrance. "Watcher girl!" he cries, raising a hand in greeting. "You made it!"

Hodge turns sharply in his seat, and then his face brightens. Before I know it, he's coming toward me.

"I'll catch you later, honey," Melody says with a knowing pat on my arm. I smile back as she makes her way to another group of Sirens, then I turn to Hodge, feeling a strange sense of shyness. He might be disguised as a street sweeper, but there's no hiding the build and grace of a warrior in the way he walks. That's the kind of detail only a Watcher would notice, though, so I try and push away my sudden flash of anxiety.

Hodge leans down to give me a hug. "How have you been?" he asks, pulling away to look intently into my face. "I missed you."

I flush and glance down. "It's been a weird time," I say quietly. "How about you?"

Hodge pulls a chair around in front of him and waves me toward it. "Tell me about it." He sits down at another chair and leans forward, ready to listen.

Taking his lead, I sit down, thankful that someone is genuinely interested in my problems. "Crucible sent me a Coding exercise, and I'm not sure what to do about it," I begin, feeling the weight of my discovery all over again. "I think . . . I think there's something wrong in the Hall of Love, but I don't know whether I can say anything."

"Sounds bad."

I nod. "I don't know whether I'm right. But if I am, then there's something massive going on up there."

"Something dangerous?" A crease between his eyes deepens in worry.

I nod.

"Bigger than the bomb?"

In my mind, there's a flash of memory from that Triumph festival years ago: Hodge's arms at the truck wheel, steering it forward. Wil disappearing out of the open door as the truck turns a corner into the forest. An enormous thump and shudder as lake water explodes into the sky. I push the memories away, then nod again.

"As big as it gets," I say. "As in," I lean forward, dropping my words to a whisper, "*I think Supreme Lover Midgate is an AI*' kind of big."

"What?" he exclaims.

"It was in the code." I begin to describe what I found, being careful not to descend too far into Coder jargon.

Hodge stares at me for a few seconds, absorbing what I've just said. "Viola?" he calls over his shoulder. She pushes away a strand of silky black hair from her eyes and looks at us. Hodge waves her over. "Could you come here a minute?"

Looking a little surprised, she heads over to where we're sitting. Hodge pulls across another chair. I smile at my old friend, glad that we've been able to keep up since her transfer back to Love City.

She sits down. "What's up?" she says brightly, looking from Hodge to me and back again.

"Quick question," Hodge says.

"Shoot."

"What would you say if you heard that Supreme Lover Midgate wasn't human?"

Viola's eyes widen. "I'd ask where you got that information first."

"Crucible sent it," I reply. Her face pales. I rush to explain. "Said it was an advanced project before I start in the Hall of Love."

"Riiight." She bites her lip, looking rattled.

"That's what I thought." Hodge shares a look with Viola that leaves me feeling distinctly uncomfortable.

"What?" I ask tersely. "What am I missing?"

Viola taps a slender finger against her mouth. "How many days until graduation?" she asks in an unnaturally calm voice.

I don't even have to do a mental calculation, because I've been carrying the answer in my head all day. "Seventy-four. Why?"

She clicks her tongue. "Too long." She turns away from us. "Hey, Danse!" she calls. "Can you . . ." She waves him over. The older man smiles and comes our way, but his smile slowly fades as he takes us in.

"Viola, Harper, Cadence, good to see you three here this morning. What can I do for you?"

I dip my head in greeting, but don't get a chance to say anything because Hodge speaks up.

"How soon can you organize an Exodus?"

Danse looks thoughtful. "I could probably make it happen in a week or two. Who needs it?"

"Cadence," Viola says.

"What?" I cry in alarm.

Viola gives me a look of sympathy. "That code is a death sentence, Cadence."

"Even if it's not intentional," Hodge continues quickly, seeing the protest rising to my lips. "Finding out information this sensitive is way above your Elite status."

"No way," I bluster. "He specifically gave me the code as a practice exercise."

Hodge looks stricken. "Then it's a setup."

I feel the blood drain from my face. "No. He wouldn't . . ." But my words fail. Of course he would. That's exactly the kind of thing Executive Lover Crucible would do.

Viola reaches over to touch my knee. "Cadence, I know this is hard, but we need to get you out of here before he makes his move."

"No, you're wrong," I say, even though deep down I know

she's right. "My results were off the charts. Crucible just wanted to see me stretch myself before I . . . before I . . ." But I know the words are false. I look at my friends and see concern in their eyes.

"I don't think he wants you to work in the Hall of Love, Cadence," Hodge says.

"He plays a long game," Viola adds. "I've read about it before. When a Security Sub Commissariat Chief Lover crossed him in a meeting once, he waited ten years before getting his revenge. Set the Chief Lover up with false information so the guy humiliated himself in public. Then when the Chief Lover tried to retaliate, Crucible made everyone think that the guy was insane. He's lucky he didn't end up on the Haters' Pavilion Show."

"Crucible waited ten years for that?" I feel a little sick.

"You've worked with him." Viola lifts her hands in a shrug. "You know what he's like."

Hodge puts a hand on my shoulder. "We have to get you safe."

I shake my head. "No. Not yet. I'm not a dropout. Besides," I rub at my wrist. "I can't leave without my full ID." *Especially not when Fuschious would love me to fail too.*

"Crucible's unpredictable," Viola says. "Who knows when he could strike?"

"I'll take my chances," I declare. "I don't have much choice."

"You need to stay with us," Hodge says quietly, looking into my face with an intensity that makes it hard to refuse.

I break away from his gaze. "I can't do that. Without my full ID I can't even get a maid's job, let alone survive out here."

"If we get you to the Exodus," Danse says, folding his arms, "that won't be a problem."

"What if you can't, though? What if I escape the Academy, miss graduation, and then the Exodus doesn't work out?"

"You don't trust the Composer very much, do you?" Viola remarks.

I glare at her. "I'm not going to burn my only way to survive."

Danse smiles. "Cadence, you know the Composer will be with you."

Forcing my face into what I hope looks like confidence, I stare at them all, hoping I can hold myself together long enough to convince them. The truth is, I can't accept what I know is true about Crucible. When I pulled out of the Watcher cadre, I could tell I made him mad. It would be just like him to spring this kind of cruel twist to my Elite career, to stop me from graduating at all. But I don't want that to be true. Not when the end is so close I can nearly touch it.

They care about you.

It's a struggle to ignore the Muse, and I feel a little stab of guilt as I squash the feeling down.

Viola's brows furrow with concern. Hodge's face is solemn, and there's so much sorrow in his eyes that I can't look at him. Danse ruminates for a few moments, letting a soft musical hum emanate from his lips. I know the words that go along with it.

Composer go with you no matter
Where your feet will tread.
With Lyric's life we live and breathe
And find our daily bread.
The Muse will guide you onward, child,
So let him lead ahead,
As Sirens we will trust and go
Wherever we are led.

The words just make me feel even more guilty about ignoring the Muse's prompts. So I roll it all up in a little ball of stubbornness. It will be fine. I know there's a seat reserved for me at graduation. Crucible wouldn't let that happen if he was going to do something despicable.

After a few moments, our Siren chapter leader stirs. "If

you go back today, how long until you get leave from the Academy again?"

"I saved this one up for about eight days, so the next one will come in twenty-two."

"Too far away," Viola says quickly.

Danse tilts his head. "It could give us enough time to get a plan in place."

"But—" Viola protests.

I talk before she can go on. "If the Exodus is where I should be, then the Composer will keep me safe. The Song says so."

"That's not—" Hodge begins.

I hold up a hand to stop him. "I have to stay."

"You'll be arrested," Viola says flatly. "Embraced."

It's hard to ignore the frustration in her voice, but I won't give in. "If Crucible plays a long game, maybe he won't move until right before the graduation ceremony."

"We are all here until the Composer decides our mission is done," Danse says. "It doesn't mean we act foolishly. So let's open an Exodus for Cadence to escape, but let her go back to the Academy for now."

Not looking entirely pleased, Viola gives a reluctant nod. Hodge sits stiffly in his chair, but I can tell he wants to argue, and for a moment, I feel a little anxious. Then he looks me in the eye, and I see what he's really thinking, and my heart starts to beat faster. For in those eyes, I see worry and more than a hint of fear.

7

Have You Had
Your Beauty Sleep
Today?
Beauty Sleep Hours 2300 – 0430
We'd Hate To Detain You.

The Love Collective
Love All. Be All.

NEARLY A MONTH PASSES, AND CRUCIBLE doesn't have me arrested. At first I feel smug, but a vague sense of unease settles in, and I begin to fear something other than Fuschious's semi-regular bullying sessions. I delete the code he sent me, making sure to remove all trace of it. But I keep the transcript of my messages from him, just in case.

It takes another twenty days before I finally convince one of the administrators to give me a city pass under the excuse of house hunting. Bearing my pass in my ID like it's gold bullion, I head into Love City's riverside parklands. The coordinates for our meeting were sent to my Siren app weeks ago, and I've been researching ways to get there unnoticed. For an hour I wander, taking in the sights. Then, after changing into a disguise at Melody's workplace, I take a circuitous route to the loading dock of a large plush hotel, before taking the stairs to one of the unused conference rooms on the seventh floor.

The reason for their choice of this place becomes clear when I arrive. As soon as the conference room door closes behind me, the noise from the streets snaps off like a switch. It's a soundproof cocoon, just like a Watcher room. We can sing to our hearts' content here, and nobody would ever know. Unless there are cameras, in which case we're done for. But Danse is such a careful planner that I'm sure he's got even that covered.

A couple of eyes snap up in alarm as I enter. I nod my apologies and slip into the remaining empty seat at the end of the semicircle. Hodge smiles as I sit beside him, and a riot of butterflies erupts in my stomach. I know he must be upset about my quick exit last time, but I hope he can forgive me. At least I made it today. No Realignment or arrest yet.

Danse starts up a Song fragment, and we all join in. Then he sits down to explain the meaning of the Song, guiding us again to Lyric's way. We pray. We clasp hands. Then one by one the Sirens begin to depart. All, that is, except for Viola, Danse, Hodge, and Loa, who remain behind, waiting expectantly for me to speak.

Melody stands guard at the doorway, ready to escort me back to the hotel. Another Siren steps up beside Danse. I haven't seen him around all that often, but I know his name is Alto. Like Danse, he wears a rainbow janitor's uniform, with the sleeves rolled up to his elbows. His sleek black hair is swept from his face, and his hazel eyes twinkle like he's thinking of some secret joke.

"Cadence," Danse says. "It is good to see you. How have you been?"

I cough slightly, feeling as if I've landed in some kind of job interview. "Good, I think. Still here." I chuckle with nervous energy. "But that's kinda obvious, so . . ."

A small grunt from Hodge says exactly what he thinks about

that, and with a sinking feeling, I know I'm going to have to talk to him about this soon. But I pretend that I didn't hear the displeasure ooze from every fiber of his being.

"I asked Alto here to get the Exodus route ready," Danse says to me. "He's put together a trail for you."

Confused, I look from him to Alto, who hurries to explain. "Safe houses. Every Exodus needs to be different. I've set up a series that will get you to the border wall."

"How far is that?"

"Two hundred miles. Since you'll be doing it on foot and at night, it can take a while to get the right travel window."

"Oh."

Viola comes up beside Alto. "Night makes it more dangerous, so you have to be super careful to avoid the Squads." She darts a glance at Alto and then blushes. "At least, that's what I heard anyway. Not having . . . not having been on an Exodus or anything."

Alto gives her a patient smile and then continues, "There are twelve safe houses along the way. Each one will tell you the next one."

"Why not just tell me all of them?"

Alto looks a little shocked at that thought. "Twelve is a lot to remember, along with the directions."

Hodge almost laughs. "You haven't met Cadence before, have you?"

"She probably already knows a map of the entire Collective, street by street," Viola adds, tapping her forehead significantly.

I feel embarrassed at the compliment behind their words. "You guys . . ."

Alto hesitates. "But if she were caught, then all twelve safe houses would be at risk."

"What if she were caught at the border?" Hodge asks. "Wouldn't that result in the same problem?"

"I guess." From his back pocket, Alto pulls out a small,

outmoded infotab. Danse, Viola, and Hodge lean forward to try and get a look at the screen.

"Wait," I say. "I haven't even agreed to this Exodus yet."

"What?" Viola exclaims, her eyes wide. "You have to!"

"Cadence." Hodge moves away from Alto's screen to take one of my hands. "Please see sense in this. Crucible—"

"Crucible is no problem," I say, gently disengaging my fingers from his. "And I only have fifty-one days to graduation. In fifty-two days, I will happily go. But so far there hasn't been a single hint of any arrest or interrogation, so I'm pretty sure I have nothing to worry about."

Viola erupts. "Don't be naïve, Cadence. Of course Crucible wants you to think everything is okay, because that's when he will pounce. Having nothing to worry about is exactly when you *should* start to worry."

Danse places a hand on Viola's arm. "Viola, I understand your fears. But don't be so fearful you forget Lyric."

She looks up at him and then back down, blushing. Danse turns to me. "Cadence, we have this Exodus ready in case of emergency. But the decision is yours. If you want to remain at the Academy and graduate, that is your choice. If you decide to escape, then we will provide the means to do that. But remember," his eyes are fixed on mine, "no matter what happens, the Composer won't forsake his Sirens."

"Exactly," I say. "Which is why I'm going to keep going to the Academy."

Hodge startles. "But you could die."

"Then I'll sing with Lyric," I reply. "If we feared death, then we would hide in our beds all day and never do anything."

"But the Song—" Viola says, a hitch in her voice.

"The Composer could make the trees sing his Song if he wanted to. I don't think he'll let his Song go quiet. Even if all of us here were arrested, he would make sure people were able to sing his Song into the future."

She looks even more displeased. "But all those fragments are held in your memory."

I give a slight shrug. "I'm just a little note in his symphony. I don't matter much in the scheme of things."

"You're the Songbook," Hodge states flatly.

"Maybe. Or maybe I'm just another Siren. My time at the Academy is nearly done. Once I get my full ID, I can take the Song out there." I wave in the direction of the door. "Danse said it. The Song is meant to be sung. And I think it's time we stopped letting the Supreme Executive tell us what we should and should not do."

"You're right, Cadence," Danse says. "But you forget that your knowledge could condemn more than just yourself."

"Then I'll just have to avoid getting caught," I remark more confidently than I feel.

"Don't be selfish," Viola snaps. She starts counting on her fingers. "You know about the Academy Siren operations. You know the Song. You know about this meeting place. Us. Everything. What do you think the Collective would do for that sort of information?"

She stares at me, eyes flashing, and I stare back. I know she's right. But that stubborn, proud part of me refuses to give in.

"I need my ID," I say.

"No. You don't," Viola says, her face hardening. "Outside of the Collective, nobody needs those things. The only reason you'd want one is if you wanted to stay here."

Against my will, my gaze flits to Hodge, betraying my thoughts.

"He can come too," she says. "If that's what it takes to get you to safety, then Hodge should go too."

Hodge raises a hand in protest. "Wait just a minute."

"See?" I say to Viola, feeling a perverse sense of justice. "It's not easy to just run away from the Collective, is it?"

Hodge blinks. "I'm not the one Crucible wants to arrest," he says. "But you—"

"Will be fine," I finish, daring any of them to disagree.

Alto looks uncomfortable and slowly puts his infotab back into his pocket. Viola looks like she wants to murder me, and Hodge isn't much better. Only Danse looks at me with anything like compassion. But I can tell he's not totally on board either, the way his eyebrows are furrowed with concern.

"I don't think you'll be fine." Viola heaves a resigned sigh. "But it appears I'll just have to let you kill yourself."

"Here," Alto says, holding out the infotab screen at me again. He points to a spot on the map. "Just remember this first house. Just in case."

Frowning, I debate for a second whether to avoid seeing it. But Alto smiles at me with such sincerity that I decide at the last second to take a quick glance. It's a shopfront across the river somewhere. But I make sure to act as if I'm only doing it to humor them all.

Leaning back from the screen, I cross my arms and do my best impression of relaxed confidence. "I'll be fine," I repeat, wondering if I even believe myself.

"WHAT WAS THAT KERFUFFLE?" MELODY asks me in the hall after we leave the conference room. Viola passes us with barely a look, followed by Alto. I wait until they're out of the door before I speak.

"Nothing," I whisper. "Forget it. When does your shift start? We should get back to work."

It's code, and Melody knows it. "Absolutely. It's our privilege to do the work of the Collective."

"Mmm." I am too busy thinking of Hodge to reply properly.

"Cadence?" his voice echoes down the hallway towards me.

I slow, feeling a nervous zing across the back of my neck. When I turn, Hodge is there, still wearing his rainbow janitor disguise. I still haven't seen him in a Love Squad uniform—not really. The Hodge I remember is the Elite Apprentice, strong and tall in grey. Looking at him now, I can see that the past few years have filled him out even more. His shoulders are broader and his face has lost some of the roundness of youth. Hair bristles around the base of his chin. The scar on his cheek has faded a little. But those eyes are the same eyes that have looked into mine for years. Warm. Brown. Solid and intense.

"Can we have a word?" he asks. The gentleness of his tone should reassure me. It's comforted me many times before. But now, knowing I am disappointing him, all his words do is drive the knife of guilt further in.

"I have to go." I cock a thumb over my shoulder in the direction of the exit.

Hodge takes a tiny step toward me. "This can't wait."

Melody gives us a knowing look. "I'll be near the door." She bustles away before I can say anything. I watch her go, wondering what on Earth I'm going to do now.

Hodge takes a step closer, so close I can smell the scent of his clothes. "Please," he says quietly. "Please don't do this."

I swallow. Hodge leans toward me, and it takes an almost superhuman effort to stop myself from just capitulating and going wherever he wants. Unwillingly, I begin to blink rapidly. "Hodge, I . . ." I shut my eyes, desperate for something to say.

When I open my eyes, Hodge's expression is frustrated. "If you're going to tell me that you need your ID, then don't say anything."

I shut my mouth, then reopen it. "I wasn't," I lie.

His eyes bore into mine. "After everything we've been through," he says, "please. Can you just choose the Exodus? It's just . . ." he trails off, a faraway look in his face. He seems to be debating something within himself. Then he looks at me again. "Remember our first night?"

"That is a low blow," I say.

"But if you get arrested, I'll never see you again." Hodge reaches out for my hand, but I pull away.

"If I don't graduate, who's going to let me see you? I'll be illegal. You would be sent to Embracement for harboring an illegal non-citizen. Either way, we don't get to see each other." I hate the way I sound right now, but the harsh facts are needed.

Hodge's face clouds. "I could hide you."

"Where? Under your bunk in the barracks?"

"I'm in the officers' quarters. I have my own—"

"You live in the most heavily surveilled location in the Collective, apart from the Hall," I say. "In what universe could I even sneak in there, let alone survive for more than five minutes?"

Hodge's expression darkens. "But if you go back, you will be arrested."

"It's a risk I have to take," I say. "You would do the same."

"Don't bring me into this."

A little ball of anger bursts into flame in my heart. "Why not? You are."

The expression on his face is as if I've hit him. "Not fair," he says, voice low.

I fold my arms, but wish I hadn't been so harsh with him. "Hodge, I've thought about nothing else for weeks. The only solution I can see is to persevere until I graduate."

"Then at least take this." Hodge fishes around in his pockets and draws out a small silver chain. Lyric's tree dangles on its pendant.

"Mumma's necklace?" I say, confused. "I thought it was in the bunker."

At his expression my heart pangs.

"I was wanting to save it for your graduation. But now"—he

holds it out to me—"I don't know if I'll get to see you again. This is yours, anyway, so . . ."

"Keep it." I say with false bravado.

"But—"

"I gotta go, Hodge." With those words, I turn away.

That warm, deep voice is full of despair as it calls out after me, "I'll leave."

At his sudden outburst, I pause for a split second.

Hodge rushes on. "We could go on the Exodus together. I'll walk away from everything, and we can go."

In that moment I see a brief glimpse of what our future together could be: On the run, both hunted by Watchers and Squads, travelling by night with no one to keep us company. It almost sounds romantic, except for the fact that we would both be dead before a week was out. Desertion from the Love Squad is punishable by instant execution, no trial necessary. Hodge can't leave the Squad without bringing the entire Collective force down on his head, and both of us know it.

"It won't work," I say, looking down the hall to where Melody is waiting.

"Can't we give it a try?"

For the last time, I turn back to him and try to smile. Grief is etched into his face. Grief and frustration.

My smile wobbles a little bit. "I'm sorry, Hodge. I'll see you when I graduate." I take a deep breath to steady myself, then keep walking, feeling my heart shatter just a little more with each step.

If your Love is visible to all, you will have nothing to fear.
–Supreme Lover Midgate,
Intimate Diaries of a Loving Leader, Chapter 14

MELODY AND I EMERGE FROM THE LOADING dock of the riverside hotel just a little behind Danse and Loa. We step out into the middle of a T-shaped lane that services the delivery entrances of all the buildings in this block. Deep shadows fall along the pavement, cast by towering office blocks.

To my left and right, I can see the end of the lane, where broad roads lead down to the river. Straight ahead is another narrow lane. It's the domain of brown and navy service uniforms. Although the street is clean, the smell from the dumpsters reminds me that the "nice" people don't belong here. Theirs are the ornate, glass-filled entry foyers. Ours are the messy, hidden service routes.

Trained by years of secrecy, the Sirens fan out in a well-practiced manoeuvre–Danse and Loa to the left, Melody and I to the right. Almost as one person, Danse and Loa lift their collectors' equipment from hidden alcoves. With the equipment strapped to their sides, they transform into their invisible selves: street sweepers, beautification technicians picking up the refuse from the streets so that Love City remains the crisp face of Collective power.

I watch them go out of the corner of my eye. Their heads are bowed low, supposedly to catch the smallest scrap of garbage with their collectors' sticks. But their eyes rove around, searching for any hint of abnormality. They aren't supposed to be in this sector, but nobody looks twice at a garbage collector, especially one just doing his job.

Melody and I cross the lane and head in the opposite direction, aiming for the Collective hotel where she works. I am due back at my dormitory for graduation practice. There's not much time to change out of my disguise. But it would be worse if an Elite Apprentice were seen walking in public with a maid. That sort of novelty would bring too much unwanted attention.

A prickling of the hairs on the back of my neck makes me turn around. A man in a Love Squad suit has stopped Danse beside a dumpster and is speaking to him. I can't hear what he is saying, but our leader looks calm. He nods. He listens. He moves his head as if he is just chatting about the weather, but I know something isn't right. Loa must know it, too, for he quickly appears at the Chief's side, watching the uniformed questioner with a wary expression.

Near a dumpster I slow, touching Melody's arm. She turns around to look as well, and at that moment Hodge emerges from the loading dock. He takes one look at Danse, another at us, then gives a small shake of his head. Melody guides me back to the way we were supposed to go and pushes me toward the corner of the street.

The memory of my Siren training kicks into gear: don't look like you're running. Get away when you can, but don't draw unnecessary attention. You are a citizen of Love City, going about your daily business. Ignore the Squads. If they see your fear, they'll pick you up too.

I know what I should do, but I just can't help it. Curious, I turn back to look again. As I do, the Love Collective man holds up his hand above his head in a signal, and suddenly the road is an ocean of black suits and guns and Love Squad vehicles. Two vehicles scream around the corner in front of us and take up position between us and Danse. Loa tries to throw himself in front of the Chief Siren. But his action does nothing. A wave of Love Squad soldiers swarms over them both, and the two men disappear beneath a sea of black. Someone throws a hood over Danse's head.

Taking shelter behind the dumpster, I watch in horror as the two men fall. Beside me, Melody lets out a small cry of alarm. Hodge makes a move as if to run back, but stops. Clenching his fists, he turns and strides quickly away from the mountain of armed bodies. I know he is doing the sensible thing. Running at that army now would only mean certain death. The safe thing is to get away. But I cannot move. I stand transfixed, watching my life fall apart before my eyes.

In a gap between the vehicles, I see Loa go down, fighting in vain against the heavily armed soldiers. His fist connects briefly with the abdomen of one of them, and then he is writhing on the ground, electrified by multiple officers pointing their weapons at him. When he's motionless, the net is pulled away and soldiers begin laying into him with fists and boots.

With Loa incapacitated, the squad sets upon Danse, pummelling, lifting, pulling, punching. Chief Danse lies beneath the hood, not resisting, but not helping his arrest. Metallic voices scream through Love Squad helmets, "Get him!" "Lift him!" "We got you now, Hater!" The Chief is silent. His rainbow uniform surfaces and then disappears underneath the pile of uniforms. The frenzy goes on, until the Love Squad seems like a single, multi-limbed monster, devouring and beating the two men even though they're already silent.

I make my fingernails bite hard into my palms to keep myself from screaming. Six Love Squad soldiers lift the limp body of the Chief and carry him to a large, imposing armoured bus. When the door of the bus yawns open, they throw him into the back like a sack of laundry. Loa's motionless body is thrown in behind him.

I feel as if I might dissolve into nothingness right here on the pavement. All I can hear is the echo of the metallic voices in the distance and Melody's frantic breaths beside me. Both of us are cemented to the ground. Unable to speak. Unable to comprehend what has just happened. Unable to drag our eyes away from the scene playing out in front of us.

"Move," Hodge hisses as he walks past. But I can't. My legs have become pillars of concrete.

It is Fife's scream that wakes us up. The single cry, "NO!" echoes from a rooftop at the opposite end of the block, turning the attention of the Love Squad toward it. Groups break away from the cars, pounding across the streets toward the place where Fife's cry was heard.

We are suddenly in a panic. Melody and I break into a speedy walk, heading away from the horror at our backs. I pick up my pace, squeezing along the alley with frightened steps. At any moment I expect a shout from behind to signal that the pursuit is coming for us. But we seem to be forgotten.

My breath quickens when I catch sight of Hodge up ahead. He has already reached the place where the alley meets the main road. He stands at the corner for a moment, hidden from the squads, but visible to me. He gazes at the heaving mass, watching the action through haunted eyes.

Don't do it, I think, hoping he understands. He leans against the wall for support. He starts forward, and I almost cry out, but at the last second, he checks himself. That's when he catches me looking. His fingers resolve themselves into the familiar Siren signal. Then he mouths a few small words, his finger pointed to his heart and then to me.

"I will find you."

My heart splinters into a million pieces. Hodge turns and sprints away. I want to follow him down the wide road. But Melody grasps my elbow in a pincer grip and drags me back.

"Hodge," I breathe, looking over my shoulder in the direction he ran.

Melody just tugs my elbow harder in the opposite direction. "Come on," she puffs.

WE SPEED ALONG THE STREET, HALF walking, half running. We round another corner and another until we come into a wide boulevard. I'm still waiting for the sounds of pursuit, and it's like torture trying to stop looking behind me every few steps. But that would be suspicious, especially to any Watchers who might be looking.

Halfway along the road, throngs of commuters are spewing forth from an underground train station, filling the area with Love Collective outfits on their way to afternoon shifts. Without a word, Melody pulls me into the crushing flow of the crowd, and we are propelled along, heading for the central business district with the workers.

Almost everyone is in white linen suits. If anyone looks at us, it is only to give Melody and I the sneering kind of disdain reserved for the lowest echelons of society. Melody pulls out her maid's ID badge and fixes it to her pocket, hands trembling. Nobody seems to notice that she struggles to fit it on, or that tears stream down both her cheeks.

We walk on in silence, letting the crowds wash around us as protection. The Haters' Pavilion soon looms above us, fortress-like white walls gleaming with a flaming-orange hue in the late afternoon sunlight. Enormous banners the size of a small building hang down the sides of the central tower. The smiling face of Carell Hummer beams from one, and a group of three Love Squad guards are depicted on the other. The slogan, "Your Collective. Your Vote." garnishes the bottom of them both. With the kind of macabre clarity that seems to jump up in times of crisis, I wonder how long it will be before Danse is up there on that show, being jeered at by a nation as he dies.

"Don't think about that now," I tell myself. "Lyric will help us."

It takes more than an hour to get back to Melody's hotel. Every shadow seems to be full of soldiers, and every camera feels like it is pointed directly at us. I should be relieved when Melody draws me into the safety of the hotel service entrance, but all I can feel is a numb, paralysing fear. She has to urge me forward until we are surrounded by linen bags and beverage boxes, hidden from the cameras on the street.

At the back of the loading dock is a disused supply room, which seems to be a storage bin for centuries of outdated or useless furniture. Melody guides me into it, eyes scanning from side to side, white and fearful. Our feet kick up puffs of ancient dust as we squeeze past objects, until we're hidden from the front entrance, shrouded in shadow.

I collapse into a faded lounge that bears a large rip in the vinyl armrest. "I'm going to miss graduation practice," I worry. "They'll notice if I'm not back soon."

"You're not going back," Melody says, suddenly businesslike. She hands me the backpack I've used to hold my Apprentice uniform. "I can't watch you when you're at the dorms, and it's my job to keep you alive. You're the Songbook now. Composer help us all."

"But—" I protest weakly, not willing to accept the truth.

Melody's hands fly to her hips, and she scowls. "Do you want to get arrested?" she snaps.

I hang my head. "No."

"Then stay here," she says, moving laundry bags into position so they block the view of my seat. "Get rid of that uniform." She points at my backpack, where my Elite clothes are stashed.

After moving a few more laundry bags into place, Melody departs, leaving me with my maid's disguise, backpack from the Academy, and a ball of terror in my stomach. The ancient pipes creak and hiss, and I jump like a frightened rodent every time I hear a noise. A musty odor of age permeates everything, mixing with the clean-linen smells and the distant wafting of something pungent and smoky.

Get rid of that uniform.

I hug the backpack to my chest. Does Melody even know what she's asking? She can't know. The attack must have addled her senses. I have to go back. I have to graduate. I've been working for so many years for this that I—

Hodge ran.

Don't think about it.

He ran.

No. Don't.

Black uniforms swarmed over the two figures, pummelling, lifting, kicking, punching. Danse didn't resist. Loa went in to attack. But Hodge?

"What could he have done?" I ask myself. "There were so many of them. He would have been arrested too. He did the sensible thing. We all did."

A hollow, empty feeling tells me I don't believe a word of it.

With a sudden rush of desperation, I stand, hitching my backpack over one shoulder. I have to get to the Academy. All I have to do is change clothes, and nobody will be any the wiser.

Two memories batter against my mind of conversations I had with Viola and Hodge.

"THAT CODE IS A DEATH SENTENCE, Cadence," *she warns.*

"Even if it's not intentional," Hodge continues quickly, seeing the protest rising to my lips. "Finding out information this sensitive is way above your Elite status."

"No way," I bluster. "He specifically gave me the code as a practice exercise."

Hodge looks stricken. "Then it's a setup."

I feel the blood drain from my face. "No. He wouldn't . . ."

"HE WOULDN'T," I REPEAT. IT CAN'T BE. Crucible would attack me, not Danse. Why would he even know? I've been so careful. It must have been a coincidence. A horrific, sick kind of coincidence, sure. But surely Crucible wouldn't be *that* twisted?

My memories answer my own question. Of course he would. *Remember that time he ordered the entire Love Squad cadre to fight just because he felt like it?*

What was it Viola said? *Having nothing to worry about is exactly when you should start to worry.*

"She's wrong," I say out loud.

I reach the doorway of the storage room and peer out, hiding behind the door jamb. A deserted utility hallway leads back into the hotel in one direction. In the other direction, the loading dock opens out onto another service road that curves away from the side of the hotel building. Once, many years ago,

Wil walked toward there, and I was so young that I believed him when he told me I was special. I know better now.

A flicker of movement in the distance catches my eye, and I freeze. Two black uniforms hover in the road a few buildings away. They lean casually against the wall of an office block, their backs to my hiding place. But their presence sends a cold chill down my spine. Slowly, I back away into the storage room again, careful not to draw their attention with any sudden movements.

With trembling fingers, I zip open my backpack, pulling out my infotab and fitness tracker. Finding a large metal paperweight on a dust-ridden table further back in the storage room, I smash the screens until they are crazed with fine white lines and won't turn on anymore. Then I rummage around in the laundry bags for a different disguise. A driver. The cap fits snugly over my head, hiding my hair, and the blue jumpsuit covers my legs. Trying to avoid thinking about what I'm doing, I shove the Elite uniform into a disused filing cabinet at the back of the room. Then I force myself to walk away without looking back.

I am too numb to cry.

PART 2

They have left the bodies of your Sirens
As waste upon the earth.
Our voices are become ash and dust.
Our songs like those of criminals.
How long, Composer, will you let destruction reign?
How long will you leave your servants alone?
Hear our plea, hear the voiceless Sirens.
Return to us, that we may sing your praises forever.

–Lament of the Exodus, 24.7

9

There are no dark times for those who live in the light of the Collective.

−Supreme Lover Midgate

IT'S ONLY HALF AN HOUR BEFORE BEAUTY sleep when Melody smuggles me into her fifth-floor apartment. We climb the stairs cautiously, avoiding the common areas, and I wait behind the fire escape door while she swipes her ID over the lock sensor. When the door to her apartment swings open, she waves me hurriedly across the small landing, and I slink in.

Beckoning me to silence, Melody bustles around her infotab-sized apartment. It's a studio, with a miniature, L-shaped kitchenette in one corner that consists of two cabinets, a sink, and a tiny stove. Near the single window, a lounge area nestles beside a wall-length vidscreen, and behind the entrance is a small hallway that leads to a bathroom and laundry. It's tiny, but immaculate.

While she tidies her already tidy home, I perch on one of the old-fashioned armchairs near the window. Outside I can see other residential towers, their balconies rising high above us. Lights shine out from the rectangular complexes, and silhouettes of residents move like shadows in front of them. Down below, manicured gardens line the walkways between blocks, their hedges trimmed so short that nothing can hide in them. A subway station entrance sits at the far end of the row, the only brightly lit feature in the whole precinct.

"Don't sit so close. Someone might see you," Melody whispers, and I shrink back from the lounge area. She hurries over and draws the curtains closed, then turns on a small bedside lamp. It looks like one of the old ones from the hotel storage room, ancient and cracked. The light it gives is a warm orange, tinted too low to hurt our eyes, but not quite bright enough to stop lengthy shadows from gathering in the corners of the room.

"Sorry, sweetheart," she sighs. "After today, we can't be too careful."

I hang my head. "This is dangerous for you," I say. "I should go."

"You're not going anywhere just yet." Hands on her knees, she lowers herself wearily into one of the armchairs. "Lyric help us all."

I take another sweeping glance around the room. Small bed. Small lounge area. Tiny closet and a barely there kitchen. It's not enough for one person, let alone two.

"I can't stay here."

Melody shakes her head. "There are no Watchers' cameras in menial housing. At least, not in the residences. Out there—" She purses her lips. "Well."

Fear and shock have had their way with me all afternoon, and my body has reacted by numbing my emotions. I am an empty husk. Unable to cry. Unable to feel anything. The images of Danse and Loa and the Squad's attack have replayed so many times in my memory that it seems like the only memory I own now.

"So," Melody says, standing up. "I should get us some dinner."

I'm about to protest, but my stomach rumbles loudly at the mention of food. In the kitchenette, Melody pulls out some packets from one of the cupboards, which she cooks up on the stovetop in a small aluminium saucepan. The smell makes my mouth water, even though it's a basic protein meal. Together we sit in the armchairs, sipping our food from large mugs. Outside the windows, the inevitable chimes ring out, and a brief message appears on Melody's vidscreen.

"Ten minutes to Beauty Sleep, my Lovelies," says the unmistakable voice of Supreme Lover Midgate. The screen shows a countdown clock, flashing red as it flows backward toward zero. This rouses Melody from her seat.

"You take the bed," she says, disappearing into the narrow hallway. From a cupboard nestled into the wall, she retrieves a large quilt and pillow. "I'll take the floor."

"No," I protest. "If you're going to go to work, you need the rest more than me."

"Nonsense," she says, but lets me lift the quilt from her arms. I lay it out quickly on the small patch of carpet beside the bed, and Melody washes up the mugs. Then she hands me a toothbrush and towel she's retrieved from the cupboard.

"This will do for now," she says. "I'll have to buy you some more tomorrow."

"What are we going to do?" I ask, feeling a sudden rush of pain.

"Only the Composer can answer questions like that," Melody replies. "Let's hope he tells us after we've had some sleep."

We mime our nightly routine in silence, making it to bed just as Beauty Sleep arrives. Outside there's a muffled chime as the clock on the vidscreen reaches zero. The bedside lamp shuts off, and we are left in complete darkness.

MEMORY DATE: 2285.108 (THREE YEARS AGO)
Memory location: Coding Room A92, Elite Academy
My mind seems to have shrunk until I can only think three words.
"Lyric, save her."

The console screen blurs.

"Lyric, save her."

I come to my senses, and the room sharpens back into focus. Ten banks of consoles. Three other people staring at their screens. Nothing to stop my brain from having a meltdown.

It's been a hundred days since she went missing, and she hasn't appeared on the Haters' Pavilion Show. Surely by now they would have crowed their triumph over her in the most violent way possible. Why no news? I could get on with life if I only knew where she was.

"Lyric, save her."

I WAKE FEELING STRANGELY BLISSFUL, BUT the feeling fades as I become aware of my surroundings. There's an armchair beside my head, a small fridge in the far corner humming, and soft breathing noises coming from the bed above my left shoulder. A split second after I work out where I am, the memories from the day before rush in like a tidal wave, replacing the warm waking feelings with a sharp, acrid fear.

"So that's what it's like," I whisper, and that hollow, numb sensation threatens to overwhelm me again. It doesn't seem real. It can't have happened. I'm still at the Academy, not hiding out in Melody's apartment.

But then I remember the image of Loa's determined expression as he threw himself in front of Danse, and I know it's real. I stifle a sob and let the tears flow down my cheeks. All of my worries about graduation seem stupid now.

More tears. I lie there in the dark, thinking equally dark thoughts until Melody stirs with a groan. Shortly afterward, the soft trill of an alarm rings out, and she sits up.

"Morning, sweetheart," she whispers through a long yawn.

"Morning." I set aside the quilt and sit up.

Melody rolls herself to a sitting position. "Let me get you some breakfast."

"No need."

She gets up anyway and shuffles across to the kitchenette, pulling ingredients out of the fridge. "Use the bathroom first, and I'll follow. Don't flush, though. The neighbors downstairs will get suspicious if they hear sounds of two people up here."

Feeling slightly squeamish, I do as she suggests, washing my face at the sink. When I return to the living area, she's laid out a bowl of breakfast meal for me. There's a small apple beside it.

When she sees me staring at it, she smiles. "We get rations every now and then. I thought you'd need it more than me." She pats her rounded stomach.

"Thank you." I smile, grateful, and begin scooping food into my mouth. Melody heads in to the shower room to get ready for work. When she's gone, I pick up the apple, staring at its red surface. It feels strange to the touch. I remember what it is, of course, but this fruit was a privilege reserved for Lovers in the Nursery Dorm, not for Apprentices. I take a tentative bite, savoring the sweet tartness of the apple's flesh. Then my mind flits and the taste turns to ash. I shouldn't be enjoying this kind of food. Not when Danse and Loa are gone.

Feeling agitated, I push away from the table and wander over to the window. But I stop short of opening the curtains. A simple glance at the weather could be deadly, if the wrong person happened to be watching.

I clean up the remnants of my breakfast, careful not to set the kitchen tap going while Melody's using another one, and then fold up my quilt and put it away in the closet. Melody emerges, hair neatly done up and maid's uniform on. She gives me a look that I think is supposed to be sympathetic. But worry is creased into every part of her expression.

"You'll need to stay here today." She shoos me into the living space. "I've got to go to work. I'm sorry."

"But it's dangerous for you." I clasp at the sleeve of her uniform.

She tenderly disengages my hand, reaching for the hotel name badge that she left on a small shelf beside the door. "No more than usual, my dear. Stay hidden."

I take the badge from her and pin it onto her uniform. "You shouldn't have to do that for me," I say.

"I've been doing this longer than you've been alive, sweetie." Melody reaches out to give my cheek a soft pat. "Long enough to know that the Composer holds us, no matter what. So there's no point moping about the things I can't change. I just need to do the things I can and leave the rest up to him."

She looks at me with a kind of determined brightness, and I can't help but be swayed by her certainty. "Anyway," she continues, "don't go anywhere near the windows, and try not to use the plumbing while I'm gone. The folks downstairs are the nosy type, and they'll be sniffing round here before you can say 'love all, be all.'" With a final cheerful wave, she departs.

I stand there for a while, frozen. Whether it's because of the constant rush of traumatic memories that keep on threatening to overwhelm me or the hollow silence of this deserted apartment, I don't know. But I lose track of how long I am hovering in the little open space behind the front door.

I am with you.

You are not alone.

The Muse's whispers echo noiselessly through my head.

TIME PASSES WITH SLOW AGONY. WITH MELODY gone, it becomes obvious how little I can actually do in this shoebox of an apartment. I can't use the vidscreen (the neighbors might notice). Can't open the windows (someone might report me). Can't even flush the toilet (because why would an empty apartment use the plumbing?). Even walking around the apartment is dangerous,

as my feet make the floorboards squeak. So I spend a great deal
of the day in complete stillness. Every noise and bump from
elsewhere in the apartment block makes me jolt in fright. It's only
when I start rehearsing the Song fragments that I can finally calm
myself down.

You are not alone
When the Muse sings with you.
Lyric's love will hold you close
And teach you all that's true.

Late in the afternoon, I'm dozing fitfully in the armchair when
an electronic beep nearly makes me jump through the roof. It's the
sound of the front door unlocking.

In a flash I am up out of the chair, desperately searching for
a hiding place. But there's no need to worry. Melody fills the
doorway, and places a fingertip over her lips in what seems to be
her new favorite gesture.

"Come in, come in," she says over her shoulder, her voice a
little too loud. "I don't know what's been happening with my VS,
but I'll be glad if you can fix it before the broadcast tonight." When
she moves away from the door, a familiar figure comes in.

Viola gives me a wave, but she's not smiling. Dressed in a red
electrician's uniform, she carries a small blue metal case. Tufts of
mouse-brown hair poke out from beneath her cap. She waits until
the door closes before giving me a thin, displeased smile.

Feeling guilty, I cross the room. Viola stiffens a little. I have to
bite back tears.

"What are you doing here?" I whisper.

"Viola's here to fix you." Melody leans in between us, clearly
pleased with herself.

"Wha—" I look from Melody to Viola and back again, confused.

"Take her over to the table, V." Melody smiles brightly. "I'll fix
us some tea." She backs away, heading into the kitchenette.

We sit with the small table between us, and Viola lifts my left
wrist. "When you didn't go back to your dorm, an automatic hold

would have been placed on your ID," she explains, patting my arm right above the little black tattoo. Her whispered tone is businesslike. "Any time you step into an Overcar or try to buy anything, they get an alert. You would be arrested straight away."

My mood sinks to a darker shade of depressed.

She turns my hand over, looking at the marks at various angles. "I know you wanted your full ID. And I'm working on a way to get you one. But it's going to take some time."

"What? How?"

She reaches for her little blue box. "The less you know, the safer you are," she says, echoing one of Akela's favourite sayings.

I'm overwhelmed by a rush of gratitude. "I-I don't know what to say."

Viola puts down the box and looks me in the eye. "I'm still mad at you," she says, her face confirming her words. "You should have taken the Exodus when D–" she falters and swallows hard. "Danse worked hard to get you a way out of here, and you refused to take it."

"But it was the only way–"

"Don't give me that." Viola's hissed whisper is furious. "If you hadn't stayed in the Academy, then Danse wouldn't have been arrested."

Melody interrupts us. "Now, V, I know you're upset. But it's not her fault that Danse was –" she pauses, and I can tell she's battling to hold back tears. "Please don't blame her."

Viola raises an eyebrow. "The timing is a bit of a coincidence, don't you think?" From the blue metal box, she pulls out an apparatus that looks a little like a chubby silver pen. She also brings out a small, square plastic box. When she opens this on the table, I see a row of sharp needles nestled into white plastic spacers. She selects one and clicks it into the end of the pen. Then she puts on a pair of dark glasses and hands me a matching pair.

"This is going to hurt," she says, grabbing the underside of my wrist and exposing my ID.

I put the glasses on, and the room dims to a dark blur. She hunches over my arm and presses a switch on top of the device. The silver pen begins to hum with a soft, high-pitched whine. When she points the needle at the top left corner of my provisional ID badge, a concentrated beam of light shoots out from the tip. At the same moment, an unbearably sharp pain shoots up my arm. I gasp.

"Told you," Viola says, her head bent over my arm.

"I remember this feeling," I manage.

Viola gives a tiny nod. "I'm sure you do. But this will take longer."

Just like it had back in the ID booth at Elite Academy, it feels as if my arm is being ripped off at the wrist. Pain sears down every line of my ID, overwhelming my senses. I have to fight the instinct to pull my hand away, but I can't stop flinching.

"Sorry," I say when a burst of pain makes me pull my hand almost completely out of Viola's grip.

This only brings a frustrated gasp from Viola. "Melody," she calls. "A little help?"

The older woman appears beside me. She looks at me with sympathetic eyes.

"I'm sorry, dear," she says as she tentatively reaches forward to clasp my arm below and above the ID mark, pressing it down to the table. It's not as firm as the ID booth was, but it reduces the amount of thrashing I can do.

"It's okay." I manage to spit the words through gritted teeth.

The process takes a long time, and my body begins to float in a state of disconnection, no longer able to register the severity of the pain. I become an observer, watching the black marks slowly disappear under Viola's care. It's as if I'm no longer sitting in the chair, but watching from a distance as the little white light erases me from the Collective.

After I've lost all connection with time, the little pen stops whirring, and Viola leans back in her chair.

"Done," she says. "For now."

Melody releases my arm and begins rubbing her hands and wrists. "Whew. I lost all feeling in there for a moment." She looks at me. "How are you, sweetie?"

I stare blankly into the distance, barely registering the release of her weight from my arm.

"Get her something sweet to drink." Viola's voice is muffled. Through a distant haze, I can vaguely register shapes moving around in the darkness. Something cold is pressed into my right hand.

"Drink, sweetie." Melody sounds like she's speaking through a pile of blankets.

Robotically, I lift the cold glass and take a sip. Whatever it is, it's unbearably sweet. But after a while, reality begins to coalesce again. I'm in a room with Melody and Viola. My hand feels like it's been torn off one sliver at a time. There's a pink scar where my ID used to be.

"As soon as I can source a new one, I'll fix you up," Viola says, packing away the torture device into the little blue box. "You'll be able to get out into the city after that."

"How long will that take?" I ask, staring down at the pink rectangle on my wrist. Melody reaches over to remove my glasses, and the pink flesh becomes even more vivid.

Viola snorts. "How long is a piece of string? It's not like I can just buy one in a loveshop."

"So I'm stuck here?" Panic laces the edge of my voice. I can't take my eyes off my wrist, looking at the void that will permanently mark me as an illegal non-citizen.

"It will be different someday. You'll see." Melody gives my shoulder a little rub.

"Composer willing," Viola says, packing the glasses into the blue box. She pushes back her chair and stands.

"Thank you for everything," Melody says. "Can I get you some dinner?"

Pausing near the front door, Viola shakes her head. "No, but thanks. Your rations are under enough strain as it is." She gives me a significant look, and my misery only grows. Now I'm not only illegal, I'm a burden.

I slump down in the chair, head bowed.

"You okay, C?" Viola asks, now concerned. I give her a noncommittal shrug in reply.

Melody's voice is hushed. "You just get yourself home safely, sweetie. I'll take good care of her."

There are whispered words between the two of them, which only serve to reinforce my misery. Then Viola is gone.

Melody returns and, shortly afterward, forces me to put some food into my stomach. I obey like a machine, not a human. My arms feel heavy, my movements too difficult to even try. I give up after a little while, and just sit there with my left arm out on the table in front of me.

Nothing matters anymore. Everything I was worried about has happened. A little square blob of pink is all that is left of my glittering career as an Elite. After all of my stubbornness, all of my protests that I had to see graduation, all of my reassurances that I'd be fine if I just left it for a few more days, all I am left with is this raw, aching emptiness.

Viola was right. If I hadn't resisted the Exodus, Danse wouldn't have been arrested, and I wouldn't be hiding in Melody's apartment without an ID, and everything would be fine. It's my fault he's gone. My fault Hodge had to run instead of fight. My fault I'm burdening Melody instead of being out there in the world doing something good.

How long can I stay hidden here? How long until the squads find me too?

10

True Lovelies
Call Out Haters
Report A Hater Now.
Love All. Be All.

MEMORY DATE: 2287.239 (THREE MONTHS AGO)
Memory Location: Secret

The room is small, but the people around me are smiling. We're waiting for the all-clear signal—word from the sentinel that our soundproof room is safe. A few stand with their eyes closed, faces turned upward in silent prayer. There are only twenty of us now. Twenty souls brave enough to risk disappearance for the sake of eternity.

Melody stands near the door, mouth pursed in an anxious knot. Danse could not make it today. I have never led the meeting before, and Melody has fussed over my hair and my nails as if I were about to appear on Collective News. At first I think she worries too much, but as the moments stretch to minutes, even I begin to feel tense. Fife should be here by now.

Movement at the back of the room catches my eye, and I see the door creak open. A scrawny figure in brown overalls slides into the room, closing the door gently behind his back. It's Fife, our sentinel for the day, all unwashed hair, greasy neck, and bony shoulders. When he gives me the thumbs-up signal, I know we are safe for the moment.

I begin.

"My people hear my words . . ."

It is a simple call and response. I sing the first line, and the Sirens repeat the melody back to me. As we sing, sweet harmonies swell around us, and we cease to be a small, bedraggled bunch of misfits. We soar, flying above this grim existence to become a part of a greater story than our own. We are the Sirens. But even more than this, we are met in the Song by the Someone. The Composer's Muse pulls away the curtain so we can see the Lyric of our Composer.

When the words of our Song cease, we sit in wordless prayer. I know that in a few moments I will have to finish this meeting. But here and now, I want us to know the Composer's power and presence.

Don't make them late.

"Go out in the Composer's love," I say, "through the sacrifice of our Lyric and in the power of the Muse."

The music ceases, and one by one we melt away into the dawn. Melody and I are the last to leave the shelter and emerge in the street. As the yellow slit of light on the horizon widens into a bright-blue morning, she clasps my hand.

"Don't let them get you," her fingers say.

"They won't," I squeeze.

I LIE ON THE FLOOR OF MELODY'S APARTMENT between her bed and the window, counting cracks in the ceiling. Today is a long, difficult day. It's about as mind-numbingly irritating as listening to a leaking tap drip at random intervals.

I know this because one of Melody's taps has a leak that lets out a single drip of water in an off-kilter rhythm.

Drip, drip.

That sound will send me insane in a few more days.

Sing the fragments.

Drip.

I can't see Melody's alarm clock from down here. Can I be bothered to lift my head and check the time? Probably not.

Sing the fragments.

How long will I be here? This apartment is really small.

Drip, drop, drip.

There is a draft of air that puffs under the door. Sometimes the draft carries the sounds of people going in and out of their apartments. Occasionally I hear a whine from the elevator.

Drip.

Someone is playing a vidscreen somewhere. I can hear the distant voices and soundtrack of a drama stream. It sounds violent. Screams punctuate loud slaps and cracks, with the occasional roar of machinery. They must be playing it loudly if I can hear it through the floor.

Sing the fragments.

Where is Hodge? He must be devastated. Has he been able to go back to his barracks? Oh I hope he doesn't end up arrested like—

Drip.

Sing the fragments.

Huh. There's another crack in the plaster up there. I didn't notice that one (drip) before.

Drip drop.

I wonder what Melody is going to bring home for dinner. It's ration night tonight. I hope she's safe. It's a long way from her hotel to this place, and anything can happen in the dark.

Drip.

What would I do if something happened to Melody?

Sing the fragments.

Somewhere out beyond the curtains, a Love Squad siren screeches down the streets. I shift my weight a little, and a tiny burning pain sparks in my scarred wrist.

Drip-ip drip.

Not fair. Why do they get to go out and enjoy life while I'm stuck here in the dark? It's not my fault this all happened, so why is Viola mad at me? It's not like I reported Danse or anything.

Drip.

Danse, is he even alive? Wait. Don't think about it. Don't think about what they could be doing to him. Don't—

Sing the fragments.

THE FIRST NOTES OF THE SONG LIFT ME OUT of my dreamless void, but I can't tell whether I'm dreaming or awake. Somewhere beyond me, a soft tune dawns like the first light of day on a green hill. Harmonies intertwine themselves around the melody, filling the music with a depth and richness that I've never heard before. The music wraps itself around me like a secure embrace. I feel warm and comforted and . . . held.

My eyes flutter open. He stands in front of me, but I cannot tell how tall he is. His face is kind and caring, wrapped in beams of glorious light. The music swirls around him like a cloud. It seems to be coming from within him, and it fills the meadow around me with a glorious, pulsating light. He reaches out for me, and when he speaks, I want to cry with the joy of the love that pours from his voice.

Cadence.

Lyric.

An image flashes across my mind. A small house in a back

street, somewhere on the edge of the city. A candle in the window, sputtering against the dark night.

Come find me.

A TRILLING BEEP WAKES ME. I AM STILL LYING on the floor beside Melody's bed. The front door opens, then closes. Footsteps.

"Sweetie? Hello? Are you—oh." Melody walks around the base of her bed and finds me lying there, staring at the ceiling. "Cadence?" she asks, a hint of worry in her voice.

I lift my right hand in a lethargic half wave. "Hi."

"Are you okay?" she asks.

I close my eyes. "Mm."

A few seconds later, I hear her footsteps retreat. The vidscreen flicks on, and a chirpy announcer's voice begins to read out the evening news.

"Good evening, Lovelies. Here is the news . . ."

So that's what time it is.

Beyond the bed, I hear water running in the kitchen sink, and the stove begins to hiss. Melody's footsteps wander down the hall, and then the water in the bathroom flows. I lie there, listening to it all like a surveillance microphone.

"Dramatic news today from the Love City Central Barracks, where—" My eyes shoot open as I register the news announcer's words. Jolted by a shock of fear, I sit up.

"That's where Hodge is posted," I exclaim. On screen, the entrance to the barracks is projected with a news ticker running below it. Two squad guards stand on either side of a high gate, protected by razor wire along the top of what looks like an impenetrable wall. The news ticker scrolls by, proclaiming:

HATERS FOUND IN LOCAL LOVE SQUAD. My hand flies to my mouth and I gasp, unable to believe what I'm seeing.

"Sources say a major Hater ring has been busted today, following months of careful surveillance and an anonymous tip-off. After the arrest of one conspirator, other members of the traitorous gang have been taken into custody for pre-Embracement questioning."

A panicky dread seeps into me. Loa has to have been the first, and Hodge the second, but a gang? Who would be in this gang of conspirators? I swallow. What has happened to my Siren family?

"Executive Lover Worthing today said he was shocked and appalled by the news, stating that this kind of behavior has no place in any Love Squad operations," the announcer continues.

My brain jumps into a host of nightmare scenarios: Hodge being led out in cuffs from the barracks, heading for the Haters' Prison. Loa and Hodge as a double bill on the Haters' Pavilion Show. All of them giving up my location under torture, and the squads pounding down Melody's door in the middle of the night.

Onscreen, the picture flicks to an older man in a Hall of Love office. Executive Lover Worthing's face is puffy beneath a thin white beard, and his rounded body overflows the edges of a white armchair. A thin golden band lines the high neck of his linen suit.

"We are saddened to hear that Haters have infiltrated even the highest echelons of our beloved Love Squads," he says in a sonorous, distinguished accent. "I have ordered a full inquiry into the matter immediately. The Collective will Embrace everyone we must until no Hater lives."

I am on my knees, horrified. Melody draws closer.

"That's not who I think it is, is it?" she says in a tremulous voice.

Fear has constricted my throat.

The news report ends and moves on to a banal discussion of local weather. I look at Melody, my mind reeling. She looks back, her face a mask of shock and fear. I wonder if my face wears the same expression.

"You can't stay here," she says.

"Don't give up." I am speaking to myself as much as her. "The Composer will save us. I know it."

She says nothing for a minute. Then with a heaving breath she pushes herself toward the kitchen, running the back of her hand across her wet cheeks. "Well, whatever you know, we still need to get you out of this apartment before the Squad comes." She turns on the tap to wash her hands.

"Will you come with me?" I ask. Out there are the Love Squads.

She comes over to me, clasping my hands in hers. They're still damp from the water. "Oh, child, I would wish nothing else, but I can't. If we travel together they'll swoop in and pick us up in less than a minute. You'll be safer on your own, much as it tears my heart out."

It occurs to me that her reasoning makes no sense, but I'm not going to argue. I'm here on borrowed time anyway.

"You're kicking me out." I feel betrayed.

"No, sweetie," Melody's voice breaks, and more tears shine on her cheeks. "The Exodus is where you belong now. You need to get out of this Collective before they find you. There's nothing for you here except trouble."

We stand there for a moment, the truth of my peril hanging between us. Melody's eyes well up again. She walks into the hallway, and when she returns, she lays a bundle of items across the edge of her bed, spacing them out neatly. A small backpack, along with a pile of fresh clothing: Sturdy pants for travel. Good running shoes. Warm rain jacket and a blanket for sleeping.

"This should get you safely onto the Exodus," she says, showing me a bundle of travel rations which she slots into a pouch in the backpack. "I'm not sure how long it will take you to get across the river, but you're going to have to move carefully. Those bridges are watched. I've packed some cleaning wipes and a first aid kit, so you'll have everything you need for the trip. There's a torch, and a couple of heat packs to keep you warm overnight."

"Are you sure this is the only way?" I ask, stalling for time. "I mean, how can we be sure that report was about Hodge? We didn't see any faces. It could have been completely different people."

The look Melody gives me tells me she knows what I'm doing. "Cadence," she says in a give-me-no-nonsense voice, "Danse and Bell were arrested. It was only a matter of time before the Collective found their secrets."

Loa's Siren name is like a punch to my stomach. I'm nearly derailed by grief right then and there. But I keep on fighting. "Then you're in danger too."

Melody gives me a rueful smile. "Danse knows nothing about my job, sweetie. He thinks I wear this uniform as a disguise. He only knows my Siren name, and that's enough."

"But Sirens are family," I protest. "How could you—we—know so little about each other?"

"We love each other," she says, a hitch in her voice. "Which is why we know so little. You can't betray what you don't know."

I battle against myself for a while. Fear is turning to anger, which is quickly becoming a volatile mess of emotion and irrational thought. A stupid part of me wants to blame Danse for this situation. I want to rush into the barracks and find Hodge just to prove that Melody is wrong. I even want to blame Viola for being mad at me. It's all unfair and upside-down and dangerous, and why couldn't I just graduate, for Love's sake?

"I know it's hard," she says softly, reaching up to pat my cheek. "But you're not going alone. The Composer will go with you."

Something in me twists. "He let them arrest Danse and . . . and Bell," I say in a strangled, sulky tone.

Melody nods. "I know. I'm sure even now he's preparing a great welcome home for them, if they aren't there already. But you—" She points at me, a determined smile pasted over her tearful face. "The Composer has other plans for you. And I just know it isn't to be silenced and hidden. You've got the words to the Song, Cadence. You need to get somewhere safe so you can sing it for everyone."

Taking my silence for acceptance, Melody lifts the clean travelling clothes. "Here," she pushes them into my hands. "Go and change."

In the back of my mind, soft lilting music begins again, and part of me wants to reach for it. But a little ball of anger that burns in my heart won't let me sing just yet. This can't be happening. I can't be standing here, getting ready to step out as a fugitive, hunted by the group I was once supposed to join.

11

United We Stand
Divided We Hate.
The Love Collective.
Your Only Alternative.
Love all. Be all.

THEY WANT ME DEAD.

Don't think about that now.

Melody's talking. "Now you know that the Safe House is all the way over on the East Quarter, don't you?"

"Yes, Melody. I saw the address."

They're trying to kill me.

Stop it. There's got to be somewhere other than this apartment where I will be safe. Anywhere.

"And you know I'd keep you here if there were any other way. Any way at all."

"Yes, Melody, I know." My mouth twists. I don't really know if this is the only way. A good thing Melody is too busy teaching me directions to notice I'm lying.

"Cadence, you must remember this: When you get to the East Quarter, find the third street after Triumph Park. Halfway down you'll find a loveshop. It's really a hub for the underground. We always—"

"Used to smuggle our illegals across the border after the Silencing. You said that. But how will I know it's the right one?"

"You'll know." She shapes her wrinkled fingers into the Siren signal. I nod and my own hands slide into the limbs of Lyric's last tree. The sign of the sacrifice. The sign we use to find safe people in this big, unsafe city. Not that I've ever been brave enough to use it on strangers before.

An awkward silence spreads out like a mist around us, filling the small, tattered apartment. I can't abandon Melody to face the Love Squad alone. They haven't targeted her yet, but I'm almost certain they'll find her one day. As certain as that compulsory photo of Supreme Lover Midgate is hanging crooked in the apartment foyer. If Melody hasn't straightened it yet, the world really must be ending.

"Can we pray?" I say. Right now, I can't think of any other way to delay *goodbye*.

Melody smiles broadly at me with such tenderness my heart is calmed for a moment.

She puts her arm around me as she lifts her head. "We thank you, Composer, for all things. Even when we don't understand, we trust you. Help us, Composer. Protect us. Send your holy Muse to be with your little Songbook here. Give her safe passage through this dangerous city, and get her safely to the Exodus. Bring her to that place where she will be hidden from those who want to destroy her and keep your Song singing for generations to come. Help us face this refining trial. In Lyric's name be it."

"Thank you," I say as her eyes meet mine.

Her arm tightens around me. "Well, time to go," she says in a clipped, businesslike tone. She takes a step away and her gaze sweeps up and down my dark street clothes. She reaches out to straighten one strap of my backpack, arthritic fingers trembling. I catch the edge of her mouth tightening as she smooths out the fabric.

"You said I'll be okay, Melody."

She takes a deep, shuddering breath, and then her wide shoulders begin to shake under the weight of held-back tears. All of the air rushes out of my lungs as she gives me a suffocating hug. I breathe the floral scent of her cheap perfume and the brittle, acrid scent of fear that clings to her clothes like smoke. Strands of grey hair have fallen loose from her tight bun. They tickle at the edge of my nose.

"My little Songbook," she whispers. "We're going to be lost without that big brain of yours."

She releases me, holding my shoulders at arms' length. I want to stay for a few moments more in the safety of her apartment, but we both know that can't happen.

Melody shoos me out of her door, whispering hurried warnings, "Don't take the transit or the Overcars. They'll try to scan where your ID was, and then you'll be trapped. Keep your eyes down. Don't let the recognition progs get a lock on your face. Stay away from the main streets. The Love Squads are thicker there. And don't forget your protein bars. You'll need to eat on the way. I've put them all in your pack, so you should have enough to get there and a little more. Oh, and please be careful."

"I will, Melody. I'll be careful," I say. Normally I'd be tempted to roll my eyes, but after Danse's arrest I'm not arguing anymore.

"Composer, send us a thousand new Songbooks, someday," she whispers, upward. She gives me a final nod of farewell, and then disappears with the sliver of light behind her closed door. And I'm left standing alone on the dim landing outside.

Behind me, the lift doors shudder as the ancient elevator whines. I know I should be making a run for it, but my feet won't move. It seems so unbelievable that my world would be falling apart surrounded by the ordinary smells of stale cooking and musty hallways.

Through the other apartment doors waft sounds of everyday Love Citizens preparing meals, readying for the compulsory evening broadcast. A clatter of plates. Muffled conversations. The Love Collective anthem blares through the cracks, followed by Supreme Lover Midgate's voice. I shudder. Our leader's warm and soothing tones once seemed motherly to me, before the Squads showed us the knives of steel hidden in her words.

Precious time ticks away. But all I can do is stare at Melody's closed door as if my eyes could draw me back into the past. I'm still standing there when a familiar feeling sends tingles along my shoulders.

I will be with you
Until the end of the age.

Lyric's words bolster my spirit as I pull the black hood over my head. Then I push against the fire door that will lead me down the stairwell and out into the big, dangerous world outside.

**LOVE COLLECTIVE OFFICIAL
COMMUNICATIONS CHANNEL
VILE HATER ALERT
HATER ALERT
ALERT**

Good evening, my Lovelies. May you live your dreams and reach for the universe. I love you all. No really, I mean it.

Tonight I want to thank our loyal Love Squads for the way they care for each and every one of you.

Nobody in the Love Collective is ignored. Our eyes are on all of you.

It is unfortunate, but I'm afraid that I cannot celebrate tonight. You see, no matter how many Triumph of Love festivals we run across all of our cities, no matter how well we feed and clothe you all, there are some lunatics who just want to bring us all down. So as much as it pains me to tell you, I have upsetting news to report:

Haters are active tonight.

Yes. I am sure you are as disappointed by this news as I am.

Now here in the Love Collective, we want to love all of you, all of the time. But we can't love Haters. Haters do not deserve to live in this beautiful world we have made for ourselves.

I am about to show you IDs of our Haters this evening. If you see them, don't touch them. We do not want you to be infected by their nasty hatefulness. Their names are flagged, so if they try and buy anything from you, the LoveSys will let us know straight away, and we'll be right there to whisk them out of your sight. Do not worry. We have it under control.

I'm sure that you, just like me, cannot wait to see those Haters get exactly what they deserve in the Haters' Pavilion.

Sleep well, my Lovelies. And remember: Love all. Be all.

Supreme Lover Midgate, signing off for the evening.

It takes me a while to walk out of Melody's neighbourhood. I skirt around the blocks, avoiding the well-lit subway entrance, and keep to the smaller paths as much as I can. After an hour or so, I reach the edge of the central business district, where the high-rise apartment blocks glitter with sparkling prestige.

Traffic thins, and the crowd of people slows to a trickle. It's getting late. In the dorms, you could be penalised for being awake past Beauty Sleep. I guess it's the same out here too.

Melody's instructions play over and over in my head: *Hurry around the corners. Look as if you're nearly home. Do not make it look like you're lost. Surveillance cams are always big black eyes above you, so keep your head down. Use the corners of your vision to check whether you've been seen. Composer protect you long enough to get the Song out of here.*

I manage to get within several blocks of the river in another hour. I stride along the back streets and two linen-clad citizens bustle past me, casting worried glances to the left and right. They know what's coming. When Beauty Sleep curfew kicks in, the city lights will be extinguished, and nobody will be allowed out.

"Are you all right, miss?"

I stop with a jolt. The speaker, an older man with a sparsely whiskered chin, leans out from the window of his sleek silver Overcar. A driver's cap hangs crookedly off his head. He must have pulled up beside me while I was lost in thought.

"Pardon?" I say, startled. Then I remember myself and salute with my right hand. "Love all. Be all." I keep my left wrist hidden against my backpack strap.

He salutes back. "Need a ride?" His tone is light, but I can see the edge of suspicion in his gaze. Few respectable citizens are on the streets at this hour. He knows that as well as I do.

"Hm? Oh, I'm okay. Just a . . . a lot of overtime at work." I shrug, shoving back my panic. "You know how it is."

"You better let me take you home, miss. Getting late." He

cocks his thumb at the vidscreen behind him. It forms a thin collar-like band around the entire building, announcing the countdown to curfew. Big orange clocks flash on and off as they scroll around the walls. *2230 . . . 2230 . . . 2230 . . . 2231 . . .*

Only half an hour until Beauty Sleep. At 2300 the Love Squads will emerge for the night patrol, and anyone stupid enough to be outside will disappear without a trace.

"Uh . . . thanks, but I'm nearly there." I lift my chin vaguely in the direction of the corner up ahead. "It'd be a waste of your time. Need the exercise, anyway."

"Well, okay. But don't blame me when you're up there on the Haters' Pavilion Show."

I force out a laugh, which sounds way too fake. "Don't worry. I'd only have myself to blame if I were that stupid."

"You got that right. You take care now."

The Overcar glides away with an electric whine, and it takes every ounce of strength I have not to break into a run. I'm still too far from the East Quarter to reach the safe house before the squads come out to play. I'm just going to have to find somewhere to hide until morning.

Know any refuges nearby? I ask the Composer.

In the distance, a boat's horn echoes off the apartment blocks. It gives me an idea. I hitch my backpack up on my shoulders and walk faster. If I can move quickly enough, I might be able to get to the river and find some shelter before it's dark.

The vision screens become more insistent as the minutes tick by, switching from bright orange to a deep, dangerous red: *2246 . . . 2246 . . . 2247.* I start to jog. I'm alone on the streets now. Apartment blocks loom above me like silent sentinels, watching, judging. Occasional Overcars hum by, their silver forms reflecting the red glow of the clocks in long, thin streaks.

"Two more blocks," I huff to myself, hoping my aching feet don't give out first.

By the time I reach the Heartstroke Bridge, the warnings

have switched to a countdown. *BEAUTY SLEEP IN 0305 . . . 0304 . . . 0303.* I have just enough time to climb under the enormous concrete pylons into a shadowy alcove before the lights across the river begin to wink out, one by one.

I've never been out during Beauty Sleep before. It's a stunning, eerie sight. Love City, vibrant hub of the Love Collective nation, is slowly wrapped in darkness as every bulb and beam shuts off. Lights in the high-rise buildings go out like a multi-eyed creature closing its eyes. Streetlights dim, then disappear. Transport grinds to a halt. And as the lights go, a silence descends that feels unnatural and wrong.

"Apprentice Flick, you have disobeyed curfew."

I shiver against the imagined chastisement and pull the blanket from my backpack. Laying it over my knees, I stare out at the moonlit river below.

There is a river whose streams make glad the city of the Composer . . .

My mind recalls the beginning of that Song fragment.

The Composer is our refuge and strength,
Always present to help in trouble.
Therefore we will not fear,
Though the earth collapse to rubble.

I didn't think I had any tears left, but they still track their way down my face, leaving cold, salty trails.

12

Love City
Is A Clean City.
24 Years Crime-Free.
Keep It Up!

MEMORY DATE: 2285.349 (TWO AND A HALF *years ago)*

Memory Location: Elite Academy dining hall.

I drag my depressed feet into the dining room and fall into line behind other Apprentices, letting my hands receive the tray of breakfast goop without a sound. Hodge's words echo on replay in my mind, weighing me down with each repetition. They won't leave me alone, even when I sit myself at a table of strangers and sluggishly begin to eat.

"Thank you for the offer, but I don't think I'd like to be your Triumph buddy."

Everything about last night stings. I feel stupid and unlovable and a whole bunch of other bad things all at once.

"I don't want a couple of weeks."

I've ruined everything.

A spoonful of food is halfway to my mouth when I stop, mouth open in an embarrassingly large O. A jolt of uncomfortable electricity shatters through my system. Hodge, the cause of the uncomfortable

*feelings, strides into the room, looking around above our heads. I
duck my head to hide behind the larger Apprentices around me.*

*In a rush of shame and embarrassment, I wait until he's nearly
at the front of the line and then make a sudden dash. Pushing myself
off the table, I speed-walk over to the return console, dropping my
plate down into the slot and then turning for the door. I aim for the
exit that's furthest away from the servery, and bolt there without a
backward glance. I don't know whether he sees me. All I can think
of is that for as long as I live, I will never want to speak to him again.*

THEY ARE COMING.

The words whisper themselves into my mind before I am fully
awake, and I am standing as soon as I hear them. No, not standing.
Running. Even if the streets are darker than the Supreme Lover's
heart, I will not fear. The Muse is with me, guiding me away
from danger.

At least, I hope it's the Muse speaking to me and not just my
own random nightmares.

The full moon gives just enough light to run by. Long shadows
loom down the side of the buildings, and I feel like a ghost, gliding
in and out of the darkness. I am four streets from the bridge by the
time I hear footsteps thudding toward the river. The Love Squad.
Their heavy boots clatter along the road in the distance, echoing
over the empty streets like an out-of-tune symphony.

The further I get from the river, the denser the buildings
become. Apartment blocks and decaying tenements crowd together
toward the sky like curious onlookers around a playground brawl.
The long shadows they cast across the streets coalesce into deep
blobs of pitch black. It doesn't take too long before I'm completely
disoriented. I can't tell where I'm heading anymore. But I have to
find the safe house before it's too late. Before . . .

Left.

Without thinking, I obey and flit sideways into an alley I hadn't noticed. How did they find me? The sounds of bootsteps are closing in.

"There it is!"

The voice is harsh and metallic, filtered through one of the black Love Squad helmets with electronic precision. I push ahead, almost flying over the pavement and around a bend at the end of the alley. By the sound I am being pursued by four, maybe five soldiers. I wonder why they haven't deployed the nets yet. Maybe the close alley walls make it too risky, or perhaps they were counting on snatching me while I slept. I speed around another corner, hopping over some upturned recycling bins that a careless Lovely will need to pay for in the morning.

This new street is too open and wide to provide any safety. I search for a better exit. The moonlight seems to be shining more brightly now, which is even more dangerous. But in the growing light, I spot another alley to my right, halfway down the block. I duck inside it, speeding toward the other end.

The Love Squad footsteps are almost around the corner. If I can get to the next corner, then I might be able to lose them. Five paces, four, three, two . . . and then I emerge on the wide avenue leading straight through the middle of the city, up the hill to the Hall of Love.

The sky is lit by sun-bright floodlights, which illuminate the vividly colored flag that always flies above the central tower. The silent road is wider than a football field. How did I end up running south to the middle of the city? I've just run from a bear into the jaws of a lion.

Trust me.

I push down my doubts, which threaten to turn my inner music into some sort of death march, and dash across the road. My backpack bounces uncomfortably. A row of Overcars lines the far curb. If I duck behind them, the Love Squad won't see me when they emerge from the alley.

Beyond the Overcars, the arched entrance to the Central Market yawns like a laughing mouth. It's too much to ask that there won't be surveillance cameras here. My only hope is to use the thousand little vendor carts lining the market's central court as a temporary cover.

"Please let the Watchers be looking elsewhere. *Please.*"

"Alert!" comes the metallic voice from the edge of the alley I just left. "All available units to Heartstrong Avenue! All units!"

My heart sinks. One squad, I can perhaps outrun. Two, I might be able to fool with a miracle. But there is no way on the Composer's green earth that I will be able to lose the entire Squadron. In a few minutes the avenue will be swarming with hundreds of black-suited soldiers, like an army of ravens hunting a lone beetle.

Passing the cars, I hunch down and bolt through the gates of the market, entering a wide square filled by a grid of small market stalls and antique-style carts. Most are shuttered closed, but some are open, their empty tables shining in the moonlight, or covered by the shadow of their canvas canopies. I flit from cart to cart, aiming for the exit at the rear.

Behind me, the boots of my pursuers have entered Heartstrong Avenue, and there's the sound of cries and commands as they fan out. I wonder when the Watchers will come online. Maybe they've already started searching from camera to camera until they find me, brought out of their barracks in the dead of night by the Squad's request. If they send commands to the squads while I'm running, I'll be dead.

"Focus," I tell myself. Heart racing, I hide behind a cart to take a quick glance backward. None of the soldiers have entered the market yet. I might be in luck.

Keep going.

I bolt forward again, listening for the sounds of pursuit. Somehow, I make it through and run into a large loading dock toward another alley. But this alley is a straight concrete passageway. There is no way to outrun the Love Squad here. The exit is too far distant, and they'll see me long before they catch me.

"Well . . . this . . . is it," I pant. "I'm . . . done."

Down.

The beat of music within me hiccups, and I falter.

Down. Now.

I spin around, confused. There is not even a doorway or alcove where I can hide. Behind me, bootsteps enter the market. In another twenty seconds they will be around the corner, and I will cease to exist.

Then I see it. Twelve feet along the path lies a derelict road grate, almost hidden beside a tall grey wall, an ancient relic leading to the disused sewers below. A bar of the grate has snapped clean off, and there is enough room for a small body to fit through. My small body. I send up a silent prayer of thanks to the Composer and leap toward the drain.

I lower myself in and land in a small, square, concrete box, a little patch of blackness hidden from the street above. As my head dips, Love Squad shouts echo from way back in the market. I crouch lower, making my body as small as I can.

After a few moments, boots trample heavily along the pavement above. I hold my breath, pressing myself down into the darkness. I see a brief cloud of black-uniformed figures pressing forward, and then they are gone. Somewhere in the distance, an ominous alarm sounds. I wait for seconds, minutes. The alley above me remains empty and silent.

What now? It's obvious that I can't stay in this stink-hole forever. Once the Love Squad realizes I'm gone, they'll be everywhere, combing the streets for any biological evidence of my existence. If I stay, it will only be a matter of time before they find me.

I reach out my right hand out to lean against the concrete wall, and almost fall into a large, circular opening. Cool, fetid air swirls at me. I hear the sound of trickling water to my left. More careful pats in the darkness tell me that two pipes open out into my hiding spot, a straight line through this boxy road drain. One to my left, the other to my right.

It suddenly occurs to me why the Muse might have sent me here. Not a pleasant thought, of course. I pinch my nose against the smell. Why couldn't there have been a nicer way to lose the squads? Why did it have to be this horrible, stinky pipe?

I look from one dark void to the other, trying to make a decision.

Without further thought, I dive to the right. Seconds later I am enveloped in darkness, blindly feeling my way through the putrid, forgotten underbelly of Love City. I squash down the doubtful memories, the faces of those faithful Sirens who have already vanished without a trace.

MEMORY DATE: 2285.313 (TWO AND A HALF *years ago)*

Memory Location: Secret

The meeting over, Sirens thank me, but I can tell they're being polite. Danse comes over.

"I was too nervous. My voice went thin. There was a spot in the second fragment where—"

Danse smiles. "Nerves are normal when you're starting out."

"I'm mostly scared that I'll get the words wrong."

"Ah. Hold on to that, Cadence. That's good fear."

I look at him, confused.

"As long as you're worried about the words, you're going to keep working to remember them correctly. The minute you stop caring is the minute you get sloppy. The Song is too precious for that. Our people need the truth, exactly as it was delivered."

"I hadn't thought about it that way. That makes me even more nervous."

"Don't let it get you down. Remember, the Composer wants his Song to be sung. He's not going to let it be forgotten."

13

You cannot hide from the Collective when they are everywhere and everything.

Supreme Lover Midgate
Love All. Be All.

DARKNESS WRAPS AROUND ME TIGHTER than a blanket. I've been crawling for hours, and my eyes are still trying to make out shapes in the inky black void. The soft sound of my hands and knees hitting concrete is the only noise I can hear, apart from my own breathing. I suppose I should be happy with that. No sound equals safety, for now.

The air in this drain smells musty and wet, a pungent mix of moss and algae. After the Triumph of Love all those years ago, recycling processes made these sewers redundant. I shudder to imagine what would be flowing through this pipe otherwise. For the first time in my life, I am almost glad about something the Love Collective has done.

When my stomach rumbles, it echoes along the pipe. I stop and clutch at my abdomen, trying to stop the noise from repeating itself. But my belly grumbles and gurgles, protesting that I have ignored it for too long.

I work my body sideways so that I am sitting hunched against the curve of the pipe as if resting in an invisible hammock. Then I set my small pack on my lap and feel blindly around the inner pockets. The emergency stash of protein bars is right at the bottom. When Melody first gave me this pack, I never thought I'd really need any of this. Now I'm glad that she was far more cautious than I ever was.

"Look after Melody, please?" She'll try to be strong, but I just know the old woman won't last one day in Love Squad clutches.

Hunger overtakes me, and I swallow down a protein bar in two gulps. It's not nearly enough to fill my stomach, but, Lyric willing, it will do for a few hours more. Who knows when I'll next find a friendly face? Best to ration out the food as much as I can.

A soft breeze drifts down the tunnel behind me, sending a gentle caress of cool air across the back of my neck. Every nerve in my body suddenly zings. These tunnels must experience drafts all the time, but for some reason, this feels different. I'm not sure whether it's the Muse's prompting or whether I'm just being paranoid, but I decide that being trapped in a drain is not such a good idea after all.

I scrunch up the protein-bar wrapper, shove it into my pack and sling the bag over my shoulders. In seconds I am scrambling away from the breeze. The whisper of air follows me. An unpleasant memory tugs at the back of my mind.

MEMORY DATE: 2282.266 (FIVE YEARS AGO)
Memory Location: Watcher dorm, Elite Academy
"Executive Lover?" I call, knowing he is monitoring me from outside the Watcher room.
"Yes, Apprentice?" Crucible's voice crackles with irritation.

"*This suspect has disappeared into the drain system. How can I find him?*"

"Send in the biological measures," he commands. Confused, I look around the sphere in front of me for some kind of clue as to what he's talking about. He must be watching me because he makes a frustrated clucking noise.

"Code 50-34," he says. "Call it in with the coordinates, and the Hall will send in a tracker drone."

"Oh," I say, feeling stupid. I call it in using Crucible's instructions, waiting to hear from the Hall's communication channel. "Why have I never heard of it before?"

"They're only for subterranean work. Strictly speaking they were decommissioned a few years ago," Crucible explains. "But I've sent a message explaining that your request is at my authority, so you won't have any problems."

I DON'T KNOW WHAT *BIOLOGICAL MEASURES* are, and in that moment I decide that I never want to find out. Adrenaline surges through my system, forcing me into a speedy dash forward. But it's hard going. I'm not built for four-legged speed, and in the cramped conditions, my arms struggle to keep a proper rhythm with my legs.

"Crucible would love this," I mutter.

I crawl along for a few minutes, ignoring the pain in my knees and hands, trying to listen for any hint of what might be chasing me. In the darkness, my hearing has become more acute, and I can tell there's something other than a breeze back there. I can also tell it's getting closer. I briefly think about fishing out the torch Melody left for me from my pack, but decide against it. If Crucible really has sent a drone down the drain after me, I don't want to waste time sitting when I need to be moving.

A few minutes later, or maybe seconds, or an hour —it's hard to tell what time it is with no light around me—my hands hit a curve in the pipe, forcing me to veer right. When I turn around the bend, the light whisper of the breeze behind me is joined by a different sound coming from up ahead.

At first I think it is another gust of wind, but it's too constant, too loud. The drain is curving toward a large, rushing body of water. My heart almost leaps into my mouth.

The sound of gushing water grows—and with it my fear. Something changes in the sound approaching from behind that makes it worse. A soft, slithering rattle. Unnatural. Mechanical. Whatever it is, the thing pursuing me is closing in.

There's no need for the Muse to warn me to run this time. I bolt forward as fast as I can, my legs and arms moving in a gangly imitation of a four-legged creature. The water sounds grow louder. So do the slithering, mechanical clicks behind me.

I crawl faster. Sweat stings in my eyes. My back aches with the unnatural effort, and my breath is coming in ragged pants. Behind me, the slithering sound grows strong enough that I can hear the way it moves. It is large, whatever it is, but it doesn't seem to be an animal. In my anxiety I had been imagining a giant serpent hastening to devour me whole, but the hissing seems to be the sound of wheels on concrete. There is something else too. Some kind of unidentifiable clicking and whirring. When I hear the mechanical sounds, a single terrifying thought overtakes my whole being:

Crucible has found me.

Panic grips me like a steel vice, and all rational thought flees my head. I am all animal now, clattering through the darkness like a hunted rat. The dull rushing of water ahead has grown to the roar of a waterfall, swift and thunderous. My prayer is nothing but a wordless terror. With strength and speed I didn't know I had, I surge forward, seeking some kind of refuge in the darkness.

Without warning, something razor sharp pierces my left calf with metallic precision. Fire rips through my leg, up my back, and into my shoulder, and I almost fall face-first into the sludge at the bottom of the pipe. I stagger forward, trying to shake off the blinding pain so I can concentrate enough to escape. Stars flash across my vision. The device releases, and I propel forward, reflexes kicking in while my mind reels.

I can only take two more tottering paces before a second sharp stab pierces my leg, almost directly over the first wound. This time metal teeth drag me down, clamping onto me like a trap. I kick wildly with my free leg at whatever it is that has me.

Time slows. I become acutely aware of my surroundings. The sound of the water is a roar in my ears, but I can still hear my thudding heart. I can feel the grainy texture of the dirt and sludge in the palms of my hands. One leg feels like it's being sliced apart. The other is still free. Behind me, the mechanical thing whirs and clicks.

With superhuman effort, I push myself up with my hands and thrash with my free leg. Steel rips even further into my flesh, and I nearly pass out with the pain. But I can't collapse. Not now. I thrust my right leg backward. It connects with something soft, and my trapped leg is suddenly free. Every instinct screams at me to give up, to curl up into a ball and nurse my injury. But I cannot stop. I cannot stop. Cannot . . .

I drag myself on, limping in a strange three-legged hop using my hands and good foot. But I am slower, dragging my left leg as gingerly as I can to avoid the jarring pain that every movement brings. I hold my breath, waiting for the next attack even as I force myself on.

Just then, my hands reach thin air where they were expecting drainpipe. I grab for something to hold on to, but all I find is rushing wind. My body pitches forward, tumbling down into dark nothingness. I'm too shocked to scream. The roar of water rushes up to meet me. Then with a loud crash, I land in the gushing torrent.

In seconds I am enveloped in a cold shock of water. I somersault around and around in the powerful current, unable to breathe. The force of the water rips the small emergency pack from my back, and I cannot see to hold onto it. My lungs feel as if they are going to explode, and my injured leg feels as if it is being torn off again. But in the middle of the darkness, the ancient words of the Song come to mind.

Reach down your hand from on high;
Deliver me from the mighty waters.

"Thank you that I . . . could serve you . . . even a little, my Composer," I think as I embrace the night.

MEMORY DATE: 2286.189 (TWO YEARS AGO)
Memory Location: Love City

In the riverside park, wind softly rustles through the leaves. A wide path curves through the lawns at the top of the slope, punctuated with small benches set at regular intervals. Green slopes face the water, occasionally marked with round garden beds brimming with spring flowers. At the base of the slope sits a wide promenade beside the river. The paved promenade is protected by a fence made of laser-cut panels, decorated in abstract, wavy patterns.

I lift my face to the breeze, feeling the gentle tickle of air and smelling the floral perfume. Water laps at the pylons below as, here and there, boats gently drift along the river's surface, following the deeper shipping channels toward loading docks somewhere downriver. It's a perfect day. I'm glad Hodge convinced me to take a walk before I had to go back to the Academy.

We stroll down the promenade, and Hodge pauses beside the fence. "Imagine being able to do this someday for real," Hodge says, gazing out at the sparkling water.

A soft breeze blows, causing little waves to toss and lap in the water. I lean on the wide railing atop the fence, looking down at the river currents. The deep brown water is too dark to see any life below it, but the world above is reflected on its surface in dark shadowy outlines. Hodge and I are two statue-like blobs against a browny-white sky.

"Do you really think we'll get to?" I ask.

Hodge stares across the river. "Composer willing."

"We would have to get matching shifts," I say doubtfully.

"No problem."

"I'd have to be posted near the barracks so we can hang out together,"

"Of course."

Hodge draws closer, leaning on the fence railing beside me, his arm nearly touching mine. We stand side by side for a while, watching the water together. For as long as I've been an Elite Apprentice, he's always been there. Intimidating at first, but now comfortable. I wonder when I first began to need him near me. When did I first think of him as more than just the dependable bunk-room leader who escorted me on city missions?

"The lake," I murmur, remembering the truck explosion and my panic. That was it, for me. The thought of Hodge not being around anymore made me realize how much I had come to depend on him. But I couldn't tell him that. Not then, anyway.

"What?" Hodge says, shifting closer.

I look up at him and smile. "Nothing. Just enjoying."

Sunlight plays in his warm brown eyes. "The Composer is good."

"All the time," I say.

Every One Of You
Has Potential.

Don't Be A Hater.

Love All. Be All.
The Love Collective.

AN ICY WIND SENDS RIPPLING SHIVERS DEEP into my body. Through numbing cold, my eyelids flutter open. I have lost all feeling in my toes, but there's a harsh stinging sensation in the palms of my hands. *I am alive, after all.*

A weak, insipid light outlines stark shapes in the gloom. For the first time in ages, I can actually see. It's the kind of light that might be reflected from a tablet screen. But it's enough to show me that I am in a rectangular kind of cavern. Man-made. Concrete.

Gentle, freezing waves lap at my knees, which must be the reason I can't feel the bottoms of my feet. I am lying on a slope of some kind. My head is resting on the concrete. My feet are nearly floating.

I look down. Water flows around my legs, toward an arched outlet, beyond which is a broad, slow-moving river. The outlet is blocked by a large metal grate, which is clotted with a nest of mangled rubbish. Outside the grate and across the river, distant city streetlamps twinkle like weak stars. From the looks of the low warehouse buildings, I've travelled away from the center of Love City to one of the outer industrial zones.

Composer alone knows how I am alive.

The concrete ramp slopes upward to a small, flat walkway between two ventilation shafts. A dark rectangular void stands between them. It looks like a hallway of some sort. I should probably investigate, but my motivation to do anything is evaporating fast. Every ounce of my being wants to disappear into a slow, lazy sleep from which I never wake up. But I've learned enough about hypothermia to know that staying would mean disaster.

My palms sting as I groan and strain up out of the dangerous liquid. A couple of times I sink back, falling even further down the slope. My clothes are heavy with water, making it harder to lift myself up. It all feels too hard. I just want to sleep.

I reach out for my blanket, only to remember that I left it in a heap under the Heartstroke bridge when I had to run. Has it been only a day that I've been running? I can't tell. The streetlights turn on at the end of beauty sleep, which means it's sometime after 0430.

My head feels full of cotton wool. The water in my clothes forces the cold even deeper into my body until I feel like an icicle. My teeth chatter so hard it's as if they're going to dance out of my head. But my will to survive kicks in, and inch by agonizing inch, I scrape myself up to the top of the slope.

A soft breath of warm wind blows from one of the ventilation shafts beside the hallway. It's suddenly the most beautiful thing I've ever experienced. I reach for the warmth, stretching out my fingers so they glide in the airburst. Then I push my body until it is fully in front of the current. The heat from the air stings my frozen fingers at first, but within minutes I have dozed off, my head resting against the silver vent cover.

When I wake, my hair is completely dry, and a weak line of yellow dawn glows along the horizon beyond the river. It won't be long, and the water outside will be a hive of activity. Activity means a greater chance that I'll be found, and I don't want to be found right now.

With what feels like a superhuman effort, I lift myself from the ground and stagger to my feet. My left leg almost gives way beneath me in agony, and I fight against the urge to sink back down and cry. I can't look at it—can't face what feels like a mangled mess of flesh. If being attacked wasn't enough, floating around in putrid stormwater is a sure way to get infected. And I have zero idea of where I can find treatment. The basic first aid kit in my pack is gone, drowned somewhere in the waters.

Since the grate blocks my exit to the river, my only option is the darkened hallway. I force my body forward. I have no idea what monsters are waiting ahead. All I can do is hope I get lost long enough to survive.

MEMORY DATE: 2285.349 (TWO AND A HALF *years ago)*

Memory Location: Elite Academy Coding wing

Sun beats down on my head, pushing trickles of sweat down the back of my neck. I hasten along the path. A frigid rush of climate-controlled air buffets my uniform when I step into the revolving door. It wheels me into the Coding common room, and I walk on, my emotions in turmoil.

"Apprentice Flick!" his voice calls out from behind me, laced with anxiety. I hesitate, my foot half raised from the ground. I know it's Hodge. But I'm not the kind of fool who goes back for a second helping of humiliation. He'll have to understand.

Taking a deep breath, I lift my foot properly this time, ready to step away. The solid pounding of his footsteps follows me down the concrete path. They're coming closer. A sudden rush of fear propels me forward, and I skip quickly toward the elevators.

"Flick!" the deep voice calls, only feet away. "Please, I—"

His voice is cut off suddenly as the doors click shut. I don't look back.

THE ROUGH BRICK BENEATH MY FINGERTIPS anchors me to the world. All else is black void. Whenever I take a shuffling step, a hollow echo reverberates into the distance. It sounds as if this narrow hallway goes on forever. But I don't have forever. My body is shutting down.

With every step, fire shoots from my ruined calf muscle up into my spine. I want to collapse into a heap and sleep for a thousand years, Song or no Song. My brain is foggy. It's good this hall has only one direction because if I came on a crossroads, I'm pretty sure the decision would kill me.

A couple of times the hallway makes a sudden ninety-degree turn. Thanks to my fingers and my incredibly slow pace, I avoid smacking my face into a wall of brick. But I'm disoriented. Clouds of memory begin to play in my head, and I'm scared that I'm slowly losing my grip on reality. My left leg drags me down all the more, and my steps slow even further. I feel as if my life is ebbing away.

"Please," I whisper. "Help me, Lyric. Don't let me die here."

After another sudden turn, a pinprick of light begins to glow at the long, straight end of the passage. As I step closer, the light coalesces from a white star-point into a single lightbulb protruding from a red brick wall. Along the way, ancient signs pepper the walls, their messages decayed and rusted over the centuries:

AR ING:
GH VOL GE
RE XTI U SH R
AD OA TIV
PO SON

Along both walls, heavy-looking metal doors are set into the brick every twenty feet or so. I am barely past one of these doors when it flies open. A tiny figure explodes out of a small room straight into my side.

I cry out as my shoulder is painfully thrown against brick.

"What the—" exclaims a sharp, feminine voice.

I look at the speaker and freeze in shock. At first I think I am looking straight into the blue eyes of Supreme Lover Midgate. But the impression fades quickly. She is much younger. She isn't wearing a Collective uniform either, but blue jeans and a top. Sure, her hair might be a similar style to Midgate's, but she is most definitely not an AI. Maybe only a few years older than me.

She steps away and wipes moisture off her sleeve from where I have collided with her.

"Who are you?" Her tone is menacing.

I shrink back. "Nobody." I stare hard at the floor. My shoulders are instantly pressed back against the brick by arms as solid as steel. If I wasn't feeling so sick and cold, I might have been able to defend myself. But she's caught me at a bad time. My left leg is useless, and her wiry arms pin me back as effectively as any Love Squad restraint.

"Why are you spying on me?" she demands.

"Spying? I wasn't . . . I don't know what you're talking about!" I gasp. For a few seconds, her deep blue eyes search my own. Then with a curt nod she releases me.

"If you're not a spy, what are you doing here?"

"I was lost."

"Your clothes are wet."

"You're observant."

"What did you do—fall into a toilet?"

"Something like that." The adrenaline begins to fade from my system, and I am suddenly earth-shatteringly weary. "Please. Do you mind if . . . if I just . . . I think I need to sit down."

I don't remember my knees buckling, but I collapse to the ground. The stranger stands over me.

"You're injured." Something in her tone of voice makes me open my eyes and look up. From this angle, the light on the wall behind her is throwing a halo around the top of her head. It's very disconcerting.

She squats down near my feet and reaches toward the ragged remains of my left trouser leg. Closing my eyes right now is probably dangerous, but I can't stop myself. I am wracked with fatigue and pain.

"Let me get you some help," she says, her voice changing. "I can take you to a health station and—"

"No!" My eyes open wide in panic. "No. Please. I'll be okay. I just . . . I need to find my friends."

"What friends?" she asks, and at exactly the same moment my mind asks it too. *What friends?* Right now, I don't know where any Sirens are, and even if I did, the last thing they need is for me to bring the heat of the Collective down upon them. I scramble for an answer.

"Um, I . . . I got lost and, and . . . um . . . I just . . . just not a health station, okay?"

Her eyes narrow. "What did you say your name was again?" she asks.

"I didn't," I say evenly.

"You look familiar."

"We live in the Love Collective. We all look familiar. Even you. A minute ago, I could have sworn you were Supreme Lover Midgate."

She sits back on her haunches and stares at me. I know she's trying to look neutral, but her face has gone a whiter shade of pale. The Midgate lookalike rubs at her short hair with long fingers, as if she's trying to make up her mind about something.

"Alright," she sighs. "I promise not to ask you your name if you don't ask mine. Deal?"

"Deal."

"Okay. Well, I can't leave you down here like this," she says with a nervous glance down the hallway.

"I'll be fine. As long as I can work out where I am, anyway." I fight against my eyelids, which seem to desperately want to close.

"You seriously don't know?"

"I got lost," I explain. "I was in this drain, and then I fell down into a waterfall and woke up back there somewhere."

"How did you get in a drain? Those places are deadly."

I can't lie to her, but at the same time it would be dangerous to reveal too much. She might be a soldier or a spy, or worse. Given the expensive cut of her clothes, I'd go with "or worse."

"Homeless Lovelies need to sleep where they can."

Understanding dawns in her eyes.

"Homeless, huh? In that case, I know exactly where to take you. Come on."

She reaches out her hand to help me up, and in that moment, I do the only thing I can think to do.

I take it.

15

No Hater Can Escape
The Love Collective.
We Will Find You.
We Will Embrace You.

Love All. Be All.

SINCE I CAN ONLY TRAVEL ABOUT AS FAST AS
a snail on a salt bath, we must make a funny sight, this strange
girl and I. One of us dripping wet, bedraggled, limping weakly,
and biting back the pain with gritted teeth. Beside her, a skinny,
neater-looking figure patiently keeping pace, hands clasped
behind her back. The silence is all sorts of awkward.

"I know I can't . . . can't ask your name," I begin, my words
bouncing off the brick walls beside us. "But I can't just say, 'hey,
you!' can I?"

"True," she admits.

"So what do I call you, then?"

"Just call me Lark," she says with a shrug. "What about you?
If you won't tell me your name, how about I call you Drip?"

"Ha."

"Soggy?"

"Not funny—ow!" I wince as another shot of pain runs up
my leg. I stumble and almost fall to the ground, but her arm is

suddenly holding me upright. It seems to bring her out of her joking mood.

"That leg's pretty serious," she says, keeping her arm just below my shoulders.

I shake my head. "I'll be okay. I don't think it's broken or anything. Well, it feels broken, but not the bones, if you know what I mean," I babble, and feel like slapping myself. Why am I babbling? It must be the injury.

"How did you do it?"

"Don't know," I reply. "It was dark."

We reach the end of the hallway, where a single metal door blocks our way. Lark opens it with her free hand and leads me through it into a brightly lit stairwell. It looks like any industrial fire escape, all white walls and stark-white LEDs. Thick concrete steps rise above our heads.

Leaning me against the lower railing of the stairs, Lark ducks under the bottom row of stairs and stops at another battered metal door, pulling a large ring of ancient keys from her pocket.

"Through here, we'll get you patched up," she says, grasping a key between her fingers and fitting it into the door's rusty lock. "It won't be as pretty as a health station, but it will have to do, since you won't go legit."

My stomach sinks slightly.

"Is it safe?" I ask.

She gives me a weird look. "That's a strange question for someone in your situation," she says.

Before I can speak, she pulls the door open. It looks as if it should creak, but it swings with a quiet sigh. A rush of hot, stifling air buffets our faces. It feels wonderful.

The hallway beyond the door is crammed with even more pipes and cables than the last one. They run the length of the narrow space in untidy bundles along the walls, from floor to ceiling. Steam rises from a few riveted joints along one pipe.

"Keep away from these ones," Lark warns, pointing at the largest brass pipes. "They're just our heating system, but they'll give you a good burn if you get too close."

I edge away from the steam-spewing pipes.

Lark leads me on. Ahead, the pipes all bend left around a hidden corner. She disappears around it, not even bothering to look back. I feel like leaning against the wall for support, but a burst of steam reminds me it's not a good idea. The smells of greasy cooking, pungent smoke, and unwashed bodies waft around the corner. In the distance, I hear a rumble of voices. Lots of voices.

When I reach the corner, my jaw drops. The pipe-filled hall opens out to a high-ceilinged underground warehouse. But that's not what shocks me to the core. Stalls and makeshift cottages are stacked up beside each other in a vast shanty town. They seem to be made of cardboard, plywood, sheets of corrugated metal, and even old wooden pallets. Walkways and rows snake between them. A patchwork of market stalls lies directly in front of us. There are people everywhere.

"Welcome to the Ghetto." Lark gestures beside me like a proud tour guide. "Home for the homeless, center of the black market, and Love City's best kept secret."

I look up at her, my mouth opening and closing like some newly caught fish.

"Why did I not know about this?"

"It wouldn't be a secret if everybody knew," says Lark. "That's kinda the point." She cocks her head, inviting me into the crowded community.

We pass a hawker who thrusts a plate of greasy-looking chips in my face. "Food for trade?" the woman says. Her face is grimy and stained, but her teeth flash white in her smile, and it's all I can do to stop myself from snatching the plate. Seeing the longing on my face, Lark picks up an apple from a fruit stall with a nod to the vendor, and hands it to me. I devour it hungrily.

We move on, past haphazard clothing stalls, tables covered with all manner of old appliances, books, meat, and groceries. Everything is a riot of noise and smell. Lark comes to a stop in front of a strange-looking circus tent.

This tent is a stark contrast to the cardboard and metal shanties around it. Thick red stripes flow down from a center pole, some faded and cracked with age. I assume the rest of the tent was once supposed to be white, but the canvas has long since been coated in grey-brown grime. A set of heavy-looking velvet curtains forms the entrance door. Lark draws these curtains aside so I can limp through. The noise dies down to a low hum as the curtains settle back into place behind us.

We stand in a dark, circular room, walled with more of the heavy velvet curtains. A table sits in the middle of the floor, with a single flickering candle as the only source of light. Behind the table lies a large bundle of rags. When the rags move, I jump in fright.

"Ah, it's my little Lark, flown back to see me," a cracked, ancient voice crows from somewhere underneath the ragged pile. "And what brings you here?"

"Good to see you again, Kent," Lark says with a smile in her voice. I wonder what she can see because I can't make out much. "How's business?"

"Better than ever. Or it will be, now they know you're back in town. Everybody wants a little piece of Lark, don't they?" The shadows in the corner move and rustle, and the rotund bundle of rags bustles out from behind the table toward us.

"If they want a piece of me, they can wait," Lark replies. "I've got someone here who needs your specialty."

The rags still.

"I'm a little busy at the moment."

"Oh, come on, Kent. You owe me. And how often do I call in favors, anyway?"

"True," Kent concedes, then sighs. "You might as well bring the patient through."

The bundle of rags glides over to the middle of the back wall, and I'm blinded by a flash of light as another curtain is drawn back. It takes a moment for my eyes to adjust, but Lark's hand is firmly under my elbow, and she guides me toward a small, square room.

A large, padded chair sits in the middle of the open space, surrounded by low tables and shelves. The chair sits on a strange plinth, with cables running below and around it. Now illuminated by the harsh white light, the large pile of rags—called Kent—turns out to be an older humpbacked human. The clothes are formless and ragged, and a scarf half covers Kent's face. A deep-blue eye regards me from beneath thick grey eyebrows, and folds of skin form a kind of curtain over bloodshot eyelids.

"Let's have a look at you, lovely," Kent rasps. A wizened hand grabs my own, stroking my palm between desiccated fingers. I am led to the chair and made to sit. Then with a clank and a whir, the chair rotates and flattens into a bed.

"So where do you hurt?" Kent asks, stroking my arms in a way that makes me feel sleepy. I know I should answer, but for some reason I am finding it hard to concentrate.

I point to my leg. The bright light around me disappears behind my fluttering eyelids.

"Hm. It's on the back," Kent says, flicking at the rags that were once the bottom of my pants. "Roll over."

With great difficulty, I heave myself sideways, wearily turning onto my stomach. Kent begins to fuss around, rattling boxes and drawers. Then there's a tiny prick of pain in my arm, and the world begins to dim.

"Alright, let's have a look. We'll have to take those pants off first, though. Lark?" Kent commands.

"What? No, I—" I try to protest, but I have no strength. My mouth feels like it's full of cotton wool. The words I speak sound wrong, as if my mouth is deformed and unable to move properly.

"You'd better handle it, Kent," Lark says, her voice coming from a great distance away.

"Squeamish, eh?" cackles the old voice. "Alright then."

I should be a bundle of nervous embarrassment, but this eccentric old being strokes my head into a quiet, relaxed fog. I barely register the wet trousers being peeled from my leg, nor the cotton sheet being laid across my body. Kent makes a distressed clicking noise, but it's as if someone else is being prodded and examined, not me. A warm, comfortable sensation washes over me, and I feel like I am floating in a deep, relaxing bath.

"That's it. We'll soon have you all patched up." The cracked and ancient voice gentles. A distant part of me feels Kent's touch along the edges of my wound. Sleep tugs at my eyes, calling me to oblivion, but through the fog I dimly register a discussion happening near my feet.

"Ew," Lark mutters.

"Where did you say she was from?"

"Homeless. Lost. Why do you ask?"

"Oh, I'm sure it's nothing. I just haven't seen this sort of wound since the Purging. If I didn't know better, I'd assume this was a Collective drone. The incisions are too regular here, see?"

"Can you fix it?"

"Not with what I've got. She'll need some of the good stuff to stop that getting infected. How's your bartering magic been lately?" Kent says.

"I'll see what I can do," Lark replies just as Kent touches a particularly raw spot, and I moan. In an instant the healer is back to stroking my arms, cooing and soothing as I drift beyond all conversation.

MY DREAMS ARE FITFUL. FEVERISH. ONE moment, I feel as if a thousand hot irons are pushing their way into my flesh and I am about to incinerate in a ball of flame and ash. The next moment my body transforms into ice, shivering into a thousand frozen splinters.

The world whirls into black, and I am back in the ancient drain, trying to flee from a giant metallic serpent. The serpent's fangs clamp firmly on my ankle and rip and tear at my flesh. I fall down and down into a void, surrounded by the sound of a waterfall but never reaching the bottom. The serpent falls with me, wrapping its unnatural coils around my body, crushing the breath from my chest. I gasp for air and the vision is gone.

Voices echo in the darkness, snatches of conversation floating around my head and through my ears. In my dream, I hear a vaguely familiar voice. Is it Sif? Or is it Akela? Perhaps someone else. I cannot tell.

Suddenly I am back in the drill field, dancing in time with all of my dorm mates, reciting the love chants and practicing our hater-recognition signs in perfect marching formations. Akela stands in ceremonial robes by the side of the field, speaking with a tree. Which, of course, to a normal person sounds crazy, but in my dream feels just as it should be.

"She's not waking up. Will she live?" Akela asks. Strangely, her voice sounds younger and smaller than I remember her being.

"Love all. Be all. Don't be a Hater!" I chant with all my dorm mates.

"She'll be fine, thanks to you," the tree replies in a cracked and ancient voice.

"*Haters can't love! Lovers can't hate!*" we chant.

"She'll have a limp for a while, but if you can get that medication, she'll heal up well," continues the tree.

"Who is she?" Akela asks in that vaguely familiar girl's voice.

"Can't tell. Someone's done a number on her ID."

"Weird."

"You say she was homeless? I doubt that. She's too clean," the tree says, folding two of its boughs as if they were arms in front of its trunk. It has no eyes, but I can tell it's staring at me.

"Looks like I'll have some questions to ask when she wakes up," Akela says.

I float from the park into Akela's office, and I am still a child, learning the Song for the first time. Then like the ground tilting beneath me, the dream shifts, and I'm back to the devastating day when Akela just vanished from my life. Dorm Leader Fuschious screams at me to stop crying, but I can't move.

Before I have time to feel anything, the dream whirls again, and I am sitting at Melody's side, singing the fragment of Lyric and the Storm into her listening ear. This time, we both hide in the darkened alcove under the Heartsong Bridge. Jack-boot footsteps pound toward us. I try to run, but my feet are encased in concrete. I try to scream, but my mouth is fused shut. The soldiers wrap around me like serpent's coils, and suddenly I am looking into Supreme Lover Midgate's accusing blue eyes, standing in the Haters' Pavilion for all the world to see.

My mind fights against the nightmare. With a panicked prayer, I squeeze my eyes shut, and suddenly I am back in a familiar street, where a squad of hunched, black-suited soldiers snatch the last Chief Siren, throwing a hood over his head and hurling him into the back of a truck. My feverish twitching starts up again. Then snatches of music float through my dreams, and the Muse's gentle touch soothes my brow. I sink into silence.

Why didn't you keep them safe?

16

Why are you so sad, oh my soul?
Why so ill at ease?
Put your hope in the Composer's plan,
For he will bring songs of joy.
He will save us in our hour of need.
　　Song Fragment 43.5

COLD TO WARM. SLEEP TO WAKE. AGAINST
my will, my eyelids flutter open, then shut at the painful assault
of light. I groan.

A soft strain of music plays in the background. It sounds
like a choir singing in harmony somewhere distant. I can't tell
whether it's my imagination or not. My brain is too fuzzy.

I try to open my eyes again, more slowly this time so the
light doesn't hurt. I lift my head and glance around the room,
wincing in pain. Low tables and shelves line the wall in front of
me. Every flat surface is covered with untidy piles of haggard
and faded equipment. I'm lying face down on a cracked vinyl
treatment bed. Where am I? I slowly turn over onto my back.

A rustling sound somewhere behind me interrupts my
questions. It grows louder until a large, humpbacked bundle of
rags appears at my side.

"So! The patient is awake, is she? Good. Good," crows the
bundle. I am regarded by a bright, beady blue eye.

"Who . . . who are you?" I ask.

"You haven't forgotten me so quickly, have you?" The blue eye twinkles with amusement.

Kent. That's this person's name. I was brought here by someone . . . Lark? After all those tunnels and water. And pain. Lots of pain.

"I . . . I was asleep," I say stupidly. A burst of cold air brings goosebumps along my skin. I draw the edge of the sheet back up over my shoulder. There's a tube attached to a bag of liquid going into my wrist, taped down over the back of my hand.

"You certainly were. Two days you slept, my dear. Two days! If I'd known you'd be out so long, I would have moved you somewhere else for the procedure. It's been a challenge keeping customers out of my treatment room, I can tell you!" Kent chuckles.

"I'm s-sorry."

Kent pats my shoulder, and I close my eyes again, still unable to look at the world without pain.

"What happened?" I ask. The distant music continues, and I struggle to work out whether or not I'm just imagining it. It's a Siren tune, but Kent doesn't seem to be affected by it at all.

Ignoring my question, Kent carefully removes the tape over my hand. "This will smart a little."

I look away, seeing the long needle going into my vein, no longer hidden by the tape. It stings for a little bit, then a bandage is pasted down over the spot and my hand is patted by those soothing fingers.

Kent smiles, showing a burst of yellowed teeth. "That was the worst leg wound I've seen in a while, kid. You're lucky to have your foot."

That piercing blue eye stares at me again, and I wilt beneath it.

Somewhere outside, the soft choir music comes to an end, and a new Song begins. Another familiar Song. I must be imagining it. It almost sounds like—

Kent pats my shoulder again. "You can relax. Nobody down here is a friend of the Love Squad." The healer moves in businesslike fashion to my leg, pulling it out from under the sheet and examining the scar. My leg aches with a dull throb. As Kent rotates my ankle, the protruding black knots of twenty or so stitches swing into view. By the looks of it, I am going to have a thick, L-shaped scar for the rest of my life.

"Who's Hodge?" Kent asks, eyes on my ankle.

"What?" My pulse quickens.

"You're quite the talker in your sleep." Kent's eye closes and re-opens, and I realize that I am watching a wink.

I cross my arms against my chest, feeling exposed.

Kent chuckles, and I catch a glimpse of yellowed teeth. "Don't worry. Your secret's safe with me."

Just then, the door to the treatment room opens, and I bunch up the sheet even tighter around me. Lark rushes in, a small white bag dangling from her hand, and a larger bundle under her arm.

Her eyes dart to me. "Oh, you're awake!" She hands the bag to Kent. "Here. Your supply order has arrived."

Kent takes the bag to a table, pulling out a small metal tube. "Ah, good. Good."

With expert movements, Kent rubs cold white goo around the edges of the black stitches. It's painful, but I keep reminding myself that medicine is good for me and try not to wince too much. When it's all done, the pair steps back to survey Kent's work.

"Okay," Lark says. "Time to get yourself out of Kent's treatment room." She dumps the bundle from under her arm onto the bed, unrolling it to reveal a pair of brown industrial-workers' overalls. "Some high fashion to replace your drowned couture."

With that she hurries Kent out of the room, and I'm left alone, ankle throbbing and mind reeling.

MEMORY DATE: 2285.106 (THREE YEARS AGO)

Memory Location: Secret bunker

"She wasn't arrested." Loa's face nearly glows with his triumph.

"Wow, you're confident," says Allegra drily.

"You're surprised?" Hodge grunts.

Loa leans forward eagerly. "No, hear me out. It's been nearly a hundred days since they told us she was transferred. Right?"

Hodge frowns. "What's your point?"

"So why hasn't she appeared on the Haters' Pavilion Show yet? I mean, normally when Carell Hummer's doing his big spiel at the beginning of the show, we get that blow-by-blow account of when people were arrested and how long they took to be captured, blah blah blah."

I lean forward, too, starting to see where he's going with this. "And?"

He turns to me. "So most of the Haters are up there within seven days of their arrest. Maybe fifteen, tops. It's wham, bam, kill 'em. Done." He claps on that last word, leaning back as if he's proven his point.

Allegra shakes her head. "That doesn't mean she was transferred."

"What if they wanted to get information out of her?" Hodge asks. "I don't mean to burst your bubble, but she's a bigger catch than most of the Haters. She knows a lot about the inner workings of Elite Academy."

"Yeah, but a hundred days? I mean come on, those guys in the Haters' Pavilion are machines," Loa says. "You've seen them in action, Harper. They can extract information faster than you could believe."

Allegra's eyes narrow at him. "How do you know?"

"Field trip," comes the curt reply.

I look from Loa to Hodge, curious.

"You don't want to know," Hodge says.

Allegra is still not buying it. "Maybe they don't want to admit that the former Dorm Leader of Elite Academy is a Hater. I mean come on. If I were the Supreme Executive, I'd be disposing of her quietly so I didn't look bad."

Loa's expression is stubborn. "She was transferred. Which means she can come back some day too."

"Crucible doesn't give people second chances," Allegra says, frowning.

IT TAKES A WHILE TO GET MY CLOTHES ON, and when I finally manage it, I pad barefooted back into the circus-tent entrance room. It looks like a museum. To one side of the entrance, thick cushions and rugs mingle with a faded leather lounge setting. On the other side, a series of shelves and cabinets holds an eclectic collection of statuettes, books and decorations. The central pole of the tent rises up in the middle, ringed by tiny LEDs that give the whole place an exotic, Triumph-of-Love-carnival feel.

Kent is hunched over a large silver contraption that sits on a bench beside a leather armchair. With reluctance, I walk across the room. Under Kent's hands, the silver machine begins to hiss and whir, and a small tendril of steam rises from the top.

"Over here!" Lark calls brightly from the lounge area, waving me toward her.

I hover at the edge of the lounge, my nostrils tingling as a delicious smell floats up from Kent's machine. I have no idea what it is, but it makes me very hungry.

"Do you know where my boots are?" I ask.

"Payment," Kent says gruffly from behind the machine. "Do some favors, and you'll have no difficulty getting replacements."

I am a little taken aback and open my mouth to argue, but then close it again. What could I say? Lark rescued me, Kent took me in and patched me up, and they've even replaced my ruined clothes. It's not like I can expect all of that for nothing. If I had my pack, I probably could have bartered some of the supplies, but that's long gone now. My boots were the most valuable thing I was wearing.

Kent carries over a tray of steaming food to the small table in the center of the area. Lark picks off a bundle of something soft, biting into it. Kent offers one to me, and I sniff warily at it. When I take a bite, it melts in my mouth, setting off an explosion of deliciousness.

"What is this?"

Kent smiles through the side of the scarf. "My secret recipe."

I stare wide-eyed at the golden bundle, my heart full. "I've never tasted anything like this." I savor the rest of it into my mouth. "It's so good."

Kent and Lark share a look. Then Kent settles down into a couch. "So how long have you been in the dorms?"

I nearly spit out the pastry. "What? Who said—"

"It's not hard to tell," Kent says. "You've never tasted a simple pastry, which means you've probably been subsisting on the protein meal they serve in dorm kitchens. You've got good muscle tone. And your hair is regulation."

"And you're young. Like me," Lark adds.

I sit for a few seconds, mind racing. "I . . . um . . ."

Kent waves a wrinkled, arthritic hand. "Don't bother trying to make something up. You're a terrible liar."

"You're as transparent as a window," Lark agrees.

Mouth open in shock, I must look pretty funny. So I take another pastry.

"So," Kent leans forward, "what are your skills? Apart from marching and drill chants, of course."

"Coding," I say into my pastry, then fill my mouth so I can't give away anything else.

"Not in huge demand down here," Lark says. She looks a little unsettled, though, and I wonder what's got her so edgy.

I hesitate. "I can sing."

Kent sighs. "No good. Never mind. Once your leg heals, you can take on some work. Until then—" the ragged healer pushes up from the chair. "Lark will get you into a temporary space. The orphanage should do for now."

Lark stands up as well. "Come on," she says. "Time for the guided tour."

17

Follow Your Dreams
And They Will Lead You To Us

Love All. Be All.
The Love Collective

LARK LEADS ME THROUGH THE GREATEST
secret in Love Collective history, and I'm too busy worrying
about my bare feet to care. They're cold. And wet. Slimy goo
squelches between my toes.

"So where are you taking me?" I wrinkle my nose at a
particularly horrible heap of refuse that I nearly stepped in.

"Somewhere safe," Lark says, hurrying away without
looking back.

I follow behind, letting dark, resentful grumblings flow
from my lips. I know I should be more polite. Lark just got me
fixed up and found almost-warm clothes for me to wear, which
deserves some gratitude. But my feet are oozing through filth.

Clad in comfortable shoes, Lark almost dances through
the marketplace, oblivious to my aching leg and grossed-out
expressions. The stitches across my wound feel tighter than
ever, and with every step, I'm afraid that I'm going to break
them open. So I struggle along in a strange, hopping limp to

keep up. I'm not very successful. With the familiarity of a long-term resident, Lark is incredibly fast.

Smells and sights assault my senses: deep-fried food, rotting vegetables, unwashed bodies. I watch as one girl—who seems far too young to be alone—argues with a stall-keeper over a jar of pickles. Beside them, two men in dirty coats examine an old plastic clock with the precision and care of fine jewelers. A few stalls later, a small crowd clusters around a woman ladling soup into steaming bowls. Their hungry eyes follow every drip, and trembling hands reach for the goods being offered.

"What is this place?" I breathe.

"I told you," Lark says. "It's the Ghetto."

"Yes, but . . . why?" I ask, staring around in wonder.

Lark shrugs. "It's been here longer than I have." She reaches out and dips a finger into one of the soup bowls. "Wonderful brew, Margo," she says to the woman with the ladle. "You've outdone yourself today."

The woman beams proudly. "Thanks to you, Lark," she says, then raps the hand of a hungry customer who was about to copy my companion's finger-dipping.

When we're clear of the food stall, Lark slows her pace and turns to explain. "When the Collective outlawed vagrants, a lot of people disappeared. When Kent discovered what the Collective was doing to them, the boss found this abandoned factory and decided to hide out here. Word got out, and Collective rejects started arriving. The secret takes a lot of work, but we manage."

"The boss?"

"Kent," says Lark, pushing past a small group of men arguing over a dice game. When they see her, they hurriedly snatch at their dice, making space for us to pass. One man pulls off a cap, clutching it to his chest and ducking his head in an awkward bow. Lark just nods and passes him by.

I look from the men to Lark, feeling oddly worried. There's

some piece of this puzzle I'm missing. It occurs to me that maybe my companion is more important down here than I first thought.

Ten minutes later, we near the outer edge of the settlement. The makeshift hovels here look weaker, less refined. Instead of rickety cottages built from plywood, the building materials are all cardboard and ragged sheets. A few residents sit at the entrances to the box homes, watching us with large, hollow eyes.

Lark takes a few minutes to speak with the thin, destitute figures, crouching down beside them and smiling. They respond, nodding and speaking in voices too low to hear. When she's done, she beckons me forward.

"Nearly there." She steps into a narrow passageway between two cardboard hovels.

We walk through a narrow labyrinthine trail formed by cardboard walls, and then around a corner between corrugated metal hovels. We stop on a small patch of concrete that acts like a courtyard. Opposite the open space stands a huge cardboard wall. A corrugated sheet of metal leans against one side, threatening to topple it all over. But for all its haphazard appearance, it's the largest structure I've seen in this underground Ghetto, apart from Kent's circus marquee.

"Here we are," Lark announces, flourishing her arms out wide. "This is what we like to call the orphanage."

I back away from the corrugated metal. "Thanks, but I'm not stopping here for long." As I'm speaking, I hear a sound rising above the tall cardboard walls. I turn toward it, straining to hear.

Lark shrugs. "Suit yourself."

Music lilts across the air currents, sung by what sounds like a large group of people. The sound echoes off the ceiling far above us, a cavernous harmony. It's too far away to make out the words they're singing, but that doesn't matter. I have sung that tune in Siren meetings often enough.

Sing for joy, children sing,
Lyric's country is our home
You are known, chosen, loved
With the Composer as your king.

"Thank you," I say, but I don't wait to hear Lark's response.

I thought I was imagining this music back in Kent's treatment room. But this is no hallucination. This is voices—a lot of voices—really singing. They're not just anyone singing just anything either. They're Sirens.

The sound grows louder as I draw nearer. I step into a small courtyard beside the warehouse wall. A pipe runs down the wall, ending in a tap, which gushes water into a large, round water tank set deep into the floor. A long queue of people waits beside the tank with buckets and containers, blocking my path. I make my way past them as politely as I can, seeking the sound that seems to be coming from just behind a row of canvas tents.

"No one cuts in line," warns a rough-looking woman wearing a simple grey dress. She looks as if she wants to punch me. "If you can't get here before water ration time, you don't stop those of us who got here early."

"Sorry, I'm just trying to get over there," I say, pointing past her to a gap between tents.

The woman mumbles angrily, but steps back to let me through. But more people are heading for the water line, and so I have to slow down. I try to hold back my impatience. What if the Song stops? What if the singers leave and I can't find them again?

With impatience, I skirt around people and jump over a small heap of boxes, landing in something soft and wet. I take no notice and nearly run through a gap between tents.

Finally, after more twists and turns than I wanted to make, I emerge into a large open space at one corner of the Ghetto. With the warehouse walls behind them, hundreds of people gather around a conductor with long, greasy hair who waves his arms to the beat. The Siren Song rings out with such clear notes that I want to weep. I've never heard so many people sing like this before. This is no secret Siren chapter, sneaking around to borrowed conference rooms and hiding from surveillance cameras. This is . . . something else.

Standing in a vaguely arc-shaped curve, the crowd sings. People of all shapes and sizes are here, some wearing rags, some dressed in neat but patched Collective clothing. A group of children stands along the front, their bare feet as dirty as mine, but their faces shining.

Tears sting the corners of my eyes, and I try not to let the lump in my throat turn into loud, messy crying.

> *Sing for joy, children sing,*
> *Lyric's country is our home*
> *You are known, chosen, loved*
> *With the Composer as your king.*

"Thank you," I whisper to the Composer. If I hadn't listened to the Muse's urgings when I was running, I might never have found this hidden treasure.

The Song seamlessly moves on to another fragment, and I stand, enraptured by the harmonies.

> *You are my hiding place and my shield;*
> *My hope is only in your Song.*
> *Uphold me according to your promise,*
> *Let me live and not be wrong.*
> *Lyric gave up everything*
> *So I may sing and follow on*
> *Hold me up, and keep me safe—*
> *Make me faithful, true, and strong*

"Ah, here you are," Lark arrives at my shoulder. "I wondered what got you so steamed up."

"It's amazing," I whisper.

"You know this stuff?" she asks sharply.

"What are they doing here?" I ask, not quite willing to give away all my secrets just yet.

Lark folds her arms, showing a bare left wrist. With a start, I realize she's an illegal like me, with no Collective ID. "Kent has always let them live here, ever since the Purging."

"Purging?" The strange word draws my attention. "Kent mentioned that, but I don't know what it means."

"All that violence when the Collective took over the government and eliminated anyone who got in their way. We call it for what it is: the Purging. But the propaganda you guys hear calls it the Triumph of Love." The sarcasm in Lark's voice is impossible to ignore.

"Oh." Another piece of the puzzle slots into my head, dislodging a few thoughts. I cast a side glance at her, still puzzled by her appearance. She looks so much like a smaller, younger Midgate that it's uncanny. But what does that matter? Since I've discovered that Midgate really is an AI, any resemblance is random, anyway. "I've learned they aren't always honest with us," I say, thinking about the code that Crucible must have sent me to set me up.

"Yeah," Lark says. She nods at the choir. "Kent could see this bunch of weirdos helping out where nobody else would. So when the Ghetto was formed, our leader made sure there was a safe place for them to stay. We find they're a nice, calming influence."

"The music is lovely."

"That too," Lark concedes. "But mostly they're just good at looking after the people nobody else wants to take in. I don't understand all their babbling, but it seems to help some."

I turn to Lark, trying to think of something to say, and failing to find anything in the moment. Years of practice have made me an expert in appearing to be a faithful citizen while reserving my true identity for secret meetings. I've been so used to hiding my Siren identity in public that silence is now easier than explanation.

My sense of guilt grows. Have I built up such effective walls between Siren and Apprentice that I can no longer cross them? How do I explain to someone like Lark why Lyric is so amazing? Given what she's told me, I'm fairly certain that I could openly talk about him down here. So why can't I just open my mouth and speak?

Just then, the music comes to an end, and the conductor claps for the crowd.

"Well done, everyone," he calls, and I am rooted to the spot. I stare at the greasy-haired figure, hoping to the Composer that I'm wrong about that voice.

No. No. No, no, no, no.

The conductor stretches his arms high above his head, then does a few turns at the waist, stretching out the muscles in his back. His face swivels around to us. A reddish beard covers his cheeks, and his face is more weathered than I remember. When he sees Lark and I standing at the edge of the courtyard, he stops mid-swivel, a look of open-mouthed shock on his face.

A spike of anger boils up from my gut into a single, seething word.

"Wil."

18

Lyric said, "I came to heal the broken melodies and make the Song whole again. So love the ones who hurt you, even those who hate you. Speak words of peace to them, not words of condemnation. For the Composer created us in harmony, not discord."
Song Fragment 5.43

IN A SPLIT SECOND, MY MIND RUSHES through a thousand possibilities: Should I run? (But why? He was wrong, not me.) Do I shout at him? (He doesn't deserve to be spoken to, after what he did.) Do I accuse him? Do I pepper him with questions? (Like, how on the Composer's green earth did he get here? And why didn't he leave the Collective?) Do I expose him to everyone? (But I've been here for like five seconds. As if anyone would believe me anyway.)

Every nerve in my body is on edge as Wil crosses the space between us with a broad, welcoming smile on his face. I stand there, still debating, my fists clenching and unclenching while I try to think.

"Cadence! What an amazing surprise!" Wil calls, throwing his arms out wide.

I stand there, a mutinous expression on my face and murderous thoughts in my head. *Don't you dare hug me. Don't you dare—*

He hugs me.

The toxic combination of revulsion and anger turns me into stone. My skin crawls at the pressure of his arms over mine. I want to scream fury at him, but the just-finished singing is still fresh in my mind. It holds me back from violence. Just.

"Wil," I manage to say. My voice is as icy as I can make it. I won't pretend to be happy to see this man. Even if his face is smiling and open, and even if he looks nothing like the old scheming Apprentice with his natural-fiber grey shirt and his forest-green linen pants and his neat-and-tidy brown leather shoes. He's lost all of the rounded youthfulness I remember from Elite Academy, with his fully grown reddish beard that rasps against the side of my face as he leans down. His greasy hair has been tied back into a ponytail, but he smells clean. At least there's that.

I take a firm, deliberate step back, using every ounce of my willpower to stop myself from punching him in the face. His smile really does make me want to do violence.

That same smile fades a little. "I'm sorry. I shouldn't have presumed. I guess it's been a while since I've seen anyone familiar, and it was just so good to see you." He smiles again as if we were best friends reuniting.

"You know each other?" Lark says suspiciously. "And did he just call you Cadence?"

I sigh. I was supposed to be anonymous here, but there's no hope of that now. Wil's just completely blown everything.

"Yeah," I mutter darkly, eyebrows furrowed. A suspicious expression crosses Lark's face as she looks between the two of us.

"You were supposed to be over the border," I manage to hiss at him.

He shoves his hands into his pockets. "The Composer had different ideas, I guess."

I thrust an accusing finger at his face. "Don't you *ever* use that name."

He shrinks back, surprise giving way to comprehension. "Oh of course. You haven't been around." His face takes on the expression of a patient Lover trying to explain something to a child. "Things change, Cadence. I've changed. I'm not the same guy you knew back then."

"Yeah, and Supreme Lover Midgate lives in this Ghetto," I say, scowling at him. Lark snorts beside me.

A small crowd of curious onlookers have begun to gather around us. Wil notices them and sidles in to grab my elbow.

"Hey, how about you and I find somewhere private to have a little talk? We have a lot to catch up on." He lowers his voice to a purring whisper. "I'm not the same guy."

I pull away from his grasp. He puts his hands up in a gesture of surrender. The onlookers nearby begin to murmur with concern.

"I can see that," I say, pointing at his beard. "What I want to know is how you managed to fool all these people."

MEMORY DATE: 2282.365 (FOUR AND A HALF *years ago)*

Memory Location: Triumph of Love festival VIP compound

"Idiot," Wil hisses, grasping at my wrist, then losing it as I twist it violently away. "You can't get out of this." With a violent lunge he wrenches my arm back down, pinching my wrist between his fingers. I let out a cry of pain, but he just twists my hand under the central bar of the steering wheel, tying the cable tie so firmly it immediately begins cutting off the circulation.

"The Composer will stop you," I say with as much confidence as I can muster.

Wil's laugh becomes bitter. "The Composer is a fairy tale

told by people who should know better. The best thing the Love
Collective ever did was outlaw that waste of an organization."

WIL LOOKS CRESTFALLEN. "PLEASE,
Cadence. Just let me explain. I—"

"You're a fantastic actor, remember? That's what you told
me," I say, folding my arms, my fury settling into a seething
boil. "And if you think I'm going to be alone somewhere with
you ever again, you're dumber than I thought you were." I wave
my wrists at him, and the memory of those cable ties still hovers
on my skin.

"You're right," Wil says, subdued. "I'd forgotten how good
your memory was. I'm sorry. You probably hate me."

"Hate isn't Lyric's way," I say, annoyed with myself at how
close to the truth he is. "But I'm not stupid. And anyone would
remember what you've done."

"You guys obviously have a history," Lark pipes up. "I
would normally bring some popcorn for this show, but I've got
somewhere to be. I'll let you two catch up." She points over her
shoulder at the courtyard exit.

For a few moments I stand there, the anger of a thousand
nightmares raging inside. Wil stubbornly refuses to burst into
flames in front of me, or reduce himself to a grovelling heap,
which only frustrates me even further. I had hoped never to
see this guy again. I had imagined a host of satisfying ends to
the one who had tied me in emotional (and literal) knots. If
true justice existed in the world, he should be flattened under a
truck right now, not smiling and healthy and leading the largest
group of Sirens I've ever seen.

That's not Lyric's way, says a small, familiar voice in my head.
But I feel powerless and angry and unwilling to listen. Out of

all the people in this world, why did it have to be him? Why couldn't it have been Danse who found this place, or Akela?

"Siren Wil?" I turn to see a wizened old man, his back nearly bent double under a large hump. He leans on a steel walking stick, turning his head sideways to look up at us. A spindly beard lines the edges of his face, and grime sits in the wrinkles around his eyes. His head is bald, and a thin pair of wire spectacles sits on his nose. He wears a similar forest-green tunic to the one Wil wears. "Is everything alright?"

"It's fine, Tim," Wil says. "This is Cadence, an old friend. She's a Siren too. Actually, she's the Songbook I told you about."

Understanding lights the old man's eyes. "Ah! Come, my dear. You must be cold with those bare feet. Come and join us." He raises an arthritic hand toward me, beckoning me forward. "Aria?"

An old woman with long white hair plaited down her back looks up from the midst of a group of women. She smiles and murmurs something to the group before she glides over to us. Tim pats her hand as she arrives. "Aria my sweet, this is Cadence. Cadence, this is my wife, Aria."

The older woman, straight-backed and slender, looks me up and down, appraising. Looking elegant in a plain, woollen dress, she somehow manages to infuse a shrewd, piercing gaze with warmth. She takes my hand. "Welcome, Cadence, it's wonderful to meet you."

"Thank you," I say, feeling my anger soften into embarrassment. It's impossible to be furious with Wil in front of these gentle, kind witnesses. I wonder if I should tell them everything that I know. If Wil has been acting the part around these good people, they could be in danger.

Aria studies me, then smiles. "Yes. You have the Muse in you," she says, then pats the back of my hand.

"What?" I say, surprised.

Tim chuckles. "Don't mind my wife." He turns away, leaning

heavily on his metal cane as he limps forward. "Come on then," he says. "We have a lunch to prepare."

With an extra dose of caution, I follow, watching Wil from the corner of my eye. He looks amazingly undisturbed by my hostility and follows a couple of steps behind me, hands clasped behind his back. I catch him nodding and smiling at a small group of Siren girls, and my blood begins to boil again.

"Stop it," I mutter under my breath. "You're going to make a fool of yourself."

But seriously, the stubborn, angry part of me thinks back. *A guy like this doesn't deserve to be happy. Ever.*

THE HUNCHBACKED MAN SHAMBLES through a gap between two plywood hovels into another rectangular open area covered with small groups of chairs. A few people mill around, laying blankets over patches of concrete or placing soft cushions on the floor. They part ways as they see the hunched figure heading toward them, bowing heads with respect. For an old, old man, he moves incredibly fast.

The courtyard here seems to be set up for food service. A row of steel benches lines one side of the rectangle, covered with large, steaming cookers. Three people wearing soft caps work behind the cookers. My nose tickles as it catches the most delicious smells. If I hadn't just recently eaten all the pastries I could handle, I'm sure my mouth would be watering.

Tim walks over to the row of cookers and greets the three people working behind the benches. Wil stops at one of the benches where he picks up a knife to help cut a round loaf of bread. He laughs with the others, and I wonder at how none of them seem the least bit afraid or suspicious.

If you knew what he was really like, you wouldn't want to be anywhere near him, I think.

"This is our soup kitchen," Aria says. "It's hard for people to find their own food down here. So we provide for those without their own means of support."

More people arrive from the Siren meeting, forming a line beside the bench. They chat happily together. When the line has grown so that it snakes around the courtyard and back out to the Siren meeting area, Tim raises his hand. Silence ripples back along the line. People wait expectantly.

"Let us thank the Composer for his provision today," Tim says. "Great Composer of our symphonies, we thank you for taking care of us this day and for your gracious provision. May it be enough for all who need sustenance. In Lyric's name be it."

At the signal, conversation hums again, and the three workers begin serving soup, ladling out steaming bowlfuls to the waiting crowd. People move from the bench to the chairs and cushions, sitting together in small circles. Their faces are happy, content. I haven't seen those sorts of expressions for a long, long time.

"Come on." Aria beckons. "Are you hungry?"

I shake my head. "Kent was kind enough to give me some pastries earlier." I pat my stomach.

Aria's face clouds a little. "I'm glad you are not hungry. But a word of wisdom, for your future." She leans closer to my ear. "That one never gives anything without expecting payment in full. Sometimes with interest."

I nod. "That's how I lost my shoes," I say, looking down at my filthy toes. "And my jacket."

She follows my gaze. Then she touches my arm. "Wait here," she says firmly, and glides away into the crowd. Unsure of what to do, I stand and watch the soup being served.

In the middle of the kitchen, Wil lifts away an empty pot, replacing it with another steaming tub, which had been simmering on a large stove behind the serving bench. Then he takes out a cloth and wipes down benches, stopping to glance up at the line. I can't hear what he's saying, but I hear the sound of laughter as he jokes.

How dare he be enjoying himself? Doesn't he realize what he did to Hodge and Akela? Doesn't he feel any shred of remorse for what he did to me?

"He shouldn't be here." I push back a musical whisper in the back of my mind, submerged in a tidal wave of righteous anger.

"It doesn't take a prophet to see there's something between you two," Aria's soothing voice at my shoulder makes me jump. I turn to see her shrewd eyes looking at me with kindness. "Here," she says, holding up a pair of soft canvas shoes and a damp washcloth. "These are for you. Clean yourself up before you put them on, or you'll be feeling grit between your toes for months."

"Thank you," I say, "but I can't pay—"

Aria waves my protest away. "No payment required." Her cheeks dimple with a smile that leaves crinkles at the corners of her eyes. "Except perhaps for your story."

I know from the expression on her face that I'm not going to be able to avoid it. I nod and sit down to wash my feet and slip on the comfortable soft shoes. If Aria wants my story, then she's going to get all of it.

Especially the truth about Wil.

19

Sing for joy, children sing
Lyric's country is your home
You are known, chosen, loved
With the Composer as your king.
        Song Fragment, 29.11

THE SOUP SERVED, ARIA INVITES ME BACK TO
her home. I walk beside her as she ambles through the crowd,
unhurried and friendly. She stops beside an ancient woman,
who gives her a toothless smile. "Mrs. Thompson, how are your
knees doing?"

"Oh, not too bad'n there'n be all things considered," the
old woman says, looking a little troubled. "The cold always be
makin' 'em ache'n somethin' terrible in the mornin's. But that's
just the Composer remindin' me'n all'n us that this here's not
our forever home."

"Ah, Mrs. Thompson, I always think I come out of our
conversations the one who's been the more encouraged."
Aria smiles.

Mrs. Thompson smiles back, showing two grey-pink gums.
"Oh, child, it's'n the Composer what encourages us'n all."

With an affectionate pat on the woman's shoulder, Aria says
goodbye and continues on smoothly through the crowd. I spend
a little bit of time wondering how old Aria really is, and how old

Mrs. Thompson must be if she's calling Aria *child*. But I file that into "mysteries to solve later." I'm too distracted.

Instead of facing up to Wil's presence, my subconscious has created a vague, dark shadow where his body should be. A void slightly larger than a human, carrying dark moods and even darker thoughts. It's better than having to watch him smile and be so comfortable all the time.

When we reach the edge of the courtyard, Tim joins us, and Aria slows her pace to match his. They guide me through another gap between hovels into a winding alleyway. Concrete blocks sit beside timber pallets, and cardboard walls lean against plywood and drywall sheets. Small children dart around us, playing games between shelters. Occasionally an adult peeks out of their home, their curious glances transforming into welcoming smiles as they see the older couple approach. Aria and Tim nod, unhurried and relaxed in their walk. I watch them as they chat to their neighbors, feeling a twinge of envy at the comfortable intimacy between them.

The alley ends at an intersection—a T-shaped space where meandering walkways meet. My guides turn left into a small semi-circular gap. At the end of this, built up against the high concrete warehouse wall, is a tiny plywood cottage. The home is made of timber boards, with a cute little gable roof and a brightly painted garden mural across the front.

I hang back, looking at the house with wary hesitation. Tim opens the front door and waves me forward. Aria comes to stand on the other side of the door, and she beams at us.

"Welcome to our humble home," Tim says with pride.

Aria gives her husband an affectionate look. "Tim built this all himself," she says. "It's not much, but we love to welcome people whenever we can."

I walk into a cosy apartment-style room. Behind a couple of armchairs, a low daybed lines one wall, piled high with cushions to form a comfortable lounge. A tall, thin bookshelf sits in the corner beside it, overflowing with piles of tattered, faded old books. Beside the bookshelf is a small kitchen table, which sits snugly beside an equally small kitchen cabinet. Brightly colored rugs cover the concrete floor. I'm surprised to see that one wall is entirely filled with a mural of Lyric's tree, with branches that curl and spread around the walls. The only window in the room is beside the front door, and this has been decorated with bright-green curtains and a small window box of plastic plants.

"Make yourself comfortable, Cadence." Aria turns to the kitchen cabinet, pulling out a bottle, which she pours into four tumblers. She hands me a tumbler which is now full of water and ushers me across to the daybed lounge.

I sit, holding the glass between both hands. When a knock raps at the door, and Wil enters in, my whole body tenses with revulsion.

"Hi, everyone, sorry I'm late. I had a bit to do back at the soup kitchen." He smiles broadly at Aria in a way that makes me want to kick him.

"Oh, Wil, hello," Aria says, looking a little disconcerted. "We weren't expecting you."

"Sorry, my love," Tim says with a sideways smile up at his wife. "I should have checked with you before inviting him."

Wil keeps smiling as he moves to sit on the lounge beside me. I must look pretty angry, though, because he takes a look at my face and decides to sit further away on one of the armchairs.

Tim sits in another armchair, and Aria comes over to sit beside me on the daybed lounge. Her face is free of any obvious emotion, but I can tell she's watching me carefully.

"You have a large Siren group." I have to say something. I stare at the tumbler in my hands. "I've never seen so many Sirens in one place before. How did you all get to be here?"

"After the Ghetto was first established," Tim says, "our children were born here." He looks at Aria with such an open look of love and affection that I feel like I'm intruding.

"So were our grandchildren and our great grandchildren," Aria adds with a fond smile back at him.

Wil nods. "One of the benefits of never being arrested. They don't need to be so secretive about the Song."

I ignore him, giving the whole of my attention pointedly to Aria and Tim. "That's a long time to be underground."

Tim and Aria share a look. "Oh, we used to get out more," Tim remarks. "Foraging and gathering and such."

"He used to be quite the hunter back in the day," Aria says.

"How did you get here?"

Aria leans back against the cushions. "Ah, that's a long story, full of telling," she says. "You've no doubt heard about the Purging?"

I nod.

Wil leans forward. "That's what they call the Triumph of Love up top."

"I know," I say, not doing a good job of keeping the snark out of my voice.

Aria looks a little troubled by this exchange, but she continues, "Before the Purging, the Sirens had been divided as to what to do. There was a civil war, you see. Many of them fled the country, finding safety across the border. But others wanted to stay and fight."

"Not with weapons, though," Tim interjects. "We thought back then that we could get the Executive to listen to reason. We protested and wrote letters and did all sorts of campaigning."

"Tim was high up in the government then," Aria says proudly. "If anyone could have changed the course of history, it would have been him."

"I tried my best." Tim's voice drops. "But it just wasn't enough."

"We didn't know that then. It wasn't until it was too late that we realized we were never going to explain ourselves." Aria's expression is full of sadness.

"What happened?" I ask.

"They killed Lyric," Tim says. My breath catches. "He had been encouraging us to stand firm with the Composer. Built up a massive following. Gave us the Song and taught us how to care for others. Amazing things happened that no one had ever seen before or since. And just like that, they strung him up. Paraded the images around for everyone to see. Many of the Sirens just fled overnight. Got out of there as fast as they could."

"I'm glad we waited, though," Aria tells me. "Because otherwise we wouldn't have seen him again." Her face shines.

"Yes," Tim agrees. He shifts in his seat. "Unfortunately, that just made the Executive even madder. They started going from house to house, arresting and imprisoning Sirens—especially the ones who sang about Lyric's return."

"That's when the Sirens disagreed again," Aria says. "Some were so excited about Lyric that they thought we were invincible. They wanted to keep on singing in the public places. They thought we'd be triumphant then and there."

Tim leans forward. "But the writing was on the wall. The Executive weren't ever going to give up."

"We learned about Kent's plan to come down here through Tim's connections. And we brought a whole bunch of Sirens with us. The rest of our friends up on the Surface were . . ." Aria stops. Tim shares a sympathetic look with her.

I don't need her to finish. I know enough.

"Without Aria's gift," Tim says, "we'd have been dead long ago."

"Oh, Timpani Brown." Aria blushes. "You stop. It's the Composer who has looked after us all these years, not me."

"Don't be so modest." Tim looks at her with a smile. "She was the one who knew that we should come here. I was still blustering and pontificating about how we were going to win over that Executive. But she knew. And I thank the Composer every day for her."

He reaches across the space to clasp her knee, and they look at each other again with a love that could only have been built with years of patience and care.

"Well, I'm glad you're here, because you gave me a home when I really needed one," Wil says. The sound of his voice grates against me so badly, especially when he's sucking up to them. Why can't these two beautiful old people see what a fake he is?

Aria turns to face me. "So, Cadence, tell us about yourself."

"You can fill us in later on how you met this rascal," Tim adds, nodding his head at Wil.

"Oh, there's nothing special," I say, feeling embarrassed.

"She's just being modest." Wil sounds proud. "Cadence is the best Songbook I've ever seen. We used to go out together searching for Song fragments, didn't we, Cadence?"

I ignore him, pointedly keeping my attention focused on Aria and Tim.

"Oh, I would love to hear the fragments you know." Aria beams at me. "How did you become a Siren?"

"My parents were Sirens," I say carefully. I begin to explain my life, about how I remembered things in the Nursery Dorm, how Akela saved me, and how I became friends with Hodge. I try to leave Wil out of the discussion altogether. Partly because I don't want to give him any credit for anything, but also because I'm too tempted to say horrible things. I figure it would be impolite to say something like, "Hi, I only just met you, but this guy is an evil terrorist, and you need to expel him NOW." That would probably only end in me being kicked out and Wil coming out looking sparkly and fresh anyway. He always had a knack for that.

"Hodge sounds like a good friend," Aria observes, and I feel myself blush. I didn't think I mentioned him much, but I guess her discernment gift is better than I thought. She looks relaxed, but there's a shrewdness in her gaze too.

"I'd wondered what had happened with you two." Wil settles back into his armchair and crosses one leg over another. "Sounds like things have progressed nicely."

My resentment boils over. I decide to throw him a curve ball.

"Hodge and I were Elite Apprentices together." My tone is louder than normal. "It was Hodge who helped me to stop this guy from setting off a bomb in the Triumph festival." I point at Wil. "Wil nearly got both of us killed. Hodge was injured pretty badly, but he managed to get the truck out of the way."

I wait for the shock, the disbelief, or the angry responses. But they just nod.

Wil clears his throat. "I told them all about that. It was an awful time. But there aren't any secrets here." To my disgust he refuses to look the least bit embarrassed about it. "How is Akela, by the way?"

"Gone," I say, spitting the words between clenched teeth. "After you disappeared, Crucible got meaner. She was transferred, and we haven't heard from her in years."

"Oh," Wil says, and he has the sense to look upset about it. "Who took her place?"

I ignore his question, staring at my glass of water. My jaw is clenched so tightly my teeth grind together. I'm not going to give this guy any satisfaction. No matter what I say, he'll try and use it to make himself look better.

"Cadence, I'm sorry," Wil says in a sudden rush. I flinch a little, refusing to look at his face. My hands tighten around the glass.

Tim's voice is stern. "There may be opportunity for explaining later, Wil. But you need to let us hear from Cadence first. How about you go and help the soup kitchen clean up?"

Out of the corner of my eye, I see Wil nod his head. He gets up from his chair quietly and leaves.

Now that Wil has gone, I finally feel as if I can breathe again. But it takes a little while for my pulse to slow, and I stare at the floor, battling against the reflexes that make me want to cry. How can this be happening? I only just met these people, and yet they're so warm and friendly that I want to tell them everything.

Aria rests her hands on her knees. "I don't want you to share anything you don't feel comfortable sharing, but I think that you've been carrying a burden about Wil for a great while. Do you feel like sharing that with us?"

I look up at the two of them and find open, caring faces. The gentleness in Aria's voice is so inviting that I can't help myself. Words tumble from my mouth like a torrent.

THERE'S NO SUN OUTSIDE THE COTTAGE window to tell me how long I've been sitting there, but I talk until my throat is dry and my voice hoarse. Tim and Aria listen, sometimes asking questions to clarify, but never offering an opinion or disagreeing look. At the end, I feel exposed and spent. Exhausted by talking and exhausted by the memories that hover in the front of my mind as clearly as if I had just experienced them.

I hadn't realized how much I'd been holding back about Wil until I let the dam burst.

Aria and Tim sit in silence for a while, looking thoughtful. "Thank you, my dear." Aria refills my cup of water. "It was clearly a difficult time for you."

I nod, starting to feel a little foolish. Now that everything is out in the open, I feel as if I've said too much. "I'm sorry," I say, wiping at my face with my sleeve. "It sounds bad, I know."

From the bookshelf, Aria hands me a small square cloth made of clean linen. "A handkerchief," she explains at my questioning look. "We find it better not to use disposable things down here."

"Any waste we make somehow has to find its way up to the

surface," Tim adds. He moves a little sideways, looking at me from a slightly different angle. "You know, when Wil first came to us, he was exactly as you described him."

"He was so harsh and arrogant." Aria nods. "The last thing he wanted was to land in the middle of a Siren family." Her eyes twinkle. "Which is probably why the Composer sent him to us."

"You should have seen him then," Tim says. "He would stay up all night arguing with us over every little thing. 'Was Lyric even real?' 'Why would the Composer let the Collective happen?' He was fired up, that boy. So angry."

It sounds just like the Wil I remember. "What happened?"

Tim grins. "Lyric showed up."

"Not *in person*, of course," Aria tells me. "But Wil was visited by him."

"How did you know?" I say with skepticism. Wil's ability to be a chameleon is legendary in my experience. It would be just like him to fake a change of heart if he could wring some benefit out of it.

"I was hesitant at first," Aria admits. "But he asked to come and speak with us. He told us about a lot of things, including that plot you mentioned. He said Lyric had visited him in a vision and convinced him that he had been going wrong for many years."

"His whole demeanor changed from that moment on," Tim says. "He voraciously lapped up every Song fragment we could give him. Worked hard at the most menial of tasks, sought out ways to help."

I sit back a little, unsure of what to say. It all sounds too good to be true. Too sudden. Too perfect. "What makes you so sure he wasn't just pretending?" I ask.

"Oh, we've been around for a while," Tim says wryly. "Long enough to know when someone's bending the truth."

"You don't know Wil," I mutter under my breath.

Out of the corner of my eye, I catch Aria giving a swift look at

Tim. I grimace. Probably not best to contradict your hosts on the first day you meet them. I decide to try better at holding my tongue.

"Sorry," I say.

"If this will help," Tim replies, "one of the things he confessed was something he had planned for the Ghetto, which showed him in a very bad light."

"He had a lot of reparations to make after that, but he did so more than willingly," Aria says.

I still don't believe it. "Didn't you ever doubt him?"

"Never," Tim says adamantly. "I've never seen someone so heartily changed as that boy."

Aria leans toward me. "Cadence, trust can take a long time to build, and trauma takes even longer to heal. We do not expect you to be in close quarters with him if that is uncomfortable for you."

"We have seen him in action a long time now," Tim adds, "and he has more than earned our trust many times over."

Aria looks me directly in the eyes. "Wil knows that a part of his journey with Lyric is to live with the consequences of his actions. He hurt you. That is not something that can be fixed with a quick word."

I let out a breath I didn't realize I was holding, feeling a little tension seep out of my shoulders. "Thank you."

But the horrible thought occurs to me: What if Wil is running a long scam with these guys? What if he's just told them what they want to hear and done a few little things to make them trust him? That would be exactly the sort of thing he would do.

As I sit and smile at Tim and Aria, I make a decision: I am going to expose Wil for a fake and protect this Siren colony so he can't do what he did to us. Wil might have fooled them, but I'm not the trusting idiot I once was. I've learned the hard way how subtle his deceptions can be. It would be devastating if people this kind became the victims of his next con job.

I'm the only one who can stop him.

20

In this life you will have trouble and pain
But Lyric has overcome
Though the struggle is real, and darkness deep
Yet he shall return again.
  Song Fragment 152.9

ARIA AND TIM ENSURE THAT I'M SETTLED IN TO
the Ghetto within a day. Within a week, I have a place to stay,
a job to do, and hundreds of new Siren friends to meet. Across
the Ghetto, the Sirens run most of the enterprises that keep the
Ghetto safe. Apart from the daily soup kitchen, there's a school
run by two of Aria's grownup children, where kids learn to read
in between singing lessons and Song fragments. On the other
side of the Ghetto is a makeshift health center, which would have
been nice to know about before Kent extracted the payment of
my boots and jacket. There's a building crew, who help erect
homes for new arrivals like me, and surface crews to trade goods
for food and necessary supplies up on the streets above. There's
even a Siren sanitation crew, who does the work nobody else
in the Ghetto seems to want to do down here. It's impressive,
chaotic, and awe-inspiring, and Tim and Aria seem to be the ones
in charge of it all.

Wil is more problematic, though. On my first full day in the
Siren community, he sticks to me like a bad smell. I can't trust

myself to speak, so I choose the safer route of ignoring him. The Muse gives me little nudges, but I ignore those too.

On the second day, he shows up at the health center, where I've been volunteered to help for a couple of hours. He waits outside for me until I'm done, then follows me around the Ghetto until I turn on my heels and face him.

"This is disturbing. Stop following me."

"I just want to tell you I'm sorry."

"So it's fake contrition now, Wil, is it?"

"Nothing fake. I swear. This place"—Wil looks up at the ceiling—"is my home now. I was a jerk before." At my expression, his head lowers a bit. "I was horrible."

I stand there, waiting for some kind of sign to tell me what to do. But nothing speaks to me. There's just a growing sense of powerlessness that feeds my frustration.

"You're a liar, Wil." I point my finger at his chest. "And I would be the world's biggest idiot if I believed a single word that comes out of your mouth. Stay away from me."

I spin on my heels and walk as fast as I can, not caring where I'm going. I just need to be anywhere he isn't.

AT THE END OF THE WEEK, I'M INVITED TO MY first Sirens meeting, and I make my way there with what seems like half the Ghetto population. I'm accustomed to furtive, secret meetings. So as the first notes swell from the voices of the choir, I feel a rush of anxiety.

I wring my hands while my brain sends panic signals. They're too loud. There's too many of them. At any moment the fire exit doors at the four corners of the Ghetto will burst open, and a thousand Love Squad soldiers will pour through. But there seems to be no fear here.

Though there are no musical instruments, there doesn't need to be. Harmonies swell, carrying us through the words into the Composer's presence. Timpani teaches truths from the Song, and then we sing them in response.

At the end, I stand near the back, trying to process my feelings. There's peace and joy, which leaves me refreshed as if I had just swum in a warm pool. But there's also a hint of sadness. Danse never got to see this. Melody doesn't know these people are here. Instead, we all lived under the harsh glare of the Collective. Who knew there was a group of Sirens here all along, so close?

I'm still trying to process all of this when three young women approach me. Two look older, but the remaining one looks my age. All of them have long brown braids and wear simple dresses in a design I've never seen before. They smile, but they don't look exactly friendly.

"We're the Brown sisters," the tallest one says by way of introduction.

"Timpani and Aria's great granddaughters," says the younger one.

"Hi." I smile. "I'm Cadence."

"We know," the taller girl says. She stares at me coolly, her expression managing to look both haughty and unimpressed. "I'm Petra."

I notice Petra is watching Wil out of the corner of her eye. She turns back to me. "Candice, is it? How did you get here in the Ghetto?"

"Cadence. I got lost."

"So, you know Wil?" says the sister who seems to be the middle child of the trio. She doesn't bother to tell me her name. She also doesn't bother to hide the suspicion in her eyes.

"I was a student with him." I feel as if I'm being interrogated by a Love Squad.

"Oh, well you don't know him as he really is," says the younger girl. "He's different now."

"Is he?" I ask, failing to keep the cynicism from my voice.

Petra eyes me. "He's been through a lot, you know."

"I'm sure he has."

"He's been really good to us." There's such a proprietary tone in the second older one's voice that it makes her feelings about Wil as obvious as a Collective billboard. I want to reassure her I'm no threat in the same breath as I want to tell her to run as far away from him as her legs can take her. But I don't.

The youngest flicks her braid behind her shoulder. "He helped us to fix our home when Da was sick."

"Found us new fabric for our clothes," the other anonymous sister says, plucking her skirt.

Petra nods. "He's wonderful with the school."

"And helps out all the time at the health center," finishes the youngest.

A grimace is the best I can do. Because what I really want to do is to scream.

The youngest gives me a distinctly side-eye glance. "You don't like him?"

"I can tell that you do," I say carefully.

The middle girl's eyes light up. "I'm going to marry him."

Petra's hand flies up, but she restrains herself. "No, you're not."

It would be almost humorous if it wasn't so pathetic. "Well, whichever one of you he chooses," I say, "you're welcome to him. Believe me, I'm no competition. Nice to meet you all."

I get myself out of there as fast as I can.

AFTER MY CONFRONTATION, WIL SEEMS TO respect my wishes and doesn't follow me anymore. I should be relieved. But instead of being able to get on with my life, a growing obsession begins to take hold, trapping me in a weird contradictory state of mind. On the one hand, I don't ever want to talk to him again, because it feels too traumatic. But on the other hand, if I'm going to expose his evil deeds to the Ghetto down here, then I need to watch him closely.

Three weeks into my confinement, Aria conscripts me to teach Song fragments to their school. It's not my favorite pastime. Coding is a pretty antisocial pursuit, so small crowds of little kids isn't really my thing. When I first meet them, the kids fidget and roll over one another, wrestling with pent-up energy. But after a few fragments, they're singing along. Sometimes I purposely leave out a word, just to see if they notice. They're good at reminding me.

"Miss Cadence, you forgot Lyric!"

"No, silly, it goes like this!"

Today, my lessons finished, I wander through the labyrinthine alleyways. The inner glow I've been feeling at the kids' smiles has worn off, and now I'm wondering how I'm going to make this work. Wil is a chameleon down here. When I catch sight of him at a distance, he's usually smiling, often in the middle of a group of women, and always looking like he's totally in charge. It makes me want to scream.

"How can they not see?" My brain sends me unwanted memories of Wil hugging me at Elite Academy, as if to remind me that I was just like them once upon a time. I don't appreciate the reminder.

The marketplace noises ring out over the top of the hovels, and I find myself drawn to the bustle. It amazes me, still, how this little community exists. I've been so used to the ever-present eye of the Watchers at Elite Academy, and the constant feeling that I am under surveillance. So how did this place survive? I find it difficult to imagine how the Collective could never find out about a group of people this large living somewhere under their great city.

Across the small spread of stalls and open tents, I spot Lark in the distance. I raise my hand to wave, but she turns away, apparently not seeing me. Two young men step up beside her. One of them is wearing dark clothes, his eyes roving over the crowd with a practiced suspicion, as if he's ready to jump into a fight at any moment. The other one is wearing a Love Squad uniform. It looks worn and untidy, and the jacket is open, but there's no mistaking the black menace of that outfit. She greets them with a cool nod.

I shrink back into the crowd, wondering what to do. I know that not everyone here is a Siren. Kent's talk with Lark suggested that there must be some sort of black market down here too. But it still makes me nervous to see that uniform. The boys can't be more than eighteen years old, but they definitely look like the kind who would cut your throat if you ran into them late at night. Actually, the Love Squad guy looks like he'd happily cut your throat in broad daylight too.

At that moment, he glances around, and I'm chilled by the hostility in his expression. He focuses on another section of the marketplace and lifts his chin. In response, a small child in ragged clothes runs up to him. Her feet are bare, and her hair falls down her back in large, matted knots. She looks up at him with a wary kind of devotion. He says something that I can't hear and points. The girl nods and dashes off into the labyrinth of the Ghetto. He turns back to Lark, and they continue with their conversation. Lark laughs loudly at something he says.

I'm surprised at the aching sensation of loneliness that washes over me. Aria and Tim are warm and kind but might be deceived. Wil's ingratiated himself into the Sirens so well that I can't talk to anyone there. Now, Lark is mixing with some very . . . interesting people, and I realize I don't know her after all.

"Why am I here?" I ask the Muse. There's no answer.

21

Do not be imprisoned by hate!
Hate wants to destroy your freedom!
Supreme Lover Midgate's Lovelies
Are Free Lovelies Forever!

WANDERING AIMLESSLY AROUND THE Ghetto becomes a habit I can't shake. One morning, I am in the middle of one such wander when I round a corner and almost run headlong into Aria.

She greets me with a wide smile. "It's so good to see you! Are you free to walk with me for a little while?"

I hesitate, then join her.

"How did school go this morning?"

"Fine," I say carefully. "We went over the Song of Lyric and the tree again."

"Ah, yes. That's an important one down here." Her eyes twinkle at me. "You must know a lot of the fragments by now."

"There are new ones down here that I haven't heard," I say. "You have parts of the Song that I don't recognize."

Aria smiles. "We were fortunate. The Composer has looked after us in many ways."

"It was hard up on the surface to find fragments," I say.

We walk on, passing cardboard hovels and ramshackle shelters made of plywood.

"You sound like you're carrying the weight of the world on those shoulders." Aria turns her head and regards me.

I make a little half shrug.

"Is it Wil?"

Surprised, I look up at her.

"There's a storm in that head of yours," Aria says.

"People just can't see what he's really like," I blurt. "He tried to kill me. He strapped my wrists to the steering wheel of a bomb truck. If it hadn't been for Hodge, I would have been blown to oblivion."

"And it angers you he's down here living as if nothing happened."

"He was able to deceive my Dorm leader, who was the wisest person I knew. He hid right under her nose for years. I look at him here, and I know he's doing the same thing all over again."

"You think he doesn't deserve to be here?"

I blink. The idea sounds harsher when said aloud. "I don't know. I know people can change. I just don't think he has."

Aria nods slowly. "You can't forgive him. I get that."

"No, it's not that. He used me, and he made a fool out of me."

Aria lays a gentle hand on my arm. "There's no question that he did terrible things. Nobody would expect you to just forget."

"But he is allowed to conduct the singing!"

"Wil's place here has been a slow process, Cadence. We didn't allow him to do anything with the Song until he had served for nearly two years in the sanitation department. That's not a job for the faint-hearted nor the smooth-tongued con man. But he turned up every day, working as hard as anyone. Harder, even."

I snort. "Probably just trying to worm his way in while their guard was down."

I wonder if Aria's about to reprimand me. "Let me tell you

a story," she says slowly. "Timpani wasn't always as you see him now. Once he was strong and tall. Until one day, a vagrant attacked him in the soup kitchen. Oh, the poor soul was out of his mind on some substance or another. But he stabbed Tim right here." She points at a spot on her side. "Missed everything important, thank Lyric, but it took a while to heal."

I wait, unsure why she's telling me this.

Aria's eyes take on a faraway look. "He started to favor that side when he walked, bending over to stop it from hurting. The medic told him to stretch it out, but he couldn't let it go. Every time he walked, he just wanted to protect his wound. After a while, it hurt him to stand up straight. After another little while, he found that when he wanted to, he couldn't."

I stare at her, wondering what on Earth this has to do with me.

The faraway look evaporates from her eyes, and she fixes me with a piercing look. "Everyone thinks that forgiveness is wonderful until they have to forgive someone. That's because we're wounded. But we can be so focused on protecting that wound that we forget the one thing Lyric gave us to heal properly."

"It's about justice, though," I say stubbornly.

"Is it really?" Beneath the weight of her gaze, I feel as if all of my inner thoughts are exposed. The thoughts I really don't want people to know about.

She studies me. "Don't let yourself get all twisted up trying to protect that wound. And remember I'm here if you ever need to talk." She gives me a warm smile.

I know she means well, but her words are about as comfortable as sticking thumbtacks into my hands. "Thank you," I say, keen to disengage myself from the conversation. "I will."

I smile and she smiles, but it's clear from Aria's expression that neither of us believes a word I've just said.

MEMORY DATE: 2282.202 (FIVE YEARS AGO)

Memory Location: Watcher Dorm

I'm sitting in the lounge, reading the news on my infotab, when Wil emerges from his room, towel hanging over the back of his shoulders. He rubs at the back of his damp hair with a corner of the towel and strolls barefoot toward the front entrance. Not even once do his eyes flick in my direction.

"Morning," I say, loudly enough for my voice to carry clearly across the room.

He doesn't say anything and skirts around the conference table, toward the kitchen area, without even glancing at me.

"Yeah, it's a great morning this morning," I continue, making my voice deeper. When he continues to act as if I don't exist, I go on. "How are you, Kerr? 'Oh, I'm fine, thanks. It was a little rough trying to wake up, but I'm all good now. How did you sleep, Wil?' I slept pretty well, thanks Kerr. 'Okay, great conversation!'"

Picking out a bottle of water from the fridge, he cracks the lid and takes a swig, half turned so I can see his profile. He still makes no sign that he's even heard me, doesn't even bother to acknowledge my existence.

I let out an annoyed sigh, feeling the niggle of frustrated anger rising in my chest. At the soft sound, the side of his mouth—still turned up toward the water bottle—curls into a smile. He replaces the lid on the bottle and walks back to his room without a word.

A FEW WEEKS AFTER MY CONVERSATION with Aria, I'm startled out of my slumber by a change in the atmosphere. Above my little plywood hovel, there's always a low rumble. It's the echo of voices clustered near the ceiling high above our heads, intermingling with the flow of air and the sounds of footsteps until it all becomes an indistinct, relaxing kind of white noise. But this morning there's a panicked note to the rumble, a glitch in the normal flow that raises me out of my sleep cycle.

Somewhere in the Ghetto, someone is wailing. The high, keening sound is soon joined by a hubbub of other voices. Shouts, screams, clattering footsteps. It sounds close.

Alarmed, I pull myself out of my stupor and jump out of my shelter into the walkway. I hesitate, uncertain of whether to head for the noise or away from it. To my left, the walkway leads to a smaller open space beside one of the four exit doors. To my right, it meanders through hovels toward the Sirens' meeting area and then straight through to the Ghetto's water tank, which is where the sound is coming from.

I decide that I at least need to find out what's happening, so I turn to the right. As I do, two figures come running down the alley in my direction. Both are clad in black, and with alarm, I realize one of them is the guy in the Love Squad uniform. I flatten myself against my little house, leaning back so that there's enough of a gap in the narrow space for them to pass. The Love Squad guy's eyes wash over me with hostile suspicion. Up close, I can see the greasy sheen on his pale white face, and the unkempt knots in his dirty brown hair. But he and his companion pass by without slowing, and I head away from them toward the source of the noise.

It doesn't take long to find it. Around the water tank, a crowd of nervous onlookers has gathered, their eyes fixed on a bundle of rags in the middle of the water. The tank itself is large and circular, and the rags float in the center, out of reach of anyone.

Beside the tank, two women surround a girl who can't be more than eleven, who is on her knees on the wet concrete beside the tank. She appears to be the source of the keening scream, and even now, she cries with high, ear-splitting wails. Beside her, one woman pats her back fretfully, her eyes straying to the bundle and then back to the girl.

"Shame," says a skinny old man near me. He is speaking to an equally skinny woman beside him.

"Not worth it now." She turns away from the tank as if to leave. "Orphans'd have a few things to say 'bout it if'n we did."

"Hush." The old man looks anxiously around him. "They might hear."

The girl beside the tank lets out another high wail, which sends the women around her into a flurry of pats and shushing noises. Anxious murmurs ripple through the crowd.

Then from the back, near an exit that leads to the marketplace, a hush descends that flows outward. Heads move sideways, and the crowd parts for a shorter figure that I can't immediately see. But then the figure emerges, and I understand why people have quieted. It's Kent, hunched over a walking stick, the piles of cloaks and clothes making the older figure look like a giant snail.

"What's going on?" Kent asks, leaning on the stick. The girl lets out a quivering sob, then falls silent. Her face goes deathly pale. The women who had been trying to calm her also pale, looking terrified.

"D-Drowned," the girl finally heaves, raising a trembling figure to point at the tank. All the hairs on my arms stand on end. I start forward, as my rescue instincts kick in. But then I remember the rolling, plunging sensation of my fall into the drain, and fear turns me to stone. I'm helpless against it, frozen to the spot by traumatic memories. My leg twinges in sympathy.

Kent peers at the surface of the water and makes a noise of irritation. "Why hasn't anyone fished it out yet?"

There's no immediate answer. It's almost as if the entire crowd is holding their breath, waiting to see how Kent reacts.

Then one little boy, who I recognise from the Siren school, speaks up. "The Orphans did it."

Shocked gasps echo around the gathered throng. As if by secret signal, the people in the crowd begin to dissipate, stepping quickly away from the trio beside the tank walls. Eyes dart sideways, anxious glances directed at every walkway that opens onto this courtyard space.

Kent's gaze fixes on the little boy. "Really?"

The boy nods his head, eyes wide and frightened. His mother steps forward and draws him back. For a few tense moments they are so still they could be a photograph.

"I think it more likely that it was an accident, don't you?" Kent says evenly.

The boy opens his mouth to protest, but his mother picks him up and nearly runs from the courtyard. Kent turns away from them as if they never existed.

Lifting the walking stick from the ground, Kent's gnarled fingers stab it first at the bundle in the water, and then in the direction of the child who had been wailing. "Remove them."

The girl's bottom lip quivers, but she clasps her hands into tight little fists and just stands there, staring at Kent. Kent turns and shuffles away. Just then, there's the sound of boots pounding across the ground toward us, and a small group of people in dark-blue overalls erupts into the space. Wil is at the front.

"Someone called the Sanitation crew—" he begins, then catches sight of the bobbing rags in the water, just as the bundle begins to sink below the surface. In a split second, Wil dives into the water, reaching out for the bundle and dragging it to him. The water must be deep, and the bundle heavier than he was expecting, because his head dips below the surface for a couple of moments. Then, face stony with determination, he resurfaces and drags the bundle to the edge of the tank, flipping it to reveal the almost blue face of a small girl, barely visible beneath a mat of long, tangled hair.

The rest of his crew leap into action, and within seconds, two of them have retrieved the girl from the water and laid her gently out on the floor. The others help Wil out of the tank.

"Get the medic!" shouts a small woman of the crew.

Wil turns the girl sideways into a recovery position. He opens her mouth, sticking two fingers down her throat, which brings up a small flow of water. Then he begins a first-aid maneuver I remember from engine-room training. Pressing down on her chest with the heel of his hands, then blowing into her mouth, he tries to revive her. The rhythm is mesmerizing. The rest of us stand around helpless, unable to do anything. Seconds seem like minutes. Minutes seem like hours.

Two Sirens appear, who I recognize from the Health Center. They crouch down beside Wil, who leans back, exhausted.

"I couldn't —" His shoulders sink. "I'm sorry."

That's when the drowned girl coughs.

22

Supreme Lover Midgate is our friend!
Supreme Lover Midgate is our hope!
Supreme Lover Midgate shows us love!
Supreme Lover Midgate is all we need!
        –Nursery Dorm Chant #33,
            completed in butterfly formation.

THE ENTIRE GHETTO IS LIT UP BY THE NEWS of Wil's miraculous effort, which shoots from group to group like fireworks. I can no longer move anywhere without hearing about the mysterious attack and the noble hero who jumped in to save the day. Even worse, the story gets more and more embroidered the longer it goes.

"Did you hear about the man with the miraculous powers?" I hear one dirty-faced urchin say to another one morning as I'm heading for the school.

"I heard he zapped her back to life like that!" replies another urchin, snapping his fingers.

"I heard he flew through the air and floated her out of the tank without touching the ground!" says one of the girls at the school.

One of the boys puts on the patient, condescending expression of the true expert in all things. "No, silly. He doesn't have wings. But he was so fast I didn't even see him jump. He's got super speed!"

I force a smile. "That's great, kids, but can we get back to the lesson?"

That week at the Siren meeting, it's easy to know where that dark Wil-shaped cloud is, mainly because it's grown to enormous proportions. There are so many people lining up to shake his hand or clap him on the shoulder that he's impossible to miss.

I'm not sure about anything anymore, but it's disturbing the way these people fawn over him. Everybody wants to say they know the hero of the Ghetto. I have to admit, what he did was amazing, but I'm conflicted. I know he's a lying traitor, capable of unimaginable evil. But then, would a lying traitor save a little girl who looked already dead?

The time arrives for the next Siren meeting, and I go reluctantly. When Timpani begins the first Song, I can't concentrate on anything. I spend the whole time talking to myself in my head, rehearsing all the arguments I won against Wil in my imagination, even though they never really happened.

After the meeting, the chatter strikes up again as we head toward our regular lunch. My irritation burns away at me, erasing any happiness that might have lingered after our singing. As my bad luck seems to be in excellent form today, the three Brown sisters just so happen to slot into line just in front of me. I'm grateful at first that they seem too engrossed in their own conversation to notice me, but that fades as soon as I comprehend what they're talking about.

The youngest says something too low for me to hear.

"I know," Petra agrees, bending her head conspiratorially close to her sisters. "So cute *and* capable."

The line moves even more slowly than normal, which is some form of primitive torture. Everyone wants to have a conversation with the hero. The line snakes around the courtyard, so I have plenty of time to watch the pathetic adulation. By the time one of the orderlies scoops a steaming ladle of soup into my bowl, I'm a hot mess.

The girls react as I predicted they would, simpering and smiling while he hands them each a bowl of soup. If I wasn't so mad at him, I'd say he looked a little uncomfortable at their attention, the way his smile is a little forced. But I am too mad to give him a break.

My turn finally arrives, and Wil is facing the retreating sisters, who wave and giggle at him as they head to a table nearby. He waves back, looking slightly embarrassed. But I decide he's just faking it. Of course he would be lapping up all this attention. It helps his fake good-guy image while he schemes behind everyone's back.

At that moment, holding my soup in the thin metal bowl, a terrible idea occurs to me. When he notices me standing there, his embarrassed smile freezes. I stare him straight in the eyes. There is a tinge of surprise in his expression, no doubt because he's so used to me ignoring him. But that surprise turns to shock when, with one determined movement, I upend the steaming liquid all over his stunned head.

"What the—" he yells, instinctively jumping back from my attack. There are shocked gasps from the kitchen hands, the waiting crowd, and Aria, who has arrived just in time to see me lose it. The greenish soup coats Wil's forehead and drips down his beard, and the orderlies beside him stare at us.

I had been ready with witty comebacks for any occasion. But I am completely unprepared for the silence that greets me. Wil doesn't look at all guilty or embarrassed as he wipes the hot liquid out of his eyes. He just looks sad. Aria's face is worse. She looks betrayed and angry.

With a growing sense of dread, I turn. Gathered around the eating area, dozens of pairs of eyes stare at me. The expressions on their faces are a mix of shock, disapproval, and anger.

"Cadence, what did you do?" Aria comes toward me.

I turn and run.

I FORCE MY WAY THROUGH THE GHETTO, cheeks burning with shame. Their expressions haunt me: Wil's shock and devastation. Aria's disapproval. The disbelief and dismay of everyone.

The alleyways of the Ghetto swallow me up, leading me further and further away. But the walls of the warehouse still loom like prison boundaries. Nowhere is far enough away from that scene. I'll carry those expressions in my memory forever.

I've ruined everything now. Of course they would take his side. They've known him for years. I've only been here for five minutes. He saved a girl's life, for Love's sake. All I've done is make myself look like an aggressive fool.

"Stupid. Stupid, stupid stupid," I admonish myself, feeling miserable.

The Ghetto pulses with life, a beating heart below the surface of the Collective. The narrow walkways past homes and shelters give way to market stalls and bartering stores. I keep my head down, trying to avoid being seen by anyone I know. News will travel quickly about my disgrace, and I would hate to be here when they find out what I have done.

The circus tent rises above the marketplace in all its stripy prominence, reminding me of the day I first arrived here in the Ghetto. It gives me an idea. That hallway, with all those doors—the one I stumbled through, half dead and delirious. It leads only to the dead end of the underwater storm drain, but maybe there will be a place behind one of those doors where I can hide while I try to figure out what to do next.

Keeping my eyes down so I'm not drawn into a conversation,

I move through the market, shaking my head at the calls to buy or trade for goods. I skirt around in a way that avoids passing Kent's home. I know Kent rarely emerges from within those canvas walls, but I don't want to risk running into Lark either.

Racing through the pipe-filled hallway, I step through the battered metal door and emerge under the concrete stairs into the sterile white fire escape. For a brief second, I think about climbing the stairs to street level. A community this big somehow hides in plain sight under the Collective's nose? It is tempting to try and find out exactly how that works. But then I remember the drone Crucible sent after me, and I rethink that option.

I turn back into the brick-lined hallway, searching for a refuge somewhere. Experimentally, I test out some of the door handles. The first one opens with a loud, rusty creak. It reveals a small broom cupboard, now empty, save a moldy bucket and long-perished mop. A disgusting smell wafts out like a decaying cloud, which makes me close the door quickly.

The next few doors won't budge at all, but I finally hit pay dirt a few rooms further along. The room beyond is dark. Suddenly nervous, I look to my left and right and then step inside, flicking the light switch as I close the door behind me.

This room doesn't smell bad at all. Enclosed by walls of light-brown brick, the space is illuminated by a single lightbulb hanging from the ceiling. Diagonally across the room from the doorway sits a large desk, covered with mounds of untidy documents and an ancient-looking computer. I remember seeing one like it in a museum on one of our virtual dormitory field trips. Bundles of wires travel from the back of the computer up through a hole in the ceiling that is possibly wide enough to fit a hand, but not much more. Beside the door is a brass-framed bed, covered with a faded patchwork quilt. A small metal cabinet stands against the brass footboard of the bed, forming a screen to the far corner. A second door sits in the wall beside the desk, at right angles to the entrance door.

Curious, I tiptoe over to the desk, drawn by the computer. It's older than the one Wil used in the bunker to return my memories. A large black rectangular box hums at one side of the desk, and a console screen with chunky black edges looms above it. I sit down on an old, squeaky office chair and pull the keyboard forward. When I tap the space bar, the screen lights up.

ENTER PASSWORD:

I turn away. If I were super keen, I'd probably be able to hack in. But I'm not that bored. Instead I swivel around, taking in the piles of paper that litter the top of the desk and the floor around it. One of the papers catches my eye, and I lean down to pick it up. The Love Collective logo is emblazoned across the top of what looks like a computer print-out:

<<<<<<<<<<<<<<< >>>>>>>>>>>>>>>
<ARCHIVE INTERFERENCE.
UNAUTHORIZED USERNAME ACCESS ALERT>
Interview Transcript Date: CE 2238.02.16
Subject: Marc Nortbert
Status: ~~Active~~ Terminated
<START TRANSCRIPT>

Interviewer: Interview time begins 0300. Suspect has waived right to representation.

Subject: No, I haven't.

Interviewer: You signed this piece of paper, did you not? Interviewer showing suspect form AC-37.

Subject: That form was different when I signed it. There

were none of these paragraphs here. They told me they just wanted to get my name and details correct.

Interviewer: It is not the Collective's fault that you can't read forms, Nortbert.

Subject: That is not the form I signed. I want a lawyer.

Interviewer: You've waived your rights to a lawyer, son.

Subject: This is an unlawful interview. I refuse to answer questions.

Interviewer: So you want us to bring your family in?

Subject: What? No, I —

Interviewer: Failure to answer questions means we need to interrogate your whole family. You really want that?

Subject: Certainly not. Look, I don't even know what I've done. What crime am I supposed to have committed here?

Interviewer: You've seen the rap sheet, haven't you?

Subject: It was all a load of gobbledygook.

Interviewer: Okay. Let's start at the beginning. Where were you on the night of the 11th of this month?

Subject: Last week?

Interviewer: That's correct.

Subject: I was . . . I was visiting with friends.

Interviewer: Friends, Mr. Nortbert?

Subject: Yes. Friends. That's not anti-love, is it?

Interviewer: Don't play dumb with me, son.

Subject: Last week on the 11th, I was at my home. We had some friends around. We had a nice visit together.

Interviewer: You "had a nice visit together." What do you mean by that?

Subject: Ah, we talked about life and stuff, ate some food, sang a few songs, had a—

Interviewer: Stop right there, Mr. Nortbert. You "sang a few songs"?

Subject: Ah . . . I . . . uh . . .

Interviewer: Are you aware that unapproved singing is a proscribed activity under Collective Regulation 13G?

Subject: No . . . no comment.

Interviewer: And what was the content of these illicit songs, may I ask?

Subject: Nothing. They were just . . . I mean . . .

Interviewer: Let me refresh your memory. According to my records, the words you sang included, "I alone am your Composer, do not worship others."

Subject: How did you get those words? Were you spying on us?

Interviewer: And "Love is how the Composer made, and love is Lyric's way. Every other foolish thought is worthless, dead, and vain." Worthless, Mr. Nortbert? You're singing songs that everyone is worthless?

Subject: You missed the rest of it. The song says the opposite of that. It—

Interviewer: These hateful comments are a long way from where the Collective wants to be, son.

Subject: But if you'd just listen to the whole song, you'd understand they're not hateful, they're—

Interviewer: It's people like you, son, who are trying to set back the progress of our society by thousands of years.

Subject: No! We are peaceful citizens. We don't break any laws.

Interviewer: Oh, but you already have, Nortbert. These songs are proof of that.

Subject: They're just songs.

Interviewer: Just songs? These are incitements to hatred, son. Your subversive society is trying to bring down the peace our government has fought so hard to attain. You are insurgents. Rebels.

Subject: No! I'm not. We don't want to hurt anyone.

Interviewer: And yet you sing your illegal anti-love songs.

Subject: They're not anti-love. They're songs of praise.

Interviewer: I think you've said quite enough, Mr. Nortbert. Let the record show I am recommending the subject for permanent reassignment to—

Subject: No! Please! Don't send me away. I can't. I can't be sent away.

Interviewer: You've only yourself to blame, son.

Subject: My kids. They're only babies. I can't [sobs].

Interviewer: Look. We want a peaceful solution here, Nortbert. There may be another way.

Subject: Another . . . another way?

Interviewer: We have a remediation program. We can rehabilitate you to be a good Love Collective citizen.

Subject: Remediation?

Interviewer: If you just sign these forms, here, we can send you to a temporary center. You follow the program and pass the Collective tests, and you get to be released again.

Subject: I get to go back home?

Interviewer: You don't want to be a Hater, do you?

Subject: I'm not a Hater. I—

Interviewer: Then show us. Sign these forms, and we'll send you to the Love Remediation program straight away. In a few months this will all be over, and you can get back to your work and home and life.

Subject: I don't have to go to jail?

Interviewer: You don't have to go to jail.

Subject: And I can get back home?

Interviewer: Absolutely.

Subject: Alright. Alright. I'll sign.

Interviewer: Let the record show the subject has complied with Love Collective directions. Interview concluded.

<UNAUTHORIZED USER ALERT>
<TRACING USER>

23

The Love Squad Always Has a Plan.
You Can Trust Us to Protect You.
Love all.
Be all.

THE PAPER TREMBLES IN MY HANDS. I HAVE heard about the Purging. Known firsthand how vile the Love Squads could be. But to see the record of an innocent person shakes me to the core.

With growing urgency, I flick through the other papers in the pile. I find more court transcripts, more interview files. All of them from a Love Squad server. A few familiar words catch my eye: *Siren, Composer, singing, illegal Hater.* There's another word that repeats over and over too. It chills my blood to see it in bold, stark type at the top of their files: *TERMINATED.*

"Just like the photos," I say, remembering that time all those years ago when I first saw a photo album of stark, vicious killings. But here, in such clinical black-and-white official transcripts, it almost makes it worse. These people come alive through their words. Some fearful. Some defiant. But all of them real people, answering for their membership in groups that the Collective decided were illegal. The transcripts make me feel as if I'm there, witnessing the trials in a way Wil's photos never did.

I shudder, the memory of his name bringing back more recent, shameful incidents that I would rather forget. Putting down the transcripts, I pick up yet another document, which sits on top of the antique computer tower. This document is marked by the official Love Collective logo.

<COLLECTIVE COMMUNICATIONS
DATE CE 2235.06.09>

< <<SUPREME EXECUTIVE EYES ONLY>> >

OPERATION NULLIFY: STRATEGIC PLAN
End game protocol activation date: 2236.01.01, 0300 hours.

My Lovelies,

Following our rather heated meeting of last evening, I am forwarding you an explanation and strategy for our most likely steps forward. I am aware of Supreme Lover Midgate's concerns, so I have put together a comprehensive plan for your benefit. We will continue with this strategy. Midgate will spearhead the campaign, as promised. I have not worked for so many years to see it fail just as we are poised on the cusp of complete victory. Therefore, this policy document is the final word on the matter. Any further objections will result in immediate removal from the Supreme Executive and the imposition of appropriate sanctions. -C

Aim: Permanently Eradicate aberrant behaviors from the Love Collective.

Action Plan:

* On official activation, Love Squad to immediately raid identified homes and remove occupants. All identified homes to be razed or acquired. All occupants, including guests, to be detained indefinitely in Love Squad Central. Property confiscated on Love Collective authority. Demolition and rebuilding plans to be executed immediately.

* Children found in identified homes to be removed to Dormitory accommodation. Prosecute parents for Generation of Illegal Offspring, regardless of actual legal status. Children to be reconditioned in high intensity Love Collective indoctrination programs.

* Interrogate detainees to determine evidence of anti-Collective behaviors. All guilty parties to be sent to Haters' Pavilion for public shaming, then to immediate Embracement.

* Identify possible cases for rehabilitation. Assign rehabs to Love Remediation Centers for re-education.

* Publish list of Hateful Societies along with automatic penalties for membership. Provide bonuses for informants and evidence of Love Collective loyalty to mop up any remaining fugitives.

* Any suspected leader of a Hateful Society is to be assigned immediately for Embracement. Suspected members will be examined and interrogated to assess suitability for re-education and reassignment.

* Destroy all written propaganda materials propagated by said Hateful Societies. Erase records and histories.

I look forward to sharing this great achievement
with you at our special Nullify Celebration, to be held

concurrent to the operation at the Supreme Lover's Compound.

Love All. Be All.

Executive Lover Crucible.

"WHAT ARE YOU DOING HERE?"

The words startle me and I jump. A pile of papers beside my leg slides across the floor, fanning out in chaotic patterns. Lark is staring at me, framed by the second door in the room, which I hadn't investigated before now. Her face is hostile, even furious.

"I . . . I . . ." I stammer, crouching down to rearrange the papers. In a flash, Lark's fingers have closed around my wrist so tightly that I cry out.

"Leave it," she hisses vehemently. She jerks my wrist away from the documents, and I let out a cry of pain. Her blue eyes flash as she stares down at me. "What are you doing here?"

"I'm sorry. I didn't realize—"

With a shove, she sends me flying across the floor, and I land dangerously close to the brass bed frame, my forehead missing it by a whisper of air.

She looms over me. "You should not be here. You should be in the Ghetto. This is *my room*."

"I'm sorry," I say again, sinking backward so that I have space to sit up. "It was an honest mistake. I didn't mean anything by it."

"Then get out."

I put my hands up, placating. "Okay, okay. I'm going," I say, then slowly lift myself up from the floor, careful not to make any sudden movements. She watches me, her eyes narrowed, and her body in a semi-crouch as if ready to pounce on me at any moment.

Reaching the door handle, I pause. "How did you get Supreme Executive files?" I ask, waiting for her to throw something at me.

But she surprises me. Like a slowly deflating balloon, she shrinks down into her chair. "I should have known you'd understand what they were." She sighs, massaging her temple with a thumb and forefinger.

"Operation Nullify was the Purging, wasn't it?" I ask.

Lark stares at me.

I lean back against the wall beside the door. "Curious."

"You'd be one of the first," she says, voice grudging.

"I find that surprising."

"Why?" Lark retorts. "Most people down here are too busy trying to survive. Nobody cares about ancient history."

She looks as if she could switch back to hostile at any second. I speak cautiously, still wary. "But that's important information, isn't it?" I say. I want to get her focus away from the fact that I am an intruder in her room. "I mean, you must have worked hard to find classified files like that."

She looks a little pleased. "It wasn't that hard. You just have to know where to look."

"I know it's not easy to get in to Collective servers," I say, and her eyes widen a little. "But I've never seen anything about Operation Nullify."

"You wouldn't. They don't leave these records just lying around for anyone to find."

I decide that the safest option is to stop pushing. "It sounded like a pretty comprehensive takeover. The operation, I mean."

Lark picks up the paper I'd been looking at before. "Operation Nullify was top secret fifty years ago. Collective used it to get rid of minorities. Wiped millions of them off the face of the earth, and almost nobody objected."

"That's terrible."

"Yep. Everything happened the way the document said it

would. Everyone else was too distracted or too scared to stop it." Lark's jaw hardens.

"Where did you get all of this?"

"Found them." Her casual shrug tells me there's a whole lot more she's hiding.

"Found them where? Sitting on a park bench? In someone's basement?" I ask, flummoxed.

"I can't tell you." She starts to tidy the piles of papers, straightening them with care. "Not if you want to live." Something in her tone makes me realize she's not entirely joking.

"But these are my people. This is my history too," I argue.

"Your people?" She looks up at me with one eyebrow raised.

"You already knew that, didn't you?" I say with false bravado.

The crooked corner of her smile tells me all that I need to know. There's a warning alarm that goes off in the back of my head.

I decide to change the subject. "The strategic plan document there seemed to say that Midgate had some concerns. Do you know what that meant?"

Lark shakes her head, suddenly super interested in a spot on her black combat pants. "No, I don't," she says. Something in her tone makes me doubt her words.

"It makes sense that Crucible would want to keep going, I guess," I go on. "Crucible's a mean kinda guy."

Lark's eyes fly to me. "You know him?" Her voice is sharp.

I've said too much. "Everyone knows Executive Lover Crucible," I reply lightly. "He would sometimes visit Elite Academy."

"What was that like?" Lark leans forward eagerly.

I know what she's asking, but I decide to be deliberately obtuse. "Elite Academy? Oh, it was okay, I guess. Lots of drill practice, lots of coding, lots of Collective loyalty exercises. Protein meals, uniforms, dormitories. That kind of thing."

MEMORY DATE: 2285.365 (TWO AND A HALF *years ago)*

Memory Location: Elite Academy dining hall

My mouth is full of lunch, so I don't immediately register the person's arrival until they slide right up beside me. When I see who it is, my whole body tenses. I nearly choke on my food.

"Relax, it's Triumph Season," Hodge says, settling onto the bench beside me. He lays the tray down on the table with almost no sound at all. "Anyone can talk to anyone now."

"Why are you here?" I hiss, too nervous to even look him in the eye.

"Look around you," Hodge says with a soft laugh. "I think we can sit at lunch and have a conversation, don't you?"

I glance around at the pheromone-charged dining hall, then wish I hadn't. "Fine," I mutter. "Just eat your lunch."

"As you wish," he replies with far too much enjoyment for my liking. "As long as you agree to talk to me properly later."

"Do I have to?"

"Call it a favor for a guy who's graduating tomorrow."

I didn't expect the sudden lump in my throat, so it takes me a few seconds to reply. "Sure."

WHILE I'M TRYING TO FORGET MY ACADEMY days, a wistful expression crosses Lark's face. "It sounds so simple," she says, staring off into the distance.

My mind goes back to the trials Crucible put me through. The games he purposely played to stop me from graduating right at the very end of all of my years of hard work. None of it was fair, and there was nothing I could do about it. "Not so simple when a member of the Executive decides that you're his favorite chess piece."

Lark's eyes narrow at me. "That sounds like you knew Crucible personally."

Keeping my mouth shut seems to be the only option right now, so I shrug.

"So tell me," Lark says, "how does an Elite end up down here with no ID?" She gives a pointed look at my blank wrist.

I should have expected it, but I really had hoped to avoid probing questions like that. "I'd rather not talk about it," I say, shifting uncomfortably.

"Oh, come on," she scoffs.

I sigh. "I'm a Siren," I say, suddenly feeling tired. "Does there have to be any other reason?"

Lark leans back in her chair and puts her hands behind her head. "I think there's more than you're telling me."

"And you still haven't answered my question," I observe mildly.

Lark sits forward. "Alright. I'll make you a deal. If I tell you what this is about"—she waves at the pile of papers—"then you tell me what you know about Crucible."

I pretend to think about it for a second. "Deal." Inside, though, I'm hoping that I can get her talking about her passion project long enough for her to forget my part. I don't want anyone to know that Crucible was personally overseeing my Watcher training. If Lark knew that I was in any way connected with that surveillance project, I'm pretty sure my life would be over before I could blink.

I go take a seat on the end of the bed, leaning against the brass bedposts. "So," I begin, "what did you want to do with this information?" I watch her for any return of hostility.

She makes a face. "I've wanted to do something for ages, but all I've managed is to find these old files." She kicks at the pile near her feet, sending them skidding across the floor again. "I mean, they're interesting, don't get me wrong. But who wants to know about trials of people who've been dead for nearly fifty years?"

I look at her. "I do."

"But they don't help me at all. You would think . . . you would think with these genes," she gestures to herself, "I could get some better treatment."

I blink. "What do you mean?"

She suddenly looks rattled. "None of your business."

24

Embracement is not our first recourse, but our last resort. It will remain necessary for as long as Hate exists. Therefore, we use it with reluctant determination.

-Supreme Lover Midgate, Intimate Diaries of a Loving Leader, *chapter 19*

A FEW HOURS LATER, LARK AND I ARE SITTING on the floor of her room, our backs against the brick wall. The piles of papers are now fanned out across the floor, organised into vague categories: trial transcripts, official policy documents, Love Squad incident reports, and so on. All of them paint a horrible picture of the early Collective.

Both of us stare at the papers. Lark has fished out two small brown bottles of liquid that smell faintly chemical. I lift my drink to my lips, trying to work out what to do next. It fizzes satisfyingly on my tongue, but leaves me feeling a little light-headed.

"What is this stuff?" My tongue feels thicker than normal.

Lark gives a short laugh. "You've never had the delights of Buzz before?" She tilts the top of her bottle toward me. "Consider yourself educated."

I like the fizz and so raise the bottle for another swig.

Lark watches me. "So what are you doing down here, anyway?"

The fuzzy, buzzy kind of feeling in my head grows. It loosens my tongue. "I have to get out of the Ghetto." For some reason, the safe house address has been floating in front of my memory. The one I looked at briefly, just to humour Hodge. Right now, it's the only solution I can see. "Need to be somewhere else."

"Join the queue," Lark says with dry sarcasm. She takes a slow drink.

"But I really do," I insist. "I can't go back in there. I made a mess of everything, and now they're all going to hate me. I can't go back."

My mind fills with the crystal-clear memory of my rash action. By now, Wil has probably been cleaned up. Aria and Timpani are probably planning some sort of disciplinary committee, and the Brown sisters will be telling everyone about how terrible I am. I'm surprised they haven't sent an angry mob after me already.

"Hodge wouldn't have made that mistake," I mutter. I feel weirdly disconnected from my body. "He'd know what to do." My bottle is empty, and I stare at it, struggling to focus my eyes. Lark jumps up and disappears into the side room. When she returns, she's carrying two more bottles. She pushes one into my hand and sits again on the floor beside me.

"Who's Hodge?" Lark twists the bottle cap off for me.

The Buzz tastes sweet and pleasant. "Someone I know from before. We were going to be—wait. I shouldn't be telling you this. Loose lips get you on the Haters' Pavilion and all that."

"I promise I won't tell," Lark whispers. I turn to look at her, still feeling that weird sensation of disconnection. She winks at me, and a smile curves up the corners of her mouth.

"Never mind." I scowl. "I wrecked things with him, too."

"What do you mean?"

I take another sip, then wipe my lips with the back of my hand. "I was this close to graduation." I pinch my fingers awkwardly together. "Hodge and I were going to be together after that. None of this sneaking around stuff." The thought is so sad that I feel a strong prickle of tears. "But Crucible went and wrecked it."

"What?"

"He did! He sent me a 'special mission.'" I make exaggerated quotation marks in front of my face with my fingers. "Said that if I was going to be a Coder in the Hall of Love, I needed to get some extra practice in. But it was a trap. A dirty, stinking, mean, old trap."

It could just be the fuzzy effects of the drink, but it feels like Lark takes ages to talk again. "What did he send you?" she says eventually.

The buzzing feeling grows. I whisper, "Code."

We sit in silence for a little while. Lark picks up one of the pieces of paper and flutters it in the air in front of her, distracted. It's kind of hypnotic. I find myself staring at it, mesmerised.

"Can you tell me what it was?" she asks. "The code, I mean."

I shake my head and it swims. "Nope. Top secret." My voice is too loud. "You wouldn't believe me anyway."

"Try me."

"Okay. But you have to promise you won't tell anyone."

"I promise."

"Not a single person." I frown. The room begins to feel as if it's spinning. I have to stare at the furniture really hard to make it hold still.

Lark puts her hand over her heart. "No one."

"This doesn't go past these walls, okay?"

"You have my word," she promises.

"Fine." Despite a little twinge of anxiety, I take another drink of the Buzz, and I start to tell her everything. "I found out that Supreme Lover Midgate *is a robot.*" That last bit sounds slurred. I face Lark to see her reaction.

She laughs. "That's the funniest thing I've ever heard! You actually believed it?"

"Well, I—Well . . . the data looked like it was . . ."

"And that was the big secret? That's all?" She is still laughing.

"That's all? What do you mean 'that's all'?" I splutter. My head feels dizzy, and it gets harder to think. A wave of sleepiness washes over me. "That's HUGE. It could bring down the whole Collective. Lover Midgate is EVERYWHERE. All the time. On our vidscreens, up on the posters, all the nightly lectures. Every. Where."

My second bottle is empty too. The room has started to come in and out of focus, and my head feels like it's too heavy to hold up. The walls opposite me begin to shift, as if we're on a boat.

"Everyone thinks she's a real person," I still manage to talk. "But she's just a bunch of code designed to tell us what to do. Imagine finding out that she's just an AI? That would really mess everyone up."

"There's no way she's AI. Believe me," Lark says. "Anyway, how would this stop you from graduating?"

A sudden wave of grief washes over me. "They arressted my Sh-shiren leader." The heaviness in my head grows. It's hard to hold it up.

"So you're on the run?"

I take a deep, fortifying breath. I can only nod. My eyes suddenly feel super heavy.

Lark says something, but it sounds as if it's coming from a long way away. I try to speak, but my chin drops to my chest. Then I'm not aware of anything else.

MEMORY DATE: 2285.365 (TWO AND A HALF *years ago)*
Memory Location: Gardens, Elite Academy

Along the tree-lined avenue in the distance, soft orange lights twinkle through the leaves, wrapped around branches so that it looks as if the trees themselves are made of pinpoints of light. Festive Triumph decorations swoop between light poles, creating a canopy of light and color. Couples wander up and down the path, some hand in hand, some stopping to embrace. When I catch sight of a couple being a little too close, I turn away, cheeks burning. I'm suddenly far too aware of the tall Apprentice beside me, his solid presence reminding me that I have been asked out here for a special "conversation." It makes me feel less like an Elite, and more like a walking bundle of awkward limbs.

Hodge draws me over to a bench that isn't occupied, and we sit, feeling the warm summer air waft over our heads. He stays beside me for a while, and I enjoy the lights, trying to ignore the obvious displays of affection around us.

Finally, my companion clears his throat. "Triumph ends tomorrow," Hodge says stiffly. "And the day after that is graduation."

"I know." I feel a sudden sense of panic. When he looks at me, my nerves zing with crazy abandon. I look away for a moment, feeling awkward. "I won't have my Siren co-leader to fall back on." I give an exaggerated grin that is the opposite of what I'm actually feeling.

"You'll be fine," Hodge tells me. "It's the Composer you need, not me."

I don't know how to answer that. "Will you remember me?"

An odd expression passes over Hodge's face. "I know I don't have your memory gift, but that's a little extreme, don't you think?"

I laugh. "Well, you said you didn't want a Triumph fling, so I just assumed you would be in a hurry to forget me as soon as you got out of here."

He clears his throat again. "That's . . . uh . . . that's actually what I wanted to talk to you about."

I turn to him, curious at the hesitation in his voice. I can't read his face, but his hands are gripping the edge of the seat as if he's nervous.

That can't be it. My own nerves are buzzing and exploding all over the place. But Hodge has never been nervous in the whole time I've known him. Not even when we were driving a giant bomb out of the city. He's always confident, always in control. Which is possibly why I've come to depend on him so much, and why it hurts so much to think he's leaving.

In the distance, Chu wanders down the path, alone. A younger Apprentice approaches him and starts what can only be described as the most obvious flirting I've ever seen. He smiles at her, and I begin to wonder whether he's finally gotten over Sif, when Sif herself comes up the path toward them. The younger Apprentice leans into Chu a little as Sif starts speaking. I can't hear my friend's words, but I can see the cold smile on her face. After a few moments, the Apprentice looks doubtfully up at Chu, and then backs away down the path. In a graceful turn, Sif threads her hand under Chu's arm, and he responds by throwing his arm over her shoulder.

Beside me, Hodge stares out at the trees, then turns back to me. "We were interrupted the other night, and I didn't get a chance to tell you . . . I'm sorry. I was called out to do Triumph guard duty, and so I was away in Love City for weeks, and I couldn't get to you, and it made me so mad. And then you ran away and, well—"

His babbling is just confusing to me. This is so unlike the unflappable Hodge I know. The guy whose head is always cool in a crisis. I put my hand on his arm, and he jolts to a stop, mid-sentence.

"What is it?" I say gently. "You can tell me."

"I'm not sure how to say this," he says, staring at his knees.

My heart sinks a little. "Try me," I say, trying to sound carefree. Inside, I'm waiting for the bad news to drop. He's going to say goodbye now, and then we'll never see each other again.

My breath catches in my throat when Hodge reaches out to lift my hand in his own. There's a whooshing feeling in my stomach, as if my heart has gone on a Pleasure Tribe acrobatic performance. The nerves in my fingers are suddenly sending high-definition signals back to my brain, so I can feel the calluses under Hodge's fingers, and the softer pads around his hands.

"Ca—Kerr," he begins, correcting his near slip in public. "When I said I didn't want to be your Triumph buddy, it wasn't because I didn't like you."

His eyes reflect the twinkling tree-lights, and I am transfixed by his gaze. The swooping feeling in my stomach intensifies. My heartbeat quickens.

"I know it's probably too late. I know I'm about to go into the Squad. But you're allowed to choose someone when you've graduated. Someone to be more than a Triumph buddy. I want that to be you. If you'll let me."

A slightly over-enthusiastic couple stumbles through the bushes beside us, giggling and talking to each other in loud whispers. They see us and keep stumbling on, laughing to each other as they seek an unoccupied patch of shadow. I barely notice them. My head is full of fireworks.

A smile breaks across my face so wide it hurts. "You could have said yes back then, you know," I say, laughing. "It would have saved me a lot of trouble."

In that moment, Hodge's dazzling smile is everything.

WEIRD, NIGHTMARISH DREAMS FLY THROUGH my mind. I'm back to the drill fields in my old Nursery Dorm, marching in a chaotic mess beneath the familiar white walls of my former prison. On the high platform, Dorm Leader

Fuschious thumps a huge drum without any apparent pattern or regular rhythm.

Down on the artificial grass, the chants are all wrong, as if the Apprentices have all picked their own words and are shouting in a cacophony of broken noises. The children around me change direction, or stop, or suddenly dash across the space without warning. If they run into someone, they erupt in violent curses and flailing arms.

"Stop it!" I scream, but my words are lost under the hurricane of noise.

Fuschious begins pounding the drum faster, and the marching becomes more frenetic. The Brown sisters march past me, their eyes shooting hatred in my direction, even as they march along like Apprentices. Someone bumps me from behind, and I fall forward onto the ground.

"Watch where you're going, Hater!" Sif yells behind me.

Surrounded by angry faces and marching boots, I lie paralyzed on the floor. Aria comes to stand beside me. She shakes her head in a disapproving way and clucks her tongue. Shortly afterward, she's joined by Akela and Viola and Danse, who all stare down at me with disappointment.

I cower beneath them, closing my eyes so I can't see the condemnation. That's when I feel a thumping pain in my forehead as one of their boots presses down on my temple. I can't tell who it is. I cry out, and the pressure increases.

With a yell, I wake myself up. But the pain doesn't stop. My head throbs as if someone has clamped a vice around my skull. My mouth is dry, and my tongue feels like sandpaper against my lips. It's hard to open my eyes as tiny fragments of light stab like sharp knives. If anything, it feels worse than the nightmare, which doesn't help.

It takes far longer than it should for my brain to register that I'm not in Lark's room anymore. Maybe it's the darkness. Or maybe it's the cold, hard concrete beneath my back. But when an icy gust of air passes over my body, I'm dragged fully into an unpleasant reality that makes my fevered dream seem like a pleasure cruise.

Wide awake now, it becomes painfully apparent that I'm lying on a street somewhere. Far above my head, stars stretch across the sky like a thick white blanket, framed by black outlines of the buildings on either side of the road. It's a narrow road, like the industrial service roads I visited on one of my fragment-hunting expeditions. The windowless walls rise above me like a prison. The concrete beneath my back seeps cold into my clothes, making me shiver. I groan and try to move and discover then that my hands and ankles are bound by plastic ties.

A harsh male voice behind me swears. "You're not supposed to be awake yet." There's a painful thump at the side of my head, and then everything dissolves into oblivion.

PART 3

Why are you so burdened, Oh my soul?
Put your hope in the Composer,
Put your hope in him alone.

Song fragment 148.1

25

If You Are A Hater
We Will Find You.

Love All. Be All.
The Love Collective.

WHEN I WAKE UP, THE FIRST THING I NOTICE IS a violent, throbbing ache next to my left eye. I move as if to reach up and massage the area, but my hands are bound. My groan is muffled behind a thick strip of tape that covers my mouth. Frustrated, I jerk my legs and discover they're tied too.

Eyes widening, I take a look at my surroundings. It doesn't take long. Somehow I've been bundled into a storage room or something. I can't tell exactly where. To my left is a dark concrete wall. To my right is a wall of large, unmarked cardboard boxes, piled almost to the ceiling. At my head and feet are open spaces, which would provide a getaway if I wasn't tied up so well.

With supreme effort, I raise myself to a sitting position, feeling a burst of nausea. In the dim light, it's hard to make out the ties around my ankles, but I realize at once the mistake made by my captors. They've placed the plastic tie over the top of my clothes.

I feel a small surge of optimism. Maybe I'm not dead after all.

It's hard to move with hands bound, but I manage to slip off my shoes, and shimmy the pant legs up and out of the way. The plastic leaves painful scrapes against my ankle, but I don't care. Within a few minutes, I have my feet back.

Replacing my shoes, I move into a crouch. Whoever has captured me is either cocky or amateurish, because there are no sounds of guards near my hiding place.

They've never tried to capture an Elite before, I think.

The tape over my mouth is the next thing to go, but unfortunately the wrist ties are too tight for easy release. If it came to close combat, I'd be at a distinct disadvantage. Elite basic training assumed we'd always be the ones restraining others, not the other way around. But I need to get moving, so there's no point wasting time without tools.

After another quick glance around the wall of boxes, I emerge into a room about the size of a smaller coding center. Four rows of high warehouse shelves mark out narrow aisles, each one packed with nondescript boxes. My movements are a little slower than usual, thanks to the throbbing in my head, but I manage to find my way to what looks like the only exit. The door is closed, so I put my ear close to the edge to listen.

There's no sound from the other side.

After a moment's indecision, I search through the shelves for anything useful. Most of the contents are sealed inside boxes, but there's a small utility shelf where I find a collection of cleaning chemicals, a torch, and a small boxcutter. I wedge the boxcutter into a corner of the nearest metal shelf, and then saw away the remaining plastic tie. Then I pocket the torch and boxcutter, for good measure.

My mind races. How did I get here? Did Lark betray me, or is she a victim too? I won't know if I don't get out of here. If I stay, it's only a matter of time before someone comes for me, and I'll be at a distinct disadvantage when they do.

Unsure of what to do next, I return to the exit, straining my ears to hear any sign of life beyond the storeroom. A thud sounds in the distance. There's a far-off *clank*, like the opening and closing of a heavy door. Then a single set of footsteps, echoing off a concrete floor. The footsteps approach my hiding place.

I crouch behind the door, and my hand strays toward the boxcutter, but I leave it in my pocket. I don't want to maim someone. Although the pain is pounding in my head as solidly as a drum, making it hard to think, I decide to rely on my memories of Elite training. As long as the person wasn't trained in the Love Squad, I should be okay.

The footsteps slow as they reach the door. I hold my breath. The door handle turns, and the door begins to creak open. I catch a brief glimpse of black clothing and a man's side profile, and then I pounce.

Shoving the door forward, I send the man off-balance, and he pitches sideways with a cry of surprise. But he doesn't get much further. His mouth opens to shout, but I slam my palm upward into his chin, then once again. Stunned, he falls like a rock and lies motionless on the ground, out cold.

"An Orphan." I recognize the unconscious figure from the day of Wil's heroism. The last time I saw him, he was following the guy who wore a Love Squad uniform. I knew these people were dangerous, but it never occurred to me that I would register in their crosshairs.

I step out of the storeroom into a darkened hallway, pulling the door closed behind me. To my right, in the direction where I first heard the footsteps, the hall ends in a darkened recess beyond a corner. To my left, though, there's a fire escape, illuminated by a blue sign above the door. I haven't got time to delay. The Orphan won't be out for long, and he'll raise the alarm when he comes to. So I've got to move fast.

I race to the exit as quickly as I can. A horizontal metal bar forms the handle. I push on it, and the door swings open into a dimly lit alleyway.

The metal door beneath my fingers is a cold anchor to the

reality of the world around me. Every fiber of my being buzzes with anxiety and uncertainty. A soft breeze whistles between tall windowless buildings, bringing cold and oily smells that wrinkle my nose. The night is so dark that it's hard to see my feet standing on the small landing beside the exit. I am tempted to pull out the torch, but that could be dangerous.

"Where do I go now?" I wonder, looking to the right and left.

In the past, my automatic reflex was always to talk to the Muse about any dilemmas. But my tongue feels dry and empty of words. For weeks, I have bathed in anger and a desire for vengeance, and it's as if I've built a wall between the Composer and me. It's too hard to ask for protection now.

So I take a deep breath and step out into the dark alley, hurrying away from my former prison.

Out in the open street, stars fill the sky like a thick white ribbon, framed by the square black shadows of the buildings along the alley. The last time I saw a sky like this, I was sitting beneath the Heartstrong Bridge with a blanket, a backpack, and the whole world laid out before me. So much has happened since then it almost feels like someone else was under that bridge, not me.

Head still aching, I slow my pace as I come to a small intersection between buildings. Four alleys lead away from me like the points of a compass. To my right, at the end of one of the alleys, I see a dark ribbon of black where the lights twinkle and shimmer off the surface of water. It's so wide it must be the river. Beyond that, a distant Love Collective sign grins at the top of a huge factory that sits on a hill. A familiar sight, and one that brings a rush of memory.

MEMORY DATE: 2285.008 (THREE YEARS AGO)

Memory Location: Love City

The sun is so hot that sweat runs down my back. I shift my shoulders, uncomfortable at the way my uniform sticks to my skin. Beside me, Hodge straightens. The heat radiates off the concrete all around us—the warehouse walls, the road, the pavement. The shade provides no relief either.

Loa lets out a long slow breath. "Tough day for a city assignment," he says.

"We're here on orders," Hodge replies. "Not our place to question what we're told."

"Which way do we go?" I squint against the harsh sunlight bearing down on us.

Hodge nods up the hill. "Factory."

I take a closer look at the massive grey building that stretches across the top of the ridge. High black metal fences ring the property. Large trucks move up and down the roads around it. Workers mill around all over the place like ants near a nest. On top of the long, flat building, a massive circular Love Collective sign sits like a giant moon.

"Why did Dorm Leader want us to go there?" I ask, confused.

"No idea," Loa replies. "But let's go before we melt."

"Up that hill?" I ask, failing to keep a whiny note of reluctance out of my voice.

Hodge lets out a little laugh. "Come on," he says, giving me a gentle nudge.

We joke about the heat as we trudge toward our assignment destination. Our mood is light. None of us knows that Akela won't be there when we return home.

LIKE A MOTH DRAWN TO LIGHT, THE SIGHT OF that factory draws my footsteps onward. There's a river in the way, but I don't care. For the first time in months, I know where I am. No longer in an underground cavern that could be at the center of the planet for all the good it did me.

I walk on the balls of my feet, trying to keep the noise of my footsteps as quiet as possible. The river is more visible now, winding its way through the industrial area with no care for the time of day or my mortal peril. But I'm glad to see it anyway.

When I reach the corner of the last warehouse in the alley, I hang back from the edge, pushing my body close to the wall before risking a look at the riverside area. My first brief glimpse shows me a wide dock, peppered with boxes and containers and machinery. During the day, this must be a hive of activity as trucks transfer containers to and from warehouses to waiting rivercraft. In the distance to my right, a wide concrete bridge arches over the expanse of the river like a grey crescent. Beside the bridge, a lone streetlamp casts a dim glow over the docks below.

A jerky movement catches my eye, and I spot a lone figure running toward the distant streetlamp. The figure is small, wearing dark clothing that looks completely out of place up here on the surface. As the figure reaches the pool of light, I catch sight of a shock of blond hair and a face I recognize: Lark.

Two figures step out from behind a large crate and come to meet her. One of them wears a tattered old Love Squad uniform, and the other is dressed completely in black. I watch, frozen in place by fear. The Orphans huddle together with Lark in conversation. One of them points down the river in my direction, and I throw myself back around the corner.

I wait for a few seconds, wondering what to do. Fear tells me

I should get as far away from here as possible. But my curiosity won't let me leave just yet. I have to know what's going on.

I decide to take another look. Taking my time to peek around the corner, I notice the scene has changed. Lark is alone, leaning against the streetlamp, playing with something in her hand. Just when I'm wondering where the Orphans went, she moves away from the light post and begins to pace between two large crates lying beside a river wharf.

I am debating whether to step forward and call out to her when another group crosses the road leading to the bridge. Six black-uniformed soldiers march along the dock toward Lark. A Love Squad. She stills, watching them come. My heart leaps into my throat. I want to scream, "RUN!" but I know that would be suicide.

I wait for the inevitable signs of struggle: stun nets, guns, amplified warnings: *"Halt! Love Squad Business!"* But they don't come. The leader steps forward from the group toward Lark. She faces them with the stillness of a carved stone statue. I hold my breath, waiting for her to run or fight.

A few heartbeats pass. Then Lark leans forward and converses with the lead soldier for a few moments. When Lark straightens up, she gives the soldier a warm embrace.

I turn away from the dock and run as fast as I can.

26

Follow Your Heart.
It Beats For The Collective.
Love All. Be All.

I'VE BEEN BETRAYED.

The words play on repeat as I sprint away from the river. Everything is crystal clear, focused only on keeping my feet from tripping and on helping my eyes see the next corner to turn. Boxy concrete buildings fly past, but I'm too focused on the path in front of me to notice anything but the occasional detail.

I run. I run and run until I think I can't run anymore, and then I keep running.

Every so often, facts manage to float in past the fog of panic. That Buzz Lark gave me back in her room was just a trick to make me pass out. Obviously she's working with the Orphans on something that involves kidnapping me in the middle of the night. I've got no idea what the plan is, but if the Love Squad is involved, then I don't want to be near enough to find out.

The industrial area is so huge that it swallows me up. I avoid the wide roads, choosing to run along the spaces between buildings, disappearing into the expansive complex of warehouses, factories, and depots. Corners fly at me, and I choose direction by instinct more than wisdom. Everything else is dim and damp. Metallic smells mingle with rotting garbage and industrial detergent. Silent factories loom over my head, their shuttered doors and security cameras the only witness to my presence here.

Please let the Watchers be looking elsewhere, I think desperately. But I know it's a vain hope.

After a few minutes, my pace slows. The night air brushes my face with a cool, soft touch. Throbbing pain returns to my forehead, even more insistent now that I need hydration. My weary body wants to find a quiet place to catch my breath and rest, but I can't afford to stop. At any moment the black uniforms will be at my heels again. Or the Orphans will find me. Or the Watchers will flag me for arrest.

I push myself down another alley and around what feels like the hundredth corner, expecting to see a wide, sweeping road between the large industrial complexes. Instead, I find another narrow walkway, hemmed in by a dark brick wall on three sides. A knot of fear forms in my stomach.

That can't be right. I pause to catch my breath and feel along the wall for any hidden doors or catches that I may have missed. The brick is smooth and unyielding beneath my fingers.

My immediate instinct is to backtrack and find where I went wrong, but knowing my luck I would probably run straight into pursuing soldiers. Turning back now would have to be the most stupid idea in the history of stupid ideas.

I turn in a slow, tense circle, weighing my options. On the positive side, the alley isn't a complete dead end. There's a small fissure running between close-packed warehouses that makes this alley a T-shaped intersection. It's wide enough that I could inch my way sideways and find an exit at the other end of the building. On the negative side, I would be trapped like an animal if any of the Squad came after me.

I look up and down the small gap, trying to decide which way to go. In one direction, the narrow space disappears into total darkness. In the other direction, a small slit of light shines weakly. It's nothing more than a dim grey rectangle a few hundred feet away, but it's better than a potential dead end.

"Any help would be appreciated," I reach out to the Composer's Muse for the first time in days. Or is it weeks?. There is no answer. With a sinking feeling, I wonder if I am beyond help. Have I spent so long ignoring the Composer that I can't hear him anymore, even if I wanted to? I deal with it by choosing the gap that leads toward the lightened exit, squeezing myself into it.

The air around me is musty and putrid, as if a thousand rats disappeared into this small wedge to die. A frigid breeze whistles around my ears and chills me to the bone. Every time I try to inch forward, rough brick scratches the palms of my hands.

After everything I've been through, it's those tiny grazes that finally tip me over into the pit of self-pity and despair. Tears well in my eyes. I nurse my wounded palms, staring at the darkness and feeling the sting. I've survived far worse than this before. Kept my head through harsher treatment. But all of a sudden, a few shallow scratches have rendered me helpless and lost.

My life seems to have devolved into a series of betrayals all at once: Wil being lauded as a hero instead of being condemned by everyone for all the things he did. Aria and Tim taking his side instead of mine. Lark doping me up and leaving me bound and gagged on some random floor somewhere. Hodge completely failing to keep his promise to find me.

It wouldn't be so bad if I could just hear the Composer's Muse again. I want to feel that solid, loving Presence. Want to feel certainty that the Composer has me. When I knew that at least the Composer loved me, I thought I could survive anything. But even he seems to have decided that I'm not worth the effort anymore.

My bottom lip trembles, and I am tempted to dive into a deep well of tears and hopelessness. To sink to the putrid shadows at my feet and be forgotten forever. Who would care if I died here? Nobody. I could disappear, and not a soul would know.

The wind picks up its pace, sending a blast of freezing air through my clothes. In the back of my thoughts, a Song fragment tickles at my memory. Out of nearly forgotten habit I reach for it and let the music fill my mind.

You are my hiding place;
You will protect me from trouble
And surround me with songs of deliverance.

The cold wind still whistles down the narrow gap, making it hard for me to believe the words at first. I am not protected, I am cold. I am sore. But I make the effort to keep singing the words in my head, repeating them again and again, and letting the meaning soak into my consciousness. This place isn't comfortable, but it is hidden. It's not a luxury pleasure cruise, but I'm safe for the moment.

"I can't stay here forever," I whisper, feeling the cold begin to seep into my bones. But the wild beating of my heart begins to slow. I take a few steps toward the light, scraping my hands against the bricks again. Another fragment rises to the front of my thoughts.

I have hidden your Song in my heart,
That I might not turn against you.

The weight of the words hits me like a speeding train.

He wasn't silent. I had stopped listening.

The walls on either side of me embrace me like a lover, and a strange, warm feeling washes over me. I wonder if that's a small encouragement from the Muse or just my own wishful thinking.

I have loved you with an everlasting love . . .

Tears sting at the corners of my eyes. It is the Muse. The Composer hasn't forgotten me. I will be okay. Thanks to Lyric, even if I die, I will be okay.

"I am sorry," I say silently. "I've been an idiot."

Will you listen now?

"I will," I reply with all my heart. "But I don't know what I'm supposed to do."

My plea is answered by the sound of a loud cry of pain somewhere just beyond the crack of light ahead.

Go.

For the first time in ages, I obey.

MEMORY DATE: 2285.008 (THREE YEARS AGO)

Memory Location: Collective Services Union

At the top of the hill, the guards at the black gates greet us with gruff nods and large weapons strung across their shoulders. At the sight of our Elite uniforms, they step back to allow us through. We salute and walk into the compound, wending our way around the trucks and forklifts, heading for a large set of glass double doors that form the entrance to the lobby.

Inside, the air is cool and stale. A wide reception desk sits beside a series of security turnstiles, where ID scanner consoles operate, sliding transparent barriers to allow workers to enter into the complex. Beyond the barriers are banks of elevators, sleek and silvery.

"We're here for the tour," Hodge says to one of the workers at the security desk, who signs us in and hands us small plastic cards containing "VISITOR" and a barcode.

"Lover Nibbs will be with you shortly," he says and indicates the middle of the lobby floor.

A few minutes later, a thin woman with slicked-back hair and a slightly dishevelled linen outfit comes rushing out of one of the elevators.

"Apprentices?" she asks from halfway across the room. When

we nod, she swivels around and begins walking back toward the elevators without stopping. "Come with me."

Obediently we follow, scanning our visitor cards across the gate consoles, then heading into a waiting lift. Lover Nibbs mutters under her breath as the lift ascends, tight-lipped and irritated. She's so quiet that I only catch snatches of grumbling.

I glance at Loa, who gives me a slightly amused look.

We reach our floor, and Nibbs rushes out of the lift ahead of us. We emerge into a crisp, cool atmosphere inside a blindingly white hall. Our footsteps clatter loudly across the tiled floor. Nibbs goes across to an unmarked white door and scans her ID on the small scanner console beside it. The door swings open with a quiet whoosh of air, and we pass into a changing room containing shelves and storage cupboards and a row of hooks along one wall at head height.

Nibbs finally turns to us after lifting some folded bundles from one of the cupboards. "Put these on," she says, looking as if this is the last thing she ever wanted to do. The bundles are disposable white coveralls, strange fabric booties that we fit across our shoes, and disposable cloth caps for our hair. I fit mine on and then giggle when I catch sight of Hodge, his hair looking like a cloud on the top of his head.

"What?" He grins. "Don't you like my new look?"

"Come on," Nibbs says sharply. She waves her ID over another console, and the doors open into an airlock that juts into the middle of a laboratory. We follow into the airlock, and the doors to the changing room snap shut behind us, leaving me with a claustrophobic feeling. Then we're blasted with a puff of compressed air that smells faintly like disinfectant. The inner door slides open with a loud hiss, and then we are inside.

I stare around at the rows of metal benches, where robotic machinery mingles with console screens, strange-looking apparatus, and specimen jars. Lovers move around the space, busy at work at the benches, checking screens, moving specimens between machines, or talking in whispers. At the far end of the room, a row of VR stations lines the wall. Two scientists are occupied here, their faces hidden behind headsets and their arms moving with slow, sweeping movements. I watch it all, bursting with curiosity.

"Not sure why they sent you to me." Nibbs agitates a small pen in angry circles. "Anyway, here's the research and development hub for our nutrition center."

"I thought I was here to see the Coding facilities," I say quietly.

Nibbs gives a shrug and walks to a solid white door at the end of the room. Another swipe of her ID, and the doors swing inward. We enter another airlock and another white hallway (or is that the same one?). Finally, at yet another unmarked white door, she scans her ID again, and the doors slide open on a darker space.

If we had known then what was happening at Elite Academy at that very moment, would we have bothered to continue the tour? What would we have done if we knew then that Akela would not be waiting for us when we arrived home?

I INCH ALONG THE NARROW GAP, AIMING FOR the grey light glowing somewhere ahead. The knowledge of the Muse's presence helps to fight against the claustrophobia. But anxiety keeps sending thoughts into my brain like "You'll get wedged in here and stuck" or "Nobody will ever find you if you die in here."

Ahead, the exit is blocked by a large pile of packing crates, which are stacked high at the end of this fissure between buildings. As I scrape my way between the brick walls, a streetlamp swings into view. The LED casts a sterile grey glow over the top of the crates, leaving everything on my side of them in deep shadow.

I slide into those shadows, reaching the end of the buildings. The relief is palpable, but the sound of pain that I heard earlier means that there are people ahead, and the only people I've seen so far are people I don't want to run into.

A small space between the stacked crates and one of the buildings gives me just enough wiggle room to get through. I sidle along the edge of a warehouse, the high crates blocking all light into my hiding space, which I try to turn into a good thing. It's good that nobody can see me. It's great. Just me and the rats in here—and whatever bugs I can't see. I'll probably be getting spiders out of my hair for a couple of days, but I'm alive.

From the other side of the crates trickles the sound of moving water. A lot of moving water. The rotten smell is less here, which is something. It's replaced by the smell of wet pavement and timber. My earlier run was so panicked that I've become a little disoriented. I send up another prayer to the Composer. Who knows where I've emerged, now that I've run such a long distance?

As I squeeze along the gap, splintery wood scrapes across my shirt, snatching at my bare skin. It leaves a burning pain where my knuckles had already been grazed by bricks. Sucking in my stomach, I grit my teeth and force myself through the last of the gap. Light hits my eyes as I step into the open space beyond the crates.

Where the crates stop, a warehouse entrance towers over me like a cavern, flanked by enormous, open hangar doors. About ten yards into the entrance sits a forklift truck, silent and cold in the middle of the empty floor. A pair of legs juts out from behind it, motionless. When a pained moan escapes from somewhere near them, I'm so startled I nearly yelp.

I take a second to look at my surroundings. I stare straight at the source of the trickling noise, feeling a strange sense of disorientation. On the other side of my hiding place is a wide dock, peppered with piles of crates and silent machinery.

Beyond the dock, the river meanders by quietly, mocking me
with its constancy. I've come full circle and somehow returned
to the very place I was trying to get away from.

Another moan splits the silence, weaker than before. The
Composer sings me forward. I'm determined not to squash
down the Muse's promptings this time. The Composer's
presence is the only thing that has kept me safe and sane so far.

Beyond the forklift, the cavernous expanse of the warehouse
hides in shadow. Between the crates and the forklift, there is
only open space. For a few short moments, my whereabouts will
be visible to anyone out on the dock, and even across the river.

The moan sounds again, petering off into shallow panting. I
gather myself up to take the plunge. But it feels too scary to step
out of the protection behind this wall of boxes. For all I know
the Love Squad could be watching whoever that is out there. It
may be a trap.

Can any one of you by worrying add a single hour to your life?

I hold the Song fragment in my mind, then dash across the
polished concrete floor toward the forklift. Forced out into
the open, and vulnerable, I focus on the pitiful protection the
forklift may provide.

Ahead, I notice the legs stiffen. Has the person lying behind
the vehicle heard me coming and is tensing for a fight? I duck
low and reach out to touch the cool metal of the forklift cabin,
grasping it like a force field. Now that I am closer, I can see a
dark stain pooling around the light-brown trousers. I take a
small step to my right, away from the legs, and circle around
the other side of the driver's seat.

I must be crazy. Somewhere out there, a Love Squad is
searching for me, led by Lark. Any sensible person would run
for the hills, looking for the safe house. Yet here I am, creeping
in the near darkness toward a random, injured stranger. I'm not
being sensible at all.

In this life you will have trouble and pain

But Lyric has overcome
Though the struggle is real, and darkness deep
Yet he shall return again.

I head around the back of the forklift, aiming for the place where I think the random person's head may lie. Anxiety throws thought-bombs at me: He might have a gun. He could be pretending. There could be a thousand eyes watching from the shadows around here.

I take a deep breath and lean around the back of the forklift, and the injured person's features swing into view. The first thing I see is a shock of familiar blond hair. I let out a gasp, and the bearded face of Wil turns up toward me, his face a mirror of my own aghast expression. From this angle, I can see the cause of the widening pool of blood. There's a huge gash in Wil's leg.

His voice is weak. "You shouldn't be here."

27

Lover Midgate is our true Parent.
We are all her children.
Love All. Be All.

A COMPLICATED BALL OF EMOTION RIVETS
me to the spot. I left Wil back in the Ghetto, face covered in
soup, surrounded by a crowd of concerned onlookers. If the
truth be told, I had hoped I would never see him again. But
here he is, and it looks like I am the only one who can help him.

My first-aid training kicks into gear, and I look around for
something I can use to staunch the blood flow. To one side
of the warehouse, near the open door, there's a small office. I
hurry across in the darkness and try the handle. It's unlocked.
Inside, I find a large green box full of first-aid equipment and
a bag of glucose sweets, which I ferry back to Wil. I fit on the
plastic gloves that I find at the top of the box. Then I pretend
like I know what I'm doing and check out the extent of his
injuries.

The wide gash across the front of his thigh doesn't seem to
have reached an artery. Still, he's lost a lot of blood. When I
look up from the wound, I notice he is also clutching his side. I

gently pull his hand away to see a red patch blossoming across his shirt.

"What happened?"

A flash of pain that isn't entirely physical crosses Wil's face.

"Orphans," he manages. I have been unwrapping a sterile bandage from its packet, but I lean back on my haunches in surprise.

"*They* did this?"

Wil nods.

"What on Earth do you have to do with those gangsters?" I say, unrolling the bandage.

"Nothing, or so I thought. I . . ." Wil grimaces. "I guess they weren't happy that I saved the little girl."

"This seems extreme—don't you think?" I point at his leg.

Wil responds in a coughing fit, which morphs into a gasp of pain. I turn all my attention to his leg. In all reality, it needs the kind of help that only a health center can provide. But we're a long way from one of those right now.

I search the first aid kit and find a large, rectangular dressing. I lay it over the wound. It's woefully inadequate, and so I remove it again, wondering what to do next.

He shakes his head at me and tries to grab my wrist. "You have to get away from here."

I look out at the wide-open space beyond the warehouse doors, lit only by the single streetlamp. Anyone could be waiting out there, and I'd never know it. We're so exposed that if there were people out this late across the river, they'd see us for sure.

"You need help," I say, and I pad the wound with gauze, which soaks red almost instantly.

"Why would you help me?" he asks weakly. "I know you hate me."

I lean back again. "I don't hate you. I just . . ." But the words won't come out properly. I don't know what to say. What do I feel, now that the guy is lying here, looking like he's about to die?

"I don't hate you," I mumble.

Wil watches me, his face unreadable. A little pang of guilt makes it too uncomfortable to look back, so I turn to the task at hand.

With a little bit of hassling, I manage to get the large dressing over the wound, and then start to wrap Wil's leg with the bandage. It feels about as useful as trying to put out a bonfire by blowing on it, but I need to feel like I'm doing something. After a few minutes of jostling and adjusting, I turn to the slightly more worrying wound in his side.

Will clasps his torso, resisting. "You're in danger. Just go."

I give up trying to pry his fingers away and look him in the eyes. "You haven't told me why you're out here, you know."

He looks embarrassed. "I was . . . I was searching for you." His eyes dart around the floor, as if looking for something to focus on.

"You expect me to believe that?" I almost ask. But there's a little warning nudge in my mind. So instead, I say, "Sorry. Why would you bother looking for me?"

"Aria sent me to find you."

"Oh." I'm surprised at the hint of disappointment I feel. For all of the fury I had directed at him, it is still a teensy blow to my ego that he didn't want to search me out for himself. I begin tidying up the first-aid supplies.

"I didn't think you'd want to see me, and I told her that, but she insisted. Said that I had created this situation, and so it was my burden to bear to find you and help you."

"She wasn't very wise about that, was she?" I say, swallowing down a laugh.

There's a sickly sheen of sweat across Wil's forehead now. "She's wiser than you think." He grimaces.

"How did you get out here?" I ask.

He shifts then grunts. "Followed Lark."

I raise an eyebrow. When he doesn't go on, I prompt, "And?"

He gives a tiny nod to his leg.

"She did this?" I ask, stunned.

He doesn't reply. I gaze at the lamppost, mind reeling. None of this makes sense. Not Lark. Not Wil. The Love Squad. None of it.

"There's something you're not telling me," I say.

"Lark wants to go legal," Wil says between breaths. "She cut a deal to hand you over to Crucible so she could get an ID."

"You know this for sure?" I say.

Wil nods. "The rumors are she's related to Midgate somehow."

The bottom seems to drop out of my stomach. "What?" I ask, going very still.

Wil continues, not looking at my face. "It's the worst kept secret of the Ghetto," he says. "Kent is Midgate's son who tried to run away from home years ago. Of course he couldn't so his punishment was to be exiled underground. Lark is Kent's granddaughter."

"But that's not possible," I say, feeling as if I've just been smacked in the side of the head. "Midgate's an AI."

"Who told you that?" Wil sounds incredulous.

"Never mind." I fuss around with the first aid kit, turning away so Wil can't see my embarrassment. "How does any of that get you here, anyway?"

"Lark owed me some favors, so she offered me the chance to leave together. I knew I would be dead before Crucible would let me back, and I told her that. She didn't take it so well."

I shake my head, mind reeling. When I first encountered Wil, it was clear he knew Lark. But it seemed as if everyone owed Lark favors, not the other way around. I don't like the unsettling feeling this gives me. It's the old, familiar feeling that Wil always used to give me of being pushed slightly off balance.

"Well, I'm not going to let you die," I declare, resolve hardening within me. "I'm fixing you up, and there's nothing you can do about it."

"Cadence, go," Wil urges. "If you're here, it means that the Orphans have lost you. They're going to be angry."

I snatch at the wrappers and throw them into a pile nearby. "All the more reason why we have to get you out of here. If Lark did this then she'll only finish you off."

"My life doesn't matter anymore," Wil says stubbornly. "I've made my peace with the Composer."

I push his hand away from the wound in his side. "Don't be ridiculous." I say, leaning down to look more closely. "It was the Muse who told me to come here, so stop."

A small, angry-looking slit lies near the left edge of his stomach, where a knife has been and gone. Even though I'm no medic, it looks too shallow to be fatal. But just like his leg, it's too big a wound for a small plaster. "Someone's going to have to sew you up," I tell him.

"I'll be fine," Wil insists, then grunts in pain. "I always survive."

"Don't I know it." I huff a sigh, pulling out the last of the bandages from the first aid kit.

"I guess you do," he says in such a gentle tone that I look at him in surprise. His eyes are soft.

I finish plastering the wound with a rectangular dressing. "Done," I say, feeling a small sense of triumph as I look at the bandaged wounds. "They're not going to last forever, but if we can get you back to the Ghetto, Aria and Tim can take you from there."

Wil's fingers brush my wrist. "I'm sorry. For everything."

I battle against that complicated knot of emotions. "We'll talk about it later."

"We might not have later." His green eyes stare at me with deep intensity. "Cadence, I am truly sorry for everything I did to you that was wrong. Can you ever forgive me?"

I look away, emotions writhing in an internal battle. Vivid memories are seared into my brain: Wil's face in a thousand contortions of disdain, mockery, and hatred. His cruel smile. The cold, calculating glint in his eyes. A thousand moments of hurt and disappointment.

"I can't do this," I plead to the Muse. *"He has hurt me so much. I can't just pretend it didn't happen."*

Leave judging to me. Suddenly, an overwhelming feeling fills my heart, and like a torrent of water, it washes away the writhing ball of emotion, leaving only a sense of the Muse's presence. In that moment, I see a glimpse of something: a figure hanging on a tree. The figure's face is marred, but it's the same man from my dream. He is surrounded by a mob that surges toward him, spitting bile and words of hate.

Raised above them, he speaks through cracked lips, looking up at the skies above. *"Forgive them, even them."* The love that pours from his words makes me want to weep.

"Lyric," I whisper.

"What?" Wil's confused voice penetrates my thoughts.

I turn back to him, eyes blurry with tears. Lyric's face is all I can see.

"I forgive you," I say. And for the first time, I mean it.

MEMORY DATE: 2286.337 (A YEAR AND A HALF AGO)

Memory Location: Secret

In the corner of the meeting room, Hodge and I sit side by side, our knees touching. I resist the urge to reach for his hand. But he reaches for mine.

"Where will we live, do you think?" he asks.

I smile. "I'm guessing we'll have to live in the Officers' quarters, won't we?"

Hodge shakes his head. "Forget reality. Where would you live if you could live anywhere?" His brown eyes crinkle at the edges.

"I never thought about it," I say, staring off into the distance.

Hodge's smile widens, and he lifts my hands onto his knee. "I thought we'd have a house. With a yard and a tree. A porch, where we could sit in the evenings and just talk."

"Wow, you must be expecting to become a Chief Lover for a dream that rich," I say. "I thought we'd just end up in an apartment in Love City or something."

"Who knows where Lyric will take us?" Hodge's mouth quirks at the corner. "We could end up living in the Hall."

A shiver ripples down my back. "Ugh. That would be the worst."

"As long as I'm with you, I don't care," Hodge replies, staring into my eyes.

28

Lovelies Don't Hide Haters.
Report A Hater Now!

Love all.
Be all.

The Love Collective.

WIL LIES BACK ON THE FLOOR, COVERING HIS
eyes with his arm. His jaw tightens as another wave of pain hits.

"Can you stand?" I ask. "We can't stay out in the open here."

"I can try." He pushes himself upward with his hands but
sinks back again with a groan.

"It might take a while." He grimaces. "My guts feel as if
they've been stuck in a furnace."

I shift my weight so that my arm rests under his shoulders, and
with both of us grunting and straining, we manage to hoist him
to a sitting position. When I finally prop him upright, Wil puts his
hand to his forehead and turns a chalky shade of white.

"I think I might need to lie back down again."

"Soon. We have to get you somewhere safe first." I hand him
a glucose candy from the first-aid kit. "I'm pretty sure the Squad
will finish the job Lark started if they find you alive."

He sighs but pops it into his mouth.

"Fine," he says. "But if I die while we're walking, I'll blame you." One side of his mouth bulges out in the shape of the small boiled-sugar treat, making his attempted smile even more crooked than usual.

I roll my eyes. "Can we please just get moving?"

With more grunts and groans, we manage to get Wil up to a semi-standing position. He wavers and almost loses his balance, leaning back against the forklift for support. I scoot my shoulder under his armpit, holding my other hand across his abdomen. The floor beneath us is a filthy mess of blood and grime. Our footprints stand out like beacons in the middle of the grotty puddle.

"I can't do it," Wil gasps. "I'm going to pass out."

I lean back to look at him. His face is ghostly, covered in a pasty sheen of sweat. It would be sensible to find somewhere close to hide out, but there's no way I'm going to be able to fit him back through that narrow alley.

Help us, Composer! Wil lets out a weak cough.

"I need to get you to the Ghetto health center," I tell him. "You need stitches and medicine."

"But that's across the river." He sounds desperate. The implication in his words is clear. He doesn't think he'll make it.

"You tell me where to go, and I'll get you there," I say, but my voice is shaky.

Wil's eyes close, and he leans his head back.

"If the Composer can get me here to you, he can get us to the Ghetto," I state, though I wish I could be more confident than I feel right now. "But you're going to have to tell me where it is. I was unconscious when Lark brought me out here, so I have no idea where to go."

"Top of the hill." Will coughs, then clutches at his stomach.

I look out beyond the warehouse doors, unable to see much beyond the glow of the streetlamp. "Where?"

"Factory. Top of the hill. There's a Ghetto entrance, which

takes us back to the market." Wil takes a few deep breaths. "If we can get back . . . across the bridge and avoid the . . . Squad, we can get in that way. There are territory issues with Kent's crew though, so Sirens don't . . . use it."

"So how do we reach it?"

"Slowly." Wil's weak smile turns into a grimace. "Only way back is across the bridge."

"Okay, then," I say. "Wait here."

I make sure he's propped up securely against the forklift's cabin, then sneak over to the wide-open warehouse door, back to the pile of crates where I had emerged earlier. I crouch down to scout out the docks outside.

Leaning against the side of the warehouse door, I peek to my left. Long, wide docks stretch down the riverbank, punctuated by the heaps of packing crates and silent cranes. I turn to my right and nearly gasp. We're right near the bridge, which arches across the river like a wide grey ribbon.

A tiny fluttering of anxiety blooms in my stomach. That streetlamp is the same one Lark waited under before meeting the Squad. Until now, I didn't realize how close I was to danger. The Orphans could be close. They could be hiding behind those containers, for all I know.

Between this point and the road, deep shadows lurk along the sides of containers scattered along the docks. They provide a small amount of cover, but a large section of open ground glistens darkly, and we're going to have to cross it. Beyond the open space, the river shushes quietly around the pylons of the old bridge. On any other night, I might find the whole scene peaceful. Tonight it just feels ominous.

The huge problem is the bridge itself. For the entire span of the bridge, we will be exposed, and anyone in the dock region will spot us long before we could see them. In order to get Wil to safety, we're going to spend a long time in danger.

Please keep us safe. I plead with the Composer. *Just give us enough time to get Wil back to the Ghetto.*

I am with you.

I tiptoe back to the forklift to deliver the news to Wil. He nods, pain leaving a sheen of sweat across his forehead.

"Last chance to leave me here," he says. "I wouldn't blame you if you ran."

I squat down beside him. "I'm not going to ditch out on something the Composer wants me to do."

"Let's go, then," he says, a shadow of the cheeky grin flashing across his face. "What's the worst that could happen?"

The next part is awkward and uncomfortable. While I was tending to Wil's wounds, I had the bandages and equipment to focus on. But now I have to prop him up.

I offer my arm, letting it circle behind his back. He rests his weight on my shoulder, and together we push up from the ground. His body is clammy with sweat, and he smells like a guy who hasn't taken a good bath for months. But then, I probably don't smell too good either.

I let him lean into me, and together we take a few tentative steps toward the warehouse door. I can tell Wil is trying hard not to drag his injured leg. His mouth is clamped into a grim line, and his muscles have tensed with effort.

We reach the doors, and the darkened dock stretches out before us, shiny black where the light from the lamppost reflects off the wet pavement.

"Ready?" I ask.

"Just go," he pants.

I keep us close to the warehouse wall, stopping every so often to look around, to check that we haven't been followed. Wil winces in pain as I help him to hop and limp the distance between the warehouse and the bridge.

By the time we reach the bridge, Wil is panting more heavily. In a few hours, hundreds of electric vehicles will drive over this bridge to their daily work. For now, it's a wide, deserted arc over the river. My heart is thudding as I peek out from behind the last cover we will have for a while. Behind us, the road curves around into the industrial area. Ahead, it crosses the river in a lazy arc, until it breaks through more warehouses and factories on the other side. I pause for longer than I need to, checking and double-checking that there is nobody nearby.

"Clear," I whisper to Wil.

We break into a weird three-legged race to the bridge. I pull him forward, feeling his weight lean into me. Down below, the water swirls and eddies, unfazed by bridge pylons and concrete banks. With every step I am expecting to feel the bite of the electrified nets used by the Love Squad or see the blazing spotlight of a pursuit drone.

The road that crosses the bridge glistens with dew in the darkness. It slopes up to a peak at the center, then down to the other side of the river. Our journey slows as the gradient in the road begins to bite. Wil's breathing becomes more labored, but he limps on.

We make the crest of the bridge marking halfway and start the slow descent, taking care not to slip on the damp surface. We are still too far from the other riverbank when a shout shatters the darkness.

"There!" It booms with unnatural volume, in the familiar metallic voice that makes my blood run cold. I'd recognize the sound of a Love Squad helmet anywhere. I turn to my left and see two black figures at the end of the dock, near the alley where I had been hiding to spy on Lark. But they're not Love Squad soldiers. One of them wears a helmet, but his jacket is open. The other just wears black, tattered clothes.

"Orphans," I whisper.

The two figures sprint in our direction. My immediate instinct is to run, except there's Wil . . . but on his own he picks up speed, grunting in pain. My shoulder aches with the weight of his body, but we press forward in a vain hope that we can maybe find some cover before they reach us.

I scan the way ahead, searching for some refuge, some irregularity between the uniform grey warehouses that will hide us. The factory sits on top of a distant hill, too far from the bridge for us to make it in time. Between the bridge and the factory are rows and rows of concrete walls, windowless and doorless blocks lined up in neat, uniform streets. But along the docks on the far side of the river, I spot a large open lot where hundreds of machines are parked in neat rows.

"Head for the trucks," I say.

Wil's breath is coming in heavy pants as he strains for air. At the sound of his labored breathing, fear grips my heart. I sweep him along, pushing against his back as if my arm could transfer my energy into him.

Out of the corner of my eyes, I risk a glance backward. The Orphans are halfway along the dock now. One of them points in our direction, and something whizzes behind my right ear. A small puff of dust explodes off one of the bridge railings a few yards away, followed by the delayed crack of the distant gun's fire. I duck low, almost toppling Wil over in my panic.

"They're shooting!" I yelp.

We hurry forward, heads bowed low. There are two more distant cracks and two more near misses. We keep to the side of the railing that stands between us and the thugs, trying to use it as a remnant of cover. The end of the bridge is close. I hug Wil to my side and mentally urge him to keep going. As if in answer, he breaks into a lopsided, hopping run, his head ducked. Our pursuers' footsteps ring out loudly across the dock, closing in on us. It won't be long until they will have reached the bridge, when they will have a clear shot. They can't miss at that distance.

Years of Elite training kick into operation. I need to keep moving Wil forward, reaching a safe place that I'm not sure exists. My mind runs calculations on the speed of the pursuers versus our lopsided, shuffling run. My heart sinks. They're going to catch us before we get to the trucks.

Another loud crack sounds directly behind me. I brace myself for the inevitable pain, but there's only a warm, glowing feeling within. Time seems to slow down. I look back across the bridge. The two Orphans have stopped in the middle of the road. They are looking at us, but they're standing still. As I watch, the guy wearing the helmet tilts it down toward the gun they are holding, shaking his head at the smoking muzzle. His partner reaches for it, but helmet guy shoves him away.

Go, the Composer urges.

Time speeds up again. I drag Wil across the open space at the end of the bridge, and then we are finally in the shadow of another warehouse. I hear a shout from behind us, and I shudder. We are off the open road, but nowhere near safe yet.

"Can you make it?" An edge of desperation breaks out in my voice.

Wil points. "Go." I follow the direction of his trembling hand, and we make a limping run for it together.

We reach the large parking lot, where hundreds of trucks and excavators are lined up in neat rows along the waterfront. Wil lunges behind one, leaning against the wheel arch for support. His demeanour has changed. Hardened. I can tell that he's remembering he was once an Elite too.

"That guy with the helmet," I whisper. "What's his story?"

Wil leans around the edge of the truck to peer back at the bridge. "Nursery grunt. Went AWOL. Took over the Orphans last year."

I nod, but then I realize that in the Collective's eyes, I'm exactly the same. Apprentice gone AWOL. Non-citizen. Unworthy of the Elite status I'd been so close to achieving.

"Come on," I say.

We move along the dock, stopping occasionally to listen for

the sound of pursuit. Now both of us are breathing heavily, and it takes a great effort to quiet ourselves enough to listen. When I look at Wil, he is still wearing determination across his face, and I see a glimpse of what he could have been before his choices led him astray. He catches me looking at him and manages a wink.

"Over here," his finger beckons, and he leads the way between the hulking machinery. At the end of the parking lot, there's a smaller open space. We quickly cross it, heading for the loading dock of a large white concrete building. Wil stops behind a huge dumpster and leans against it, exhausted. The distant echo of footsteps has dimmed.

"How far is the Ghetto?" I whisper.

"About four blocks."

I look down at his leg. The white bandage is now a dark stain, and the blood on his leg is gleaming wetly in the moonlight. If we have to run four whole blocks, he's going to faint from blood loss before we arrive. I don't see how we're going to make it.

"Is there somewhere we can lie low for now? You look like you need a rest."

"Don't worry about me," he replies. His pale face is covered in sweat.

I raise one skeptical eyebrow at him. A corner of his mouth curls up in a grin.

"Better dead than caught," he whispers with another wink.

"Hopefully the Composer is not going to let you die. Not if I have any say in it, anyway."

"Doesn't matter. Death has no sting for me anymore." His grin actually lights up his entire face. "Come on. We got a squad to outrun."

He hops off toward a darkened warehouse, and I slow my pace to keep beside him.

Wil pants, pain brimming at the edges of his eyes. "I think . . . I know . . . how we can get home."

29

Love Is All Around You.
The Love Collective Sees All.

The Love Collective.
Love All.
Be All.

FROM BEHIND THE TRUCKS, WE TIPTOE
across to the closed warehouse. The loading-dock doors are
firmly shut, but around the corner of the building, four concrete
steps lead up to a smaller personnel entrance. It scares me a little
that as we climb those steps, Wil's movements are slowing, and
he draws every breath with supreme effort. I offer to support
him, but he just shakes his head and limps on in front of me.

We reach the personnel door, and Wil turns the handle. It
opens without complaint.

"Not even locked?" I ask, surprised.

"I thought that might happen." he says as the door swings
outward. "So naive."

"I guess you can be when crime is supposed to have been
eliminated," I observe.

The interior of the warehouse is dark and quiet, and our
footsteps hush along the paved floor. A thousand questions pop
into my head, but I'm too afraid to ask and break this silence.

What is this place? How did Wil know where to go? Where is he taking me?

We sneak past sleeping machinery and a long, large conveyor belt. I get distracted for a while, tracing the conveyor belt's path across the ceiling, down long ramps and across the floor. When I finally look back, Wil has dropped a few meters behind me. He leans against the factory wall, one arm crossed protectively across his stomach and his head bowed. His breathing is even more labored. I start back to him, and he pushes himself slowly off the wall with a small groan.

"Are you sure you're going to manage?" I whisper. "Do you need me to carry you?"

"Don't worry about me. Just keep . . . the noise down," he wheezes.

I nod, afraid to say anything more. I let him walk in front so I can keep an eye on him. His pace keeps on slowing, and eventually I quietly tuck my shoulder under his arm again. This time he doesn't protest.

It's hard to see his face, but judging by the sound of his weakening breaths, I may not have much time left. Fear prickles its way into the back of my thoughts, and I desperately hope we aren't just wasting our time.

"Come on," I urge, trying to hold myself up under his increasingly heavy weight.

We duck under a metal gantry and emerge where a series of stairs rises above us toward a mezzanine. On the level above, high glass windows protect management offices from the general hum of daytime machinery. For now the windows are dark, but in the top corner below the ceiling is a single, blinking red light.

"Camera," I hiss into Wil's ear. He nods, and we duck our heads down, hurrying below the mezzanine and out of range. I know it's too late, and I have just given the security system a full view of my face, but I can't think too much about that now. According to Wil, we're only a few streets from the Ghetto.

He points me to a green exit sign at the far wall, breathing hard. Below the green light is another standard metal door, complete with emergency-exit bar. Wil falls on it, and when the door snaps open, he overbalances and almost pulls me headlong into the night. We catch our breath on the small landing for a moment, surrounded by the eerie silence of a city wrapped in Beauty Sleep.

Heavy-lidded and sweating, Wil nods in the direction of a laneway. The lane leads past loading docks and garbage-disposal bins toward another open road.

"There," he rasps. "Up the hill." He's barely holding himself up now, and the more he leans into me, the harder I have to work to stop both of us from toppling over.

We take a few tentative steps forward. Wil's injured leg drags behind him, scraping loudly along the ground. His boot judders over the uneven pavement, and he can no longer hold back the agonized groans that escape from between his clenched teeth.

"Where to now?" I ask when we reach the open road. He can barely lift his arm high enough to point. Alarm surges through me. We can't collapse here. Not in the middle of a road like this, where anyone can find us.

"Not far now," I say, as if I'm a nurse cooing gently to a small child. "Almost there."

Wil makes no reply. I stagger with him to the other side of the road, toward a pile of low crates, and lower him to a sitting position. His head lolls back, and his eyes close in a tight grimace of pain. The bandage around his leg gleams wetly in the moonlight. Then he falls further back into the shadows along the wall, almost completely disappearing in the darkness.

"We really, really need to get you to Aria." My voice shakes with alarm.

"No. *You* need to get out of here," his voice pants from the shadow. "I'm done."

I am about to tell him not to be stupid when a flood of sharp, stinging pain courses through my body, sending shudders and spasms from my shoulders down to my ankles. Electricity drags me down until I am rolling on the ground, every nerve trying to lean away from the source of the shocks, which seem to be emanating from all around me. My teeth clamp shut, and I writhe in a rictus of agony made worse by the dew on the damp road.

Somewhere distant I hear a bird call. A fine web of brightly glowing fibers criss-cross in front of my face, blocking my view of everything else. The net tightens around me until I am wrapped in a cocoon of pain. Unable to think. Unable to speak. Unable to do anything except writhe and shake.

"Halt. Remain calm," comes an electronic voice from behind my back, and I finally realize what is happening. In a brief moment of lucidity, I wonder how the soldier could possibly expect me to remain calm under a Love Squad net, but then another wave of electricity rolls across my body, and I am paralyzed again.

I shut my eyes tightly, willing myself to survive this impossible pain, enfolded in a tomb of light and heat. Then as suddenly as it comes, it is gone. When I open my eyes, the fine mesh which wraps me from head to toe has dulled to a plain black fibre. Beyond the confines of the net, two pairs of black boots point toward me. One boot reaches in and nudges my stomach with the steel-capped toe.

"Is this the one?" drones the voice of a soldier, his deep tones metallic and sharp as a knife's edge. Face hidden beneath the glossy Love Squad helmet, he turns to his companion. A smaller soldier, similarly anonymous, leans in closer. Instead of a face, an orb of shiny black glass peers at me.

"She matches the description," the smaller soldier replies.

Her voice is also filtered through the helmet and comes out in a mangled monotone. Then she leans back. A red LED illuminates her face, and she barks commands through her helmet: "Suspect apprehended, sector 9A-14. Await confirmation." I can hear a distant growl of static, as she receives her answer, but I can't make out what they're saying.

The sleek black helmet turns to look down on me again. "Identify."

"I don't know what you're talking about," I mumble. Instead of a reply, there is a swift and sudden kick at my midsection, which leaves me gasping for air. The pain is so harsh it makes me want to vomit.

"Identify," drones the larger soldier.

"C-c-c . . . can I . . . can I stand up, first?" I manage to heave out, still gagging. Sweat breaks across my brow. I almost gave my name away.

Composer, help me!

The male soldier leans over me, hoisting me to my feet, arms yanked up behind me. Pain shoots across my back. I clamp my jaw together to keep from crying out.

Up close, members of the Love Squad are even more intimidating. Taut black uniforms cover them head to toe, showing no sign of soft edges. Dangerous-looking implements on their belts. Holstered guns. Both their red helmet LEDs are on now, giving the soldiers' faces an almost demonic glow. I used to love watching these suits in action on infotab streams. But it's totally different when their boots are at your eye level.

Reaching down, the man lifts the net off my head with one hand and clips it back into a pouch on his belt, where it retracts smoothly. With his other hand, he pulls out his gun and points it at me.

"Identify," the woman barks at me, pulling a mini tablet from her belt. I can see her angry frown under the red glow of the VR unit hidden within her helmet. I swallow hard.

"Rain," I reply through gritted teeth. My legs feel wobbly. The officer taps her tablet a few times, then looks back up at me.

"Negative," responds the woman. "Present ID for confirmation."

I shake my head. The woman grasps my wrist. With an overly rough movement, she bares my forearm beneath the tablet's scanner where my ID should be. A brief flash of a red laser line runs up and back over my wrist. Then the scanner goes dark. Thanks to Viola, they won't find what they're looking for. It's a pity she only got halfway through her job, though.

"Illegal," the soldier pronounces to her companion, the scowl clear in her voice. The male officer steps forward and grabs my wrist in a painful grip.

"Look again." He twists it so the light of the tablet falls on my wrist. I wince. The woman with the scanner presses a switch, and the light flicks from red to blue as it glides over my skin. I watch in horror as wisps of ID line reappear across the pale flesh of my wrist.

"Info is too sketchy to read, but she could be the one we're looking for," the woman says.

Her partner nods. "Who did this to you?" his robot voice drones at me.

"I don't know what you're—" Pain shoots up my arm as the man twists my elbow cruelly behind my back.

"Answer."

I can't do what he asks. I'm too busy trying not to scream. "I . . . I . . ."

"Leave her alone," rasps a weak voice from the shadows.

"No!" I say, feeling a horrible, creeping dread. But it's too late.

Wil leans forward, and his pale, sweaty face emerges into the weak light from the streetlamps. "She's just an urchin. But I'm not."

The soldier's grip on my wrist lessens, and I use the

distraction to pull away from his hand. Instantly, his gun trains back on me. I put my hands up and squat down.

Wil tries to stand. "I think you'll find that I'm a better prize than this random illegal." He nods dismissively at me.

I turn to him, in panic. "Don't!"

He ignores me, keeping his eyes on the Love Squad soldiers. "Here," he says, holding out his arm. Horrified, I see the strong black lines of his interim ID still tattooed on his wrist. I reach out to push it away, but the female Love Squad soldier is too quick. She points the scanner at his arm, and an immediate alarm goes off, screeching into the cold dark night.

"See?" Wil says with a faint smile. "I'm *much* more interesting." Suddenly he gasps, and his words peter off into a cough that wracks his whole body. Weakened, he falls back into the shadows.

The man barks a command into his helmet this time. "Unit 84-B Viper Command, this is Viper Gamma. We need backup at sector 9A-14. Over."

I hear the soft static of a reply and feel a hopeless sense of despair wash over me. We're done for. All those years of working in secret. Everything I tried to hide from the Collective's view. All those Sirens in the Ghetto. We're all dead.

I lean back into the shadows, reaching for Wil's arm. His skin is clammy. I feel for the pulse near his wrist. When I finally manage to locate the right spot, I nearly cry out in frustration. His pulse flutters weakly, like a candle flickering through fog.

Distant footfalls echo from down near the river, tramping in our direction. Another pair of soldiers jogs up the road toward us, rifles in their hands and the reflection of streetlamps glinting off the sleek black helmets on their heads. One is tall and solidly built. The other, short and stocky in the Love Squad armour. Although they are wildly different in height and build, they jog in perfect step with each other.

My spirits sink even further. If it was too difficult to escape two Love Squad soldiers, four will be impossible. I might as well just give up now.

Don't lose heart. I am with you until the end.

The Song fragment is enough to bolster my spirits just a little. I'm able to watch the approaching soldiers without collapsing to the ground in a quivering heap.

When they draw up beside us, the two soldiers who have captured us salute at the taller Squad soldier who has just arrived.

"Sir!" the woman says in her metallic voice. "Suspects apprehended as commanded. This one" —she holds her scanner up to him— "is injured. We'll need medic support to get him to the holding facility."

The taller one takes a long look at the scanner screen, and then nods. "Good," he replies, voice also robotic through the helmet. "Viper Gamma, you two go and bring the medic here. We will supervise."

"But sir—" the other man begins.

He is stopped by the curt gesture of the officer's hand. "That's an order, Gamma."

"Yes, sir." Even through the helmet, the man sounds displeased.

Two things happen at almost exactly the same time. A puff of dust erupts from the ground near the soldiers' feet, and there is an ear-splitting crack from somewhere above us. We all duck instinctively.

"Don't move!" comes a shout from somewhere high above me.

It's followed by a guttural yell. "Or we'll blow you so far into the sky you'll have to rent space on the moon!"

The voices came from the top of a warehouse across the road. I risk a look upward. Two black-clad Orphans are standing on the roof, looking down at us with what seems like rather large guns in their hands. I take a few involuntary steps back into the shadows. A soft grunt tells me Wil is still alive.

"Put the weapon down. Now," commands the female officer who scanned my arm. As she reaches for her belt, there's another loud snap at her feet, and she jumps high in the air.

"I wouldn't do that if I were you." A third figure emerges beside the others. It's the Love Squad Orphan, looking triumphant in his dishevelled uniform. "You've got our property down there. And we would like it back. Get your hands up. Nice and easy now."

The officers obey, raising their hands in the air. They're outgunned. By the looks of the weaponry in the hands of the Orphans, I guess that they've raided an armory at some point. I haven't seen guns that big since my earlier VR training days.

"Viper Gamma, engage," the officer says. "We will remove suspects to a safe location."

"Yes, sir," the pair replies in unison. Their voices are a soft buzz.

Everything happens quickly, then. The first two officers pull out their weapons, firing an assortment of gas canisters and guns up to the rooftop. A cloud of smoke erupts around us, shielding us from view. I am pulled forward by the smaller, stockier officer, and Wil is gathered up by the commander. A hail of bullets and crackling gunfire echoes off the warehouse walls.

"Die, scum, die!" screeches the Orphan leader over our heads. The world explodes in bursts of noise and light.

30

Lyric invited us to ask,
And said that we would find.
The seeker would be satisfied
In him, for he is kind.
Song fragment 7.8

THE ROOFTOP AND STREET ARE ALIVE WITH shouts, gunfire, and grunts. A piercing scream splits the air, and when I look back, the taller soldier stands in the middle of the road, his arm on a downswing. At the edge of the rooftop, two Orphans are now a writhing bundle of light flashes and dark jerking bodies. They gasp and screech in pain, immobilized for the moment by an electric net. I flinch, remembering the agony of the currents across my own skin.

The third Orphan hoists his weapon onto his shoulder, face rigid with fury.

"Come on," hisses the stocky Love Squad soldier beside me, and we stagger out of sight around the corner of the building. "I thought you were fitter than this."

The amused note in the soldier's voice draws me up short. I stare in shock at the glassy black helmet. "What did you say?"

The red helmet light switches on, and a familiar face glows at me in the night. She even has the gall to wink at me with an impish expression.

I gasp. "Sif? What the Love—"

Holding a finger up in front of her helmet to shush me, my old friend pulls me away from the corner. "You look terrible." She grins.

My mouth is gaping. "What are you doing here?"

"My job," she says, that metallic speaker completely disguising her voice.

My mind is a whirl of confusion and dissonance. Sif was at Elite Academy. What's she doing out on the streets arresting me? How can she talk about getting me safe when she's a Hater-reporting machine? I know I've been underground for months, but what on the Composer's green earth has happened?

"I guess you graduated." I struggle to keep up with her.

Ahead of us, running with wide, confident strides, the larger soldier carries Wil over his shoulder in a fireman's hold. I can't see Wil's face, but his arms droop lifelessly. I wonder if we're going to lose him. The thought speeds me forward.

Four loud cracks echo into the night, and the screaming behind us quiets. I don't want to think about what that means. But a creeping dread surges through me all the same.

Another gunshot echoes around the corner, heading in our direction. "The Ghetto entrance . . . I . . . don't know . . . where it is," I pant, feeling helpless. Wil was the one who knew how to get back to his home. Not me. We could be running past it right now, and I wouldn't have a clue.

"Keep going," Sif says, pushing on ahead.

We jog along the wide avenue leading to the factory entrance. The road is deserted, save for a single black van parked beside a warehouse driveway about thirty yards away. The sight of the official squad vehicle brings back a very unwanted memory: Loa and Danse, bundled into the back by a horde of black uniforms. *Arrest. Prison. Death.*

Already at the van, the taller officer opens the large rear doors and lays Wil down inside the back. He is unconscious.

I halt. "You're not taking me to that, are you?" Sif is Love Squad, after all. I know her history well enough to see how this is going to end.

Sif reaches for my wrist. "Don't make a scene."

"Stop." I pull away. "Sif, you can't take us in. You have to let us go. Wil—"

"Explain later," she says, grasping at my arm again.

"No!" I say, more urgently. "Sif, if they Embrace us, there's a whole lot of people who will die. You can't—"

Sif steps in front of me, her face illuminated in a fiery red glow. "If you don't come with me now," her electronic voice drones, "so help me, I'm going to have to use drastic measures."

I raise my hands, pleading. "Sif, just hear me out. We used to be friends once. Can't you just let us go? Please?"

"You know I can't do that, Kerr," Sif says, hands on hips. She pulls a small bundle from her belt.

I take a step backward, still holding my hands up in supplication. My words come out in a panicked sob. "Sif, I've never asked you for anything before. But please . . . please, I really need you to listen."

Sif raises the bundle in the air. She draws her hand back, ready to strike, but her fist is grasped by the gloved hand of the other officer, who is suddenly beside her.

"Enough," he says to her, and she stills immediately. He turns to me, his sigh robotic through the helmet. "Cadence, will you just do what you're told for once?"

I freeze.

He lets go of Sif's hand and then reaches up to lift the helmet from his head. Curly black hair springs back as it is released from the helmet's restraint, and the brown eyes I had been dreaming of for months stare at me.

"Just get in the van," Hodge says, looking annoyed. "Please?"

THE BACK OF THE VAN IS COLD STEEL. TWO metal benches line the walls from cab to rear, large enough for a dozen soldiers to sit. Sif has jumped in the front to drive, so I'm sitting on one bench, facing Hodge. Wil lies on the floor between us, still unconscious.

My heart is singing, but I fold my arms and try to glare at Hodge. "You owe me an explanation."

Hodge glares back. "You were very hard to find, you know."

"That was the point."

Hodge's voice is stern. "But we could have sorted this out much earlier if you had stayed with Melody."

"Blame the Composer, not me," I say wryly. "I just fell down a drain."

He gives me a look full of confusion, and I laugh. "It's a long story."

"Tell me after we get him to the safe house." Hodge nods at Wil.

I look down at my hands. My fingernails are dirty, and there's dried blood caked on the back of my skin. "I think he needs to get back to the Ghetto," I say, feeling embarrassed.

"What?" Hodge's tone is sharp with surprise.

I look up at him. "He won't make it to the safe house. But there's a big Siren community down there, and they've got a health center that could fix him up properly. It was his home."

Hodge looks at me closely. "With Sirens? That makes no sense."

"I know." I look back down. "But across the river . . ." I sigh, remembering the cold floor of the warehouse and Wil's confessions. I fix my eyes on Hodge's. "It took me so long to see that he changed. The Composer wanted me to forgive him, Hodge."

Hodge studies at me for a few seconds. Then he nods. "I can't really argue with that, can I?" He bangs his fist on the wall beside the cabin, and a small window slides open.

"Yeah?" Sif calls.

"Did you get the Ghetto entrance coordinates from Lark?"

"Yeah, why?"

"We need to drop the package there," Hodge tells her.

"Oh!" Sif replies, sounding startled. "Okay."

The small window slams shut. Moments later, the truck rumbles to life, and we chug forward. I grasp the bench on either side of my legs, trying not to slide with the momentum.

Their exchange has bothered me. "How do you know Lark?" I ask tersely.

"How do you think we found you?" Hodge says. "Lark's a . . . let's just say she's a 'well connected' contact. In exchange for becoming a legal citizen, Lark was going to hand you over. Sif and I planned to intercept the official handover and get you to the Exodus. It was a great plan, by the way, until Wil decided to play hero. He nearly ruined everything."

"It wasn't *you* who hurt him, was it?" I ask, shocked.

Hodge shakes his head. "No, no, that was all the Orphans. But we lost you in the chaos. If the Viper Gamma team hadn't stumbled across you back there, I don't know what we'd have done."

"Oh," I reply, still feeling a little confused.

There must be something forlorn in my expression, because Hodge moves across the truck to sit beside me. His squad armor is hard against my leg. But his fingers are gentle as they lift my hand into his.

"Are you okay?" he says. "Being away from you nearly killed me."

The truck lurches forward, throwing me at him. He catches

me with expert reflexes, holding me steady while the truck comes to a stop. Wild fluttering erupts in my stomach as we stare at each other, unmoving.

Seconds later, the small window flies open, and we jolt away from each other. I'm sure my face must be all shades of red right now. It's just a good thing the back of the truck is too shadowy to see anything properly.

"We're here!" Sif's voice floats in through the window. "Fire escape on the left."

Hodge opens the van door for me, and I jump out into a nearly pitch-black alley. The smells of wet pavement and garbage make a pungent mix. A long, tall concrete wall rises above our heads, marked only with a single fire-escape door, which has been chocked open with a small rock. A small, dim sliver of light glows through the slit.

I pull the door open and step into a sterile-looking concrete fire escape. Stairs rise above my head in what seems like an endless loop. But I turn for the stairs that head down.

"I'll go and find someone who can pick him up," I say, with a wave to Hodge.

He starts forward. "I'll come with you."

I shake my head. "No. You'll just spook everyone." I give him a swift smile, but then my face grows serious. "Really, Hodge. You would."

I leave him there as the fire-escape door scrapes closed behind me, snagging on the rock and clanging to a halt. Below, a distant clamor rises up through the fetid air of the stairwell. Sounds of shouts, screams, crashes, and cracks.

I lean back through the door, pushing it open just a little. As I do, I catch sight of Hodge hoisting Wil over his shoulder.

I give a surprised yelp. "What are you doing?"

"We haven't got time to waste." Hodge carries Wil toward the door. "By the time you find someone, he could be dead."

"But . . ."

"Come on," he says curtly.

Looking at the expression on his face tells me that arguments will be a waste of time, so I start down the stairs. The sound from below gets louder as we approach, and I begin to make out distinct voices in the hubbub.

"Get out of here!"

"My home!!"

I pause on the final landing. Down the flight of stairs is a small square of concrete beside a rusty, old metal door. The sounds ring through the doorway, loud and chaotic.

Hodge draws up beside me. "Is it always like this?"

"No," I reply, tight-lipped. "No, it is not." Taking a deep breath, I climb down the remaining steps and reach out for the door handle.

Hodge's hand covers mine, holding me back. "Let me."

"With that load?" I glance at Wil's unconscious body. "It's better if I go first."

He gives me one of his stony-faced grimaces, then nods. With a racing heartbeat and slightly shaky fingers, I pull the door open and am greeted by the ninth circle of hell.

Shouts echo off the high ceiling of the Ghetto. The fire escape door is elevated above the warehouse floor, so I get a bird's eye view of the chaos. I gasp in shock. We've arrived at the opposite end of the settlement, far away from the marketplace. At least, I think it's the marketplace. All I can see is smoke and people. People running everywhere, but strangely enough, nobody is running for the exit.

Across about a third of the Ghetto, shelters have been razed to the ground, and the concrete floor is littered with scraps of cardboard, plywood, and metal. Where the marketplace used to be has collapsed into a smoldering, smoking heap. There's a line of people snaking from the water tank to the marketplace, handing buckets of water along to douse the embers. Kent's stripy circus tent has collapsed into a rumpled circle on the floor.

"Oh no," I exclaim, aghast. I dash down the stairs and grab the arm of a woman who is running past. "What's going on?"

The woman stares back over her shoulder, eyes wide with fear. "Kent," she breathes, then pulls her arm from my grip. I have no chance to ask her anything more, because she disappears into a walkway nearby.

"Cadence!" Hodge calls, but he sounds too far away to hear properly. I rush frantically through narrow walkways, heading for the Sirens' soup kitchen, searching for familiar faces. Right now, I think I'd be happy even to see the Brown sisters.

Shouts and screams continue to echo around me. After a few chaotic minutes, I reach the water tank and pass it by, running through a narrow passage and finally entering the space where Sirens meet each week. I skid to a halt. The area is littered with bodies, some bearing burns, some with jagged cuts and open wounds. Small groups of Sirens move around the space, tending to the wounded.

I struggle to keep from collapsing to my knees. Tears well as I carefully pick my way around the figures on the ground. I search for anyone I might recognize among the wounded. Near the far corner, I spot a hunched figure bent over a long white shape hidden under a dirty cloth. His shoulders are shaking with weeping. My heart stutters. Timpani's sobs are lost underneath the frantic calls and shouts around me, but there's no need to hear his grief. It seeps through the air around him, casting a long gloom.

A young boy walks toward me, holding a bowl of dirty bandages. I stop him just as he's about to pass by.

"What happened here?" I ask desperately.

The boy's face clouds with confusion. "How can you not know?"

"I've been on the surface." Guilt lands on me like a falling rock.

The boy looks at the bundle in his hands, and then at me. "Kent lost something very important and went on a rampage. Someone had to take him out." His voice grows small.

"Wha-at?" I ask, beginning to feel sick. Was Lark the cause of all of this?

He looks around. "Those girls heard it at the beginning." He points his chin over my shoulder. "They can tell you more."

I turn in the direction he's indicated and feel the sensation of dread again. Two of the Brown sisters huddle beside the youngest, who's lying unconscious on the floor. I am glued to the spot, unwilling to move, unable to avoid the inevitable.

Petra's head turns, as if in slow motion, and her eyes lock on me. Her gaze hardens. With grace, she rises from her crouch and begins to walk deliberately in my direction. As she crosses the space between us, she raises an accusing finger and points it directly at me.

"You!" she says. "What do you have to say for yourself?"

"I don't know what you're talking about." I blink and raise both hands in defence.

"What did you say to Kent?" she persists. "What did you say to make Kent so mad at Sirens?"

"What?" I say, completely flummoxed. "I haven't spoken to Kent in months."

She falters, looking a little uncertain. "If it wasn't you, then . . ."

"Petra, what happened?" I ask. "Nobody is giving me a straight answer."

"The tent suddenly collapsed a few hours ago. Then Kent was there in the marketplace in front of everyone. Said that if Lark wasn't going to stay where she was safe, then what was the point? And then he set the marketplace on fire."

"But . . . but why?" I ask, completely bewildered.

"Who knows why a crazy person does anything?" Petra says. Just then, her eyes widen at something past my shoulder, and her hands fly to the sides of her shocked face. "Wil!" she screams.

I turn. Hodge's entrance has caused quite a stir. Small children, too young to understand, stare open-mouthed at the imposing figure in black armour. But older Sirens duck for cover, disappearing through alleyways and evaporating into shadows. A few brave souls stand to face him, fists tight at their sides.

I run through the chaos to Hodge. "I said it was better for you to wait."

Petra is beside me. "Is that Wil? Is he hurt?"

Hodge glances at me, then replies, "Yes. He's wounded. He needs stitches, and he's lost a lot of blood."

"Over here." Petra draws us to the side of the courtyard where a flat space of concrete remains. "I'll get the medics. What happened?"

"Stabbed," Hodge says in his clipped, businesslike tone. He catches sight of Petra's horrified expression and explains. "Not by me."

"Oh! Oh, I didn't think—" she stammers, but we all know she did.

"Orphans," I inform her.

Nodding mutely, she steps back. Hodge carefully lays Wil on the ground, taking care to gently lower his head to the floor. Wil's face looks peaceful, but his breathing is shallow.

"We have to hurry," I say. "He's getting worse."

Petra looks at us, then races across the courtyard to a small group of people I recognize from the health center. As I stand beside Hodge, I catch sight of the wary and suspicious glances being cast our way.

"He's okay," I say loudly, patting Hodge's shoulder. "This is Harper." I hope that using Hodge's Siren name will send the right kind of signals. It seems to work. Understanding glances pass between Sirens, and people get back to work, still casting suspicious glances.

When the medics arrive, we take a step back to let them work. Petra rolls up her sleeves as she sits beside him.

"I'm his blood type," she says and actually blushes. "We . . . donated blood together once."

Just then, a tall, willowy figure walks into the courtyard, and

I do a double take. Aria carries a load of blankets and begins handing them out to the attendants nearby. When her eyes fall on our little gathering, she gives no immediate reaction but glides in our direction.

"Cadence," she says, looking grave. "You're back."

I lower my head. "I'm sorry," I say heavily. My mind attacks me with memories of upending soup all over Wil's head and Aria's disapproval. But secretly I'm glad it wasn't her under the cloth after all.

Aria looks down at our unconscious companion. A medic has cut away his bandage and trousers, revealing the open wound. Another medic has set up a makeshift blood-transfusion apparatus, complete with a pouch of red liquid ready to transfer to Wil.

Aria hands Petra a bundle of cloth, which she puts behind Wil's head, then Aria turns to me. "You returned Wil?"

"Yes." I hesitate, but I want her to know. "The Composer made sure we made peace."

Aria's face softens. "Good," she says, then looks up. "I am Aria. And you must be Hodge."

He nods. "I am, ma'am."

Aria holds out her hand. "It is good to meet you. I have heard *so* much about you."

Hodge clasps her hand in greeting but casts a questioning glance at me.

"I'll tell you later," I say, feeling awkward.

Aria looks at both of us and beams. "You two will make a great family."

Hodge startles, and my face grows redder. I change the subject, glancing around at the mayhem. "Aria, what are you going to do?"

Her piercing gaze is steadfast. "We will rebuild."

"But Kent has removed his protection. What if the Squads come?"

Aria smiles. "Our safety has never been dependent on the good will of a mere human. Who knows when the Composer will decide to call us home? We can't extend our lives by worrying."

"The Exodus could save you. All of you," I say. Hodge is silent, his gaze fixed hard on us.

Aria shakes her head. "Timpani and I have been here for far too long to be worried now. This isn't our first disaster, and Composer knows it probably won't be our last."

"But the Song—"

"Will be sung even after we die," Aria says firmly. "Which reminds me." She turns away, catching Timpani's eyes. He gives her a nod and hoists himself up from the ground. He gestures, and within minutes, a small choir has gathered at the edge of the courtyard, and a group of Sirens begin to sing soft and low over the space.

Around us, the clamor of voices quiets. A deep bass note thrums out. Then the tenor begins a solemn dance over the top, keeping a slow beat. An alto harmony rings across the tune like a winter sunrise, cold at first but growing warmer and lighter as it goes. Finally, the soprano melody lilts in, and our hearts are lifted by the sweet words flowing through the air.

Hodge intakes a quick breath.

Nothing can separate us
From the Composer's strong, strong love.
Not height nor depth nor anything
From below or from above.
Death nor life, nor powers
Have any hold on us
For through Lyric, we have faith
In the Composer's strong, strong love.

I glance at Hodge and see tears in his eyes. He catches me looking and gives me an embarrassed smile. He clears his throat. "I haven't heard the Song in months."

"Do you want to stay?" I ask gently. "You should hear it when the full choir sings."

He reluctantly shakes his head. "I wish I could, but Sif will be wondering where we are."

I jump. "Of course! Aria, I'm sorry, we have to go. We have someone waiting for us."

She takes my hand. "Then go. Thank you for bringing Wil back home." She glances down to where the older Brown sister is sitting. The blood transfusion line is now working, and Petra is staring at Wil with open adoration. Aria chuckles softly. "I think he will be well looked after here, don't you?"

With a grudging admiration, I see that Petra really did know Wil better than I. Then it dawns on me that this will probably be the last time I see Aria and the Ghetto Sirens. All the words I had planned evaporate from my mind. "I . . . I . . ."

Aria touches my cheek. "The Composer will go with you both."

I drop my gaze to the floor. "Oh, Aria, I'm sorry. I should not have—"

"No, you shouldn't. But the fact you brought him back shows you have learned." She pats my back gently.

Tears fog my vision. "Thank you."

She waves me on. "Go."

I look down at Wil for one last time, feeling a funny mix of emotions. His eyes are still shut, but color is beginning to return to his cheeks, and the wound no longer gapes open dangerously.

"He really changed?" Hodge asks.

I nod. "I think the Composer really found him."

Transformed and in his unconscious state, there's no longer any trace of the sly old Wil. No hint of the dangerous quirk at the corner of his mouth. Just a peaceful, open kind of slumber. Beside him, Petra holds his hand, her constant and watchful gaze flicking from his face to the dressings now covering his wounds.

"Goodbye," I say, though I know Wil won't hear me.

Hodge puts an arm across my shoulders, then guides me away.

31

Death nor life, nor powers
Have any hold on us
For through Lyric, we have faith
In the Composer's strong, strong love.
      Song Fragment 52.7

THE TRUCK SHIFTS GEARS AND SLOWS around a corner, throwing us off balance. Sliding sideways, I grip the sides of the troop carrier's bench, holding on for dear life. I'm sure it's easier to ride one of these things when packed with soldiers. When it's just me and Hodge, I'm rolling up and down the bench like a ball.

We've been riding for what seems like hours, and fatigue has well and truly sunk in. All the activity of the night combined with a lack of food means that I'm fading quickly. My reaction times are slowing to the point that I'm in danger of losing my grip altogether. When we drive in a single direction for any period of time, my head begins to nod, and it's nearly impossible to keep my eyes open.

"Where are we going, anyway?" I ask.

"Not too far now," Hodge says across from me. "I know you must be exhausted."

A yawn escapes that doesn't seem to stop. "I am."

"Tell me your story," he leans forward. "It might help to keep you awake."

"You first."

He looks a little surprised. "Okay. What do you want to know?"

"The last time I saw you, you were running away from me, dressed up like a street sweeper. How did you get here?"

He laughs. "You wouldn't believe it if I told you."

"Try me."

His laugh cuts short. "I thought I was gone, Cadence." The depth of honesty in his voice makes me sit up and pay attention. "I spent hours wandering the streets and wondering if I should just head for the safe house. But in the end, I couldn't come up with anything better than going back to the barracks and hoping nobody noticed me at the scene. Then when nobody did, I felt —" He takes a deep breath. "Oh man, it was hard. Danse and Loa were gone, and then you disappeared, and I was nearly out of my mind."

"Did you find out what happened to Danse?" I ask, falteringly.

The silence at the other side of the van tells me everything.

"It was better they didn't make it," he says eventually. "They didn't have to go through the Haters' Pavilion."

I search for something to say, but words escape me. There's a lump in my throat that threatens to erupt into sobbing. I swallow, trying to keep it together.

"The Composer's got them now," Hodge says quietly.

Despite my best efforts, the tears flow down my cheeks, and our ride descends into silence for a while. Now that the panic has mostly ended, the adrenaline in my system is washing away, replaced by a heavy fatigue. A yawn attacks me again, and I shift in my seat. "I'm sure Crucible was behind it," I say, trying to stay awake.

"I thought that too," Hodge tells me, "but he wasn't."

"What?" My world tilts slightly, and it's not because of the truck.

"It was a random report from one of Danse's neighbors. We were just in the wrong place at the wrong time."

I blink. "But I thought he was after me."

I can sense Hodge's nod. "We were right about that, at least. I was on detail with some security guys a couple of weeks after the incident. You'd be amazed at how much those guys talk when they don't think the cameras are watching."

"What did they say?"

"One of them had just gotten back from Midgate's house in the country."

My mouth drops. "W-what?"

"Crucible sent you a lie, Cadence. It was a setup from the beginning. He wanted you to start fishing around in places you weren't supposed to go, so he could have you demoted for security breaches. You weren't ever going to be allowed to graduate."

I frown, feeling a helpless anger rise up at the unfairness of it all. "That . . . that man . . . that . . ." I'm surprised, though, at how muted my anger is. Maybe I'm just too tired to be furious. But there's still the sting of injustice. What did I ever do to him that made him want to wreck my future?

"That man helped me to find you, though," Hodge says.

"What? How?"

"He sent through a directive after you disappeared. The Watchers lost you, can you believe it? Our street patrols were put on alert for anyone matching your description, which gave me permission to use Love Squad resources. Eventually Lark popped her head up and bam! Operation Exodus was underway."

"But this could get you killed," I say, feeling faintly sick. "They know you're linked with me."

There's a rustle and the sound of movement in the dark,

and then Hodge is on the bench beside me, his arm around my shoulder. "I am linked with you, Cadence. I've got a plan. It'll all work out, you'll see."

His nearness is comforting and warm, and I lean into him. "He won't just give up when I don't turn up," I protest.

"Lark's given him a whole other project, so he'll be too busy to bother with us for a while."

"So she really is related to Midgate?" I ask.

"Yep. She probably doesn't realize it, but she's just given Crucible the very thing he wanted to topple Midgate from the Supreme Lover position."

"But—" The van brakes suddenly, and then the window at the front of the truck slides open.

"Delivery service! We have arrived at our destination!" Sif's cheery voice announces through the window.

THE STREETS ARE WIDE, DECORATED ON each side by avenues of broad, leafy trees. We're far away from the center of Love City now. Houses line the road. Old and tattered porches, broken-down fences, and overgrown gardens tell the story of this place. It might once have been alive with families, but now darkness deadens most of the windows. I can't tell if it's because of Beauty Sleep or whether they're actually deserted. But a lone candle burns in a side window a few houses down the street.

"I feel like I've seen this before," I mumble, staring hard at the ramshackle building. I'm so tired that the memory doesn't immediately float back into my mind.

Hodge takes my arm and guides me forward. We walk alongside the van, using it as cover. When I reach the driver's side window, Sif rolls it down.

"Are you coming?" I ask in a near whisper, looking up at her.

She leans her elbow on the truck door. "This is where I leave you."

"What? You're not coming with us?"

"Someone has to take the truck back to the depot. Chu's back there, and I've got patrolling to do. Plus," she grins, "I can't leave without ever tasting a burger!"

I look from her to Hodge. "Aren't they going to ask questions about you disappearing for a few hours?"

Hodge gives me a little nudge. "Give us some credit," he says.

"The Love Squad always has a plan," Sif adds and nods toward the candlelit house. "Now go, or you'll mess up our carefully timed execution."

I reach up and grasp her arm, overwhelmed. "Thank you, Sif."

She shakes her head. "It's the least I could do after all I put you through back then," she says. "Be safe."

I feel a sudden urge to jump into the cabin and give her a hug. "You're a good friend."

She smiles ruefully. "Not as good as I should have been."

I squeeze her arm. "I'm glad we got to be friends, though."

Sif's mouth quivers slightly, and her eyes glimmer. "Keep safe," she says.

Hodge gently pulls at me. "We should get into the house," he says. "Dawn's coming."

With one last wave, Sif puts the truck back into gear and chugs away. I watch it go, feeling again a mixed mush of emotions. Happy that old Sif is really back. Desperately sad that I won't get to see her again. Fear of what she's going to face when she returns to her barracks.

"She will be fine," Hodge says into my ear.

"This plan of yours better be spectacular," I tell him.

"Don't worry," he assures me. "We've got help."

I'm about to ask what that plan could possibly be, when a

jaw-splitting yawn stops me in my tracks. Hodge puts his arm around me, and the fatigue in my legs is suddenly so great he is the only thing holding me up.

"Come on," he says. "Let's get you into the safe house before you drop."

MY EYELIDS FLUTTER OPEN. I AM WARM FOR what feels like the first time in months. The bed beneath my back creaks as I roll over, and I tuck the thick quilt under my chin, keeping out a cool waft of air. I actually slept on a proper mattress. It was old and a little lumpy, but compared to the Ghetto, it's luxury I thought I might never have again.

Above my head, bright light dances in dust motes from a crack in a boarded-up window. The air smells musty, like an old museum. I wriggle my toes, only to find that my feet have become tangled in the quilt. When I kick them free, a cloud of dust puffs up toward my nose. It sends me into a coughing fit.

"Afternoon, sleepyhead," a deep voice says. Hodge peeks his head into the room.

I sit upright. The sudden movement sends a dull ache thudding across my temple. A sign I have been asleep for too long.

"What are you doing here?" I draw the quilt up close to my chin.

Hodge steps in, holding a glass of water. No longer in the imposing black uniform of a Love Squad soldier, he looks smaller but more comfortable in soft trousers and a rumpled, old blue shirt. The scar along his cheek is nothing but a wisp of lighter skin now. But he's still the Hodge I've known for years. When he smiles, a riot of butterflies erupts in my stomach.

"I brought you a drink," he says, handing the glass to me. "You're probably pretty dehydrated."

Gratefully, I accept his offering and sip down the lukewarm liquid. "I was out as soon as my head hit the pillow. How long was I asleep?"

"About fourteen hours."

"What?" I jerk forward and swing my feet out of bed and onto the floor. I'm hit by a wave of dizziness, and I rock back, holding my head. "Ow."

"Don't worry about moving just yet," Hodge says. His smile is warm. "We can't go until nightfall anyway. Take your time. I've got food in the kitchen when you feel like something to eat."

At the mention of food, my stomach gurgles loudly. "I would like that. Thank you," I say, groaning back against the pillows. Hodge bows out of the room, closing the door quietly behind him.

Now that I'm aware of my hunger, it quickly becomes the only thing I can think about. That and the bathroom. With an annoyed grumble, I get to my feet. The shoes Aria gave me sit neatly beside the bed. I slip them on and wonder how she's doing.

Questions multiply in my head as I find my way out of the room. How is the Ghetto going to survive now that Kent removed his protection? All these years, the citizens of Love City went about their business on the streets above, eyes glued to their AR glasses or infotabs. Everyone was too busy clocking up Love Points to bother noticing the world below their feet. Will anyone even notice if one day the Ghetto is gone?

"Keep them safe," I beg the Composer. "I don't know how, but please keep them safe."

It takes me a while to find the bathroom, but I eventually get there, splashing my face with cool water and looking at my haggard reflection in the mirror. The time in the Ghetto hasn't been kind. My skin is pale and greasy from too many days without sunshine. Dark circles ring my sunken eyes. My hair has grown so long it sticks out in all sorts of dangerous directions.

"Ugh. Can't deal." I turn away from the horror. At least Hodge doesn't care if I look like a slightly warm corpse, or does he?

The thought of Hodge makes me turn back and ransack the cupboards for any beauty products I can find. I manage to find a small tube of soap and a couple of hair ties. By the time I leave the bathroom, I'm still looking pale, but less like a zombie.

Muffled thumps and clatterings waft down the narrow hallway, and I follow the sounds to the kitchen.

Hodge looks up as I enter. "I didn't have much to work with," he says apologetically, "but here. Today's feast."

He holds out a small bowl. I accept it gratefully and spoon a lump of the goo into my mouth without thinking. "What is this?" I ask, mouth still full. "Tastes like the Academy."

"Ration packs," Hodge explains. "Hopefully I've got enough to last us to the wall."

I pause between mouthfuls. "How long until we get there?"

Hodge turns to the sink, where he runs the water. "Long enough. Let's just say there's a few more nights before we get out of the Collective, all things going well."

I nod, feeling a strange and sudden shyness. "So . . . we'll be . . . travelling alone?"

Hands poised over the sink, Hodge goes very still. "Uh . . . I'd better go and check our packs," he says and disappears down the hallway fast.

By the time he returns, I've finished my food and washed up. He holds two backpacks in front of him. He hands one to me before dumping the other one on the small, rickety table in the center of the room.

"Viola made sure these were left here for us," he says, zipping open the one in his hand. "It's got the rations but also most of the things we'll need to travel."

"Thank you," I say, looking at the neatly folded jacket inside my pack. He smiles, and I feel all tingly. It's my turn to walk away this time, but I only go as far as the chair on the other side of the dining table.

We fill the remaining hours of sunlight with talking. We catch up on what we've done for the last few months, what happened to our friends, where they are now. Hodge carefully avoids asking too many questions about Wil. Mostly.

"Did he hurt you in any way again?" he suddenly asks. I look up, and there's worry in his expression. And a hesitancy in his voice that makes me love him even more.

"No," I assure him. "I don't know that I could have survived down there if he'd been the same old schemer."

Hodge shakes his head. "I have to say, it was a pretty big shock to see him. If he wasn't so injured, I don't know what I would have done."

I smile. "I poured hot soup all over him."

Hodge's eyes widen. "Really? That would have been interesting to see."

The memory of it brings a blush of shame. "It wasn't. I made an idiot of myself in front of a whole lot of people. Some of them were really upset."

Hodge searches my face for a few moments. "You're sure he changed?"

I pause, thinking about every interaction I had with him underground. The Wil who helped out in the background, no matter how dirty the job to be done. The Wil who saved the little girl's life. Who apologized to me over and over again.

"I think the Composer really changed him," I say slowly. "And I never would have believed it if I hadn't seen if for myself."

Hodge stares into the distance. "Well, the Composer can do anything."

We lapse into silence for a while. I stare at the crack in the boarded-up windows, watching the light slowly fade from outside.

In a few hours, we'll be gone from here, and who knows what we'll face on the road.

Hodge reaches into a small pocket in his backpack, fishing out a paper packet of some sort. "Here," he says. "I thought you might feel like taking this with you."

I stare at the envelope, reading and re-reading the familiar letters on the front. "You kept Mumma's letter?"

He nods.

I reach out for the packet and give a little cry when I feel a hard lump behind the paper. "You kept . . ."

I quickly tip the contents into my palm. The silvery chain pools in my hand, bright against the dim shadows of the room. Seeing Mumma's Lyric-tree pendant brings a lump to my throat.

"Why?" I manage, voice hoarse with emotion.

Hodge's shrug is imperceptible. "I wanted to give it to you someday."

My fist closes around it. "Thank you," I whisper.

Hodge moves around the table. "Here. Let me."

He lifts the chain out of my hands and lowers the pendant in front of my neck, fixing the clasp behind my head. It nestles lightly on my clothes, sparkling. Hodge goes back to his seat, giving me quiet space for my memories.

Mumma's voice lilts in my mind, her soft, hushed tones singing to me a lullaby from the Song. Absently, I let myself hum along to the remembered music, stroking the silver pendant as if Mumma had given it to me herself.

When I come to my senses, Hodge has moved to the packs and is folding and repacking provisions.

"Do you think we'll make it?" I ask.

He holds his hand out to me. "Let's ask the Composer to protect us."

I take his hand, and it feels like the most natural thing in the world. The Muse's soft Song joins us, and we lay out all our worries to the one who brought us together.

32

LOVE CITY NEWS

SHOCK! MIDGATE'S SECRET CHILDREN

Love City was sent into uproar today upon shattering revelations that our Supreme Lover had been hiding a secret family for generations. The news came as a woman, name withheld, has come forward claiming to be Midgate's great-granddaughter. The Supreme Executive was quick to deny the claims. However, one unnamed source from deep within the Hall of Love has supported the woman's account.

"We were skeptical at first," the source said. "After all, it was our Supreme Lover herself who championed the cause against exclusive families. But DNA tests have confirmed the relationship."

Rumors of a secret Midgate family have circulated for decades but have always been vehemently denied by officials. Early concerns that the Supreme Lover had secretly given birth to a son who later "went rogue" were quashed, but stories remained of a man being held in a secret facility "off-grid" from the Collective. With the recent appearance of an alleged great-granddaughter, these rumors have now resurfaced.

Executive Lover Munsch would not be drawn on the scandal, and Executive Lover Worthing denied all claims. However, Executive Lover Crucible was public in his expression of concern.

"Questions will need to be answered," the Executive Lover for Education said this morning. "Do not worry. The Executive will not stop until we have come to the bottom of this cruel deception. Our citizens deserve no less than the truth."

Love City News will update this story as more information comes to hand.

WHEN NIGHT FALLS, WE BEGIN THE EXODUS in earnest. I follow Hodge's lead as he navigates expertly away from main roads and checkpoints and takes us through parks and back streets until there are no more roads to walk on. The security cameras thin, then disappear.

Flat suburban wastelands give way to a steep series of hills, and our progress slows. It takes us most of the night to reach the top, and we take a break at the summit, staring out at the dark black carpet that stretches out beyond the horizon below us. The night sky is hidden behind a thick bank of clouds, deepening the darkness below. Somewhere beyond that horizon is the Hall of Love, but it's too far away to see.

As we watch, Beauty Sleep hours come to an end, and lights begin to wink on across the city. I gaze in wonder as first the streets, then the apartment buildings and parks glow up to the predawn sky. In the distance, I catch sight of a circular Nursery Dorm, its walls lit up like a spoked wheel. Small specks of light start to move along some of the roads as Overcars begin their daily commute.

I take a breath, speechless at the glittering spectacle below us. Hodge glances at me. "Pretty huge, huh?"

"I had no idea the city was this big," I say. "It feels weird to be leaving."

He clasps my hand. "We wouldn't be going if we didn't have to."

I nod. "I know."

There's a lump in my throat as we resume our journey, and I have to fight the urge to keep looking over my shoulder. But after a while, the view is lost behind trees and more hills. And just like that, I have left the only home I'd ever known.

For the next few days, we travel after dark. Hodge keeps us to a route that avoids the security checkpoints along the main roads. He seems so familiar with the area that I tease him about it.

"I had an assignment out here right after graduation," he explains, guiding me along a narrow path through thick undergrowth. "The guys spent their days gambling on their infotabs and shooting stones off the wall. I had plenty of time to do research."

I push away some of the excess growth. "Where are the cameras?"

"There are only a couple to the south of here. Most of them stick to the main roads."

After the frontier outpost, we stop seeing people, even at a distance. Out here, the Collective still bears the marks of a long-dead civilization. We walk along cracked concrete roads that disappear under swathes of bracken and grass. Tangles of thorny plants choke old timber poles along the side of the overgrown path. Sweet, cloying scents fill the air.

"We can travel during the day now," Hodge says that night, as we set up camp beneath a rusting, old billboard. The posters have long since faded and hang from the metal frame in jagged slivers. "It will be safer, anyway, and we can move faster."

The next day, a sudden downpour sends large, hot drops of water teeming down on our heads, and we take shelter in an abandoned building that was once white, with a strange awning that stretches out over the pavement. That night, we sleep in a hollowed-out shelter nearly completely overtaken by piles of long-dead leaves.

Before the sun rises, Hodge wakes me, and we start our hike all over again. We walk through the grey predawn light, watching the clouds waft along above us like cotton-candy wisps. Birds sing as the sky turns pink around the edges of the horizon. Soft whispers of mist sit in hollows beneath the hills.

"It's so beautiful," I say, watching my breath create foggy clouds as it leaves my mouth.

I turn and catch Hodge gazing at me with a strange expression. He immediately looks off in the direction we're heading and clears his throat. "We need to keep moving."

He turns on his heels and strides off at a faster-than-usual walk. I trot along behind, wondering if I said something wrong. But for the rest of the day, I keep catching him out of the corner of my eye. He looks at me, and when I turn to him, his eyes flick away as if he were looking somewhere else. I plan to ask him about that look, but we walk so far and so fast that I fall into an exhausted sleep almost as soon as we stop for the night.

The hills outside of Love City give way to vast, scrubby forests, punctuated with open wastelands that leave me with a weird feeling of disconnection. My whole life, I've lived surrounded by walls and buildings and manicured gardens. Even the Ghetto was urban, crowded, and full of noise. Out here, it feels as if Hodge and I are the only two people left in the whole world. When I share my thoughts with Hodge over our lunchtime ration packs, he shakes his head.

"Don't get complacent."

"But it feels like we could just live out here, and nobody would ever know," I say.

"As long as we're in the Collective, they'd find us eventually."

"Maybe."

A day after that, we pass a whole settlement, long since deserted. Most of the buildings have been torn down, but a couple remain standing, their windows broken and doors hanging haphazardly off their frames. The buildings have been completely stripped bare, and only broken glass and fittings remain as evidence of people living here in the past. It makes a good place to stop for the night, but I don't get much rest. The creaks of rusty door hinges and banging shutters keep waking me.

Hodge takes us back into the wilderness after that night, letting the forests shield us from view. His timing is impeccable, because the following night, I wake to the sound of trucks in the distance. I listen to the sounds rumbling far away, wide awake until long after they fade into silence. Hodge sits with his back against a tree, a watchful sentinel over our darkened camp.

At the end of the second week, we step out of one forest into a swathe of open grasslands. The sun beats down on us from a cloudless blue sky. Long grass sways and sighs in the wind, rippling up and down the hills in golden-green waves. Far ahead, another ribbon of forest lines the horizon, and above the green foliage lies a long, straight white line.

"Is that . . . "

"Yes," Hodge answers even before I finish. He stares to the left and right with a grim expression. "We're going to be exposed for a long time."

"The Composer's looked after us so far," I say, staring at the sky. I step forward, and the grass rises to my shoulder.

"Can you duck lower?" Hodge says. "We're goners if an aerial patrol comes over, no matter what. But if we stay down, they won't see us from the road."

So I duck down, scurrying forward so that my head doesn't crest above the flowing waves of grass heads. It doesn't last long, though. My shoulders hurt, and I feel like I'm running in circles, instead of heading for the forest protection ahead. It's no surprise that Hodge lets out an exasperated gasp and passes me by.

"You didn't get any further than basic training, did you?" he says with a grin that is far too annoying to let slide.

"Just go," I huff.

The wall continues to appear higher and higher as we draw near. It forms an unnatural gap between land and sky, too flat and elevated to be hills, but too low and regular to be clouds. It rises above the grasslands and forest with silent menace, bordering our view as far as our eyes can see. With the sun pointing at it, the whiteness of the concrete is nearly blinding.

After an hour or so, we make it to the end of the grasslands, and step back under the cool shade of trees. I risk a glance behind us. The wide circle of grassland stretches out to my left and right like a ring. In the far distance to my right, though, I see a tiny black box-shape glide along the horizon in the direction of the wall. I shrink back, watching the truck until it disappears behind the line of trees. It's the only sign of people I can see, but it's more than enough.

Hodge stands very still, having watched the same thing as me. "Things just got complicated," he says.

It's the tiny flash of fear at the corner of his eyes that gets me. In a split second, I am at his heels, crashing through the undergrowth in the direction of the wall. This layer of forest thins out quickly, and I soon discover why. Heat radiates from the concrete, making the land beside it too hot to support thick greenery. We skid to a halt near the last line of trees, staring at a wide stretch of dust and rocky red earth. The wall towers above our heads, concrete panels too large and smooth for any finger hold. It stretches in both directions, as far as our eyes can see. Almost at the horizon, a small hiccup in the unbroken concrete shows us where a border crossing sits. It brings back a long-repressed memory of a time when I was Crucible's pawn.

"I've seen a place like this before." I pull Hodge back behind a tree. "When I was a Watcher. There will be a camera. A drone down at the checkpoint, and another one up on a pole somewhere."

Hodge looks over my shoulder, staring upward. He nods.

"It's here somewhere," he says, pointing along the wall, away from the checkpoint direction. "If my calculations are right, anyway."

"What?" I gape at him. "You left this up to a guess?"

He shakes his head at me. "Calculations aren't guesses, C. But we have to be fast. If that truck is what I think it is, they'll be sending out the drone soon."

We sneak along under the cover of the trees. Hodge keeps his face turned toward the wall, searching. I'm on the verge of calling for a rest when he halts, holding up a hand.

"There," he points.

Behind a small ridge, the rough and rocky ground dips suddenly in a half-bowl shape. At the center of the bowl, in the side of the wall, lies a circular drain, its black mouth hidden from a distance by the ridge at the side of the dirt. Hodge propels me forward, heading straight for it. Above the wall, the black dome of a surveillance-camera housing points straight down at the drain's opening.

"Wait!" I stop and stare up at the camera, shrinking back under the leaves of the tree.

"There's no time," Hodge says shortly. "If we delay any more, we won't make it."

I peer toward the checkpoint, which is now beyond the horizon. As I watch, a little dust cloud appears where the ground meets the sky. It gets larger, and a small black dot appears in front of it.

"Go!" Hodge yells and drags me to the drain. "Now!"

We dive into the bowl-like depression in the ground, crawling into the concrete circle that forms the large stormwater drain.

Hodge has pushed me in front of him, and I crawl, squashing the memories of the last time I was in a large dark space like this.

We are quickly engulfed in complete darkness, and for a few minutes the two of us press on, unable to see where we're going, and not willing to think about what is approaching from behind. Then in the distance, a pinprick of yellow light begins to shine. The pinprick grows into a small circle of sunshine. There's an opening ahead. A grate at the end of the wall on the other side.

That's when I hear it. A soft, slithering noise from somewhere up ahead. Soft and metallic, sliding and clicking over the concrete. I freeze. The sunlight disappears. In the darkness, a bulky shape fills the drain, heading straight for us. It's a sound I've heard before—and hoped never to hear again.

"Hodge!" I yell. "Back!"

My feet scramble backward into Hodge's arms. "Drone!" I squeak, panicking.

"Get down!" Hodge demands, and I drop on my belly to the floor of the drain. Moments later there's a large crack over my head. A glowing yellow bundle shoots forward, spreading out just as it reaches a horrific figure in the darkness. I see only glimpses of a glutinous shape and razor-sharp metallic pincers, and then the net lands on its target. There's a sizzle and a pop, and the drone goes silent.

"Give me a second," Hodge says, clambering over. I hear a soft squelch, and then Hodge grunting and panting as he moves whatever it was back. We continue onward, but our crawl slows. Then a sliver of sunlight reappears, and Hodge pushes the drone into the side alcove where it had been stationed.

Behind us, the sound of an arriving vehicle booms along the drain. Doors open and close, and footsteps crackle along the rocky ground behind the wall.

"You go ahead," Hodge whispers, as my hope fades.

"Don't," I say, reaching out for him. "Don't do anything stupid."

"You should know me by now." There's a smile in his voice, even though I can't see his face in the darkness.

I know I should keep on crawling forward, but I can't go without him. So I hover where I am, listening carefully at the sounds around us.

From the alcove, there's a soft, metallic slithering, then it stops. Then Hodge is at my side, touching my arm gently.

"That should hold them for a little while," he says. "It will reboot in a few minutes, so they'll have to deal with it."

With a frenzied burst of speed, we hurry on to the circle of daylight.

MEMORY DATE: 2284.039 (FOUR YEARS AGO)

Memory location: Underground bunker

"What happens if you have to leave? I can't survive without your help," I say, clasping my hands together anxiously.

"You will have someone even better than me at your back," Akela says with a soft smile. "Remember that not even death can stop the Composer."

WE EMERGE FROM THE DRAIN INTO WARM, golden sunshine. Beside a patch of sandy path that runs parallel to the high white concrete, the ground slopes gently away in grassy green hills. Rectangular fences line fertile paddocks, where animals graze in meandering ease. Small copses of trees lie in the folded valleys. In the distance, the sunlight glitters off rooftops.

I take a deep breath. "We made it."

"The Composer answered our prayers." Hodge smiles, running a hand through his hair. His shoulders relax, and he looks happier than I've seen him in a long time.

A sweet sound whispers in our ears, carried on the breeze. My spirits soar with it. "Is that . . ." I breathe, too afraid to speak loudly in case the sound disappears.

Hodge nods. "Come on."

Taking a step forward, he holds his hand out to me, calloused with years of fight training and still bearing the grime of the tunnel floor. Memories flutter into my head of the years we've had together. His silent, gruff presence in the dorm rooms. The missions we went on to the city, gathering Song fragments. The way he looked into my eyes on that Triumph night. I listen to the sweet sound coming from the town below us, and I let his warm fingers enfold my own. My other hand reaches for the silver pendant around my neck.

"Mumma would have loved to see this," I say.

Not far below us, a small copse of trees nestles into the hillside below the wall. We walk towards it, noticing the tendril of smoke that snakes up from behind the leaves. Birds sing in the treetops, heralding our approach.

We round a bend, and the trees give way to a small, neatly manicured garden that rings a cozy white cottage. A rambling vine frames the red door, I'm about to wonder if we should just keep going when the door opens, and a woman clad in a vibrantly coloured dress steps out from the cottage. Her hair is wrapped in a scarf the colour of emeralds, and her arms are bare in the sunshine. She lifts her hand and waves, and Hodge lets out a little strangled cry.

"You made it," Akela says with a welcoming smile. "I was wondering when you would come."

The words of the Song waft again on the breeze, sung by voices in the distance.

ACKNOWLEDGMENTS

Back in 2016-17, I wrote a dystopian novel and entered it into an unpublished manuscript competition in Australia. It won, and the prize was an assessment by the wonderful Iola Goulton at Christian Editing Services. Iola thought that manuscript had promise, but she felt that it started a little too quickly. She suggested that I add a little backstory. I went away, kept on writing, and that "little backstory" turned into two entire novels. That's how the Collective Underground Trilogy was born. So I owe Iola a great deal for her wonderful encouragement! Her faithful and godly outlook on my writing was incredibly helpful, and I am always a better writer after receiving her thoughtful feedback. Of course, those two novels changed Book 3 almost entirely, but that's a story for another time . . .

When *Apprentice* was first accepted by Enclave for publishing, I had no idea what the next few years would have in store either. I would go from part-time to awesome but demanding near full-time work, our town would be affected by bushfires, a global pandemic would break out, my mother would be diagnosed with cancer and go to be with the Lord, our family would embark on a quest to look after my father, and I would change ministries to serve in a Missionary Bible college. The fact that this trilogy was able to be finished in the middle of all of that is a gracious mercy from God. I am so grateful for His presence in hard and good times, and for the way He helped to guide me as I wrote.

I'm also incredibly grateful for the gracious and patient assistance from the Enclave team. I have been incredibly blessed by them: Steve and Lisa Laube, Trissina Kear, Jamie Foley, Sarah Grimm, Katie S. Williams, and Megan Gerig. I'm in awe of Kirk DouPonce's artistic gifts and the amazing work he's done on the cover once again, and I'm super grateful for the talented team at Oasis, who turned my novels into living, breathing audiobooks.

I'm grateful to my family, to my wonderful husband who faithfully reads my books and thinks they're kinda cool. To my friends who read the books and gave me helpful feedback, and to some of my Year 13 students and colleagues who were cheerleaders for me during a really hard time. (Jess D, I'm especially looking at you, mate. I still use that bookshelf mug!)

Oh, and to the always awesome Enclave street team, and the readers who've shared their feedback and reviews: I see you guys. You rock. You have no idea how encouraging it is when someone across the world actually likes the words you put on paper. Thanks for being awesome. I hope I was able to bring some good ending vibes to you with this story.

ABOUT THE AUTHOR

Kristen is an Australian author, who also ministers to young people as a lecturer and pastoral worker with a Christian gap year program. Although she loves those days when she gets to dream of faraway worlds and put them into writing, she feels blessed to be able to share the good news of Jesus in her everyday work.

THE LOVE COLLECTIVE IS EVERYWHERE.
IT SEES EVERYTHING.
BE NOT AFRAID.

 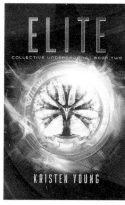 

THE COLLECTIVE UNDERGROUND SERIES

Apprentice

Elite

Flight

Available Now!

www.enclavepublishing.com